THE EXPLOITS OF ELAINE

ARTHUR B. REEVE

The Exploits of Elaine

Arthur B. Reeve

© 1st World Library, 2009
PO Box 2211
Fairfield, IA 52556
www.1stworldlibrary.com
First Edition

LCCN: 2009923340

Softcover ISBN: 978-1-4218-8812-5
Hardcover ISBN: 978-1-4218-8911-5
eBook ISBN: 978-1-4218-8713-5

Purchase *"The Exploits of Elaine"*
as a traditional bound book at:
www.1stWorldLibrary.com/purchase.asp?ISBN=978-1-4218-8812-5

1st World Library is a literary, educational organization
dedicated to:

- Creating a free internet library of downloadable ebooks

- Hosting writing competitions and offering book publishing
scholarships.

Interested in more 1st World Library books? contact:
literacy@1stworldlibrary.com
Check us out at: www.1stworldlibrary.com

1ˢᵗ World Library Literary Society

Giving Back to the World

"If you want to work on the core problem, it's early school literacy."

- James Barksdale, former CEO of Netscape

"No skill is more crucial to the future of a child, or to a democratic and prosperous society, than literacy."

- Los Angeles Times

"Literacy... means far more than learning how to read and write... The aim is to transmit... knowledge and promote social participation."

- UNESCO

"Literacy is not a luxury, it is a right and a responsibility. If our world is to meet the challenges of the twenty-first century we must harness the energy and creativity of all our citizens."

- President Bill Clinton

"Parents should be encouraged to read to their children, and teachers should be equipped with all available techniques for teaching literacy, so the varying needs and capacities of individual kids can be taken into account."

- Hugh Mackay

CONTENTS

CHAPTER I

THE CLUTCHING HAND

"Jameson, here's a story I wish you'd follow up," remarked the managing editor of the Star to me one evening after I had turned in an assignment of the late afternoon.

He handed me a clipping from the evening edition of the Star and I quickly ran my eye over the headline:

"THE CLUTCHING HAND" WINS AGAIN

NEW YORK'S MYSTERIOUS MASTER CRIMINAL PERFECTS ANOTHER COUP

CITY POLICE COMPLETELY BAFFLED

"Here's this murder of Fletcher, the retired banker and trustee of the University," he explained. "Not a clue—except a warning letter signed with this mysterious clutching fist. Last week it was the robbery of the Haxworth jewels and the killing of old Haxworth. Again that curious sign of the hand. Then there was the dastardly attempt on Sherburne, the steel magnate. Not a trace of the assailant except this same clutching fist. So it has gone, Jameson—the most alarming and most inexplicable series of murders that has ever happened in this country. And nothing but this uncanny hand to trace them by."

The editor paused a moment, then exclaimed, "Why, this fellow seems to take a diabolical—I might almost say pathological—pleasure in crimes of violence, revenge, avarice and self-protection. Sometimes it seems as if he delights in the pure deviltry of the thing. It is weird."

He leaned over and spoke in a low, tense tone. "Strangest of all, the tip has just come to us that Fletcher, Haxworth, Sherburne and all the rest of those wealthy men were insured in the Consolidated Mutual Life. Now, Jameson, I want you to find Taylor Dodge, the president, and interview him. Get what you can, at any cost."

I had naturally thought first of Kennedy, but there was no time now to call him up and, besides, I must see Dodge immediately.

Dodge, I discovered over the telephone, was not at home, nor at any of the clubs to which he belonged. Late though it was I concluded that he was at his office. No amount of persuasion could get me past the door, and, though I found out later and shall tell soon what was going on there, I determined, about nine o'clock, that the best way to get at Dodge was to go to his house on Fifth Avenue, if I had to camp on his front doorstep until morning. The harder I found the story to get, the more I wanted it.

With some misgivings about being admitted, I rang the bell of the splendid, though not very modern, Dodge residence. An English butler, with a nose that must have been his fortune, opened the door and gravely informed me that Mr. Dodge was not at home, but was expected at any moment.

Arthur B. Reeve

Once in, I was not going lightly to give up that advantage. I bethought myself of his daughter, Elaine, one of the most popular debutantes of the season, and sent in my card to her, on a chance of interesting her and seeing her father, writing on the bottom of the card: "Would like to interview Mr. Dodge regarding Clutching Hand."

Summoning up what assurance I had, which is sometimes considerable, I followed the butler down the hall as he bore my card. As he opened the door of the drawing room I caught a vision of a slip of a girl, in an evening gown.

Elaine Dodge was both the ingenue and the athlete—the thoroughly modern type of girl—equally at home with tennis and tango, table talk and tea. Vivacious eyes that hinted at a stunning amber brown sparkled beneath masses of the most wonderful auburn hair. Her pearly teeth, when she smiled, were marvellous. And she smiled often, for life to her seemed a continuous film of enjoyment.

Near her I recognized from his pictures, Perry Bennett, the rising young corporation lawyer, a mighty good looking fellow, with an affable, pleasing way about him, perhaps thirty-five years old or so, but already prominent and quite friendly with Dodge.

On a table I saw a book, as though Elaine had cast it down when the lawyer arrived to call on the daughter under pretense of waiting for her father. Crumpled on the table was the Star. They had read the story.

"Who is it, Jennings?" she asked.

"A reporter, Miss Dodge," answered the butler glancing superciliously back at me, "and you know how your father dislikes to see anyone here at the house," he added deferentially to her.

I took in the situation at a glance. Bennett was trying not to look discourteous, but this was a call on Elaine and it had been interrupted. I could expect no help from that quarter. Still, I fancied that Elaine was not averse to trying to pique her visitor and determined at least to try it.

"Miss Dodge," I pleaded, bowing as if I had known them all my life, "I've been trying to find your father all the evening. It's very important."

She looked up at me surprised and in doubt whether to laugh or stamp her pretty little foot in indignation at my stupendous nerve.

She laughed. "You are a very brave young man," she replied with a roguish look at Bennett's discomfiture over the interruption of the tete-a-tete.

There was a note of seriousness in it, too, that made me ask quickly, "Why?"

The smile flitted from her face and in its place came a frank earnest expression which I later learned to like and respect very much. "My father has declared he will eat the very next reporter who tries to interview him here," she answered.

I was about to prolong the waiting time by some jolly about such a stunning girl not having by any possibility such a cannibal of a parent, when the rattle of the changing gears of a car outside told of the approach of a limousine.

The big front door opened and Elaine flung herself in the arms of an elderly, stern-faced, gray-haired man. "Why, Dad," she cried, "where have you been? I missed you so much at dinner. I'll be so glad when this terrible business gets cleared up. Tell—me. What is on your mind? What is it that worries you now?"

I noticed then that Dodge seemed wrought-up and a bit unnerved, for he sank rather heavily into a chair, brushed his face with his handkerchief and breathed heavily. Elaine hovered over him solicitously, repeating her question.

With a mighty effort he seemed to get himself together. He rose and turned to Bennett.

"Perry," he exclaimed, "I've got the Clutching Hand!"

The two men stared at each other.

"Yes," continued Dodge, "I've just found out how to trace it, and tomorrow I am going to set the alarms of the city at rest by exposing—"

Just then Dodge caught sight of me. For the moment I thought perhaps he was going to fulfill his threat.

"Who the devil—why didn't you tell me a reporter was here, Jennings?" he sputtered indignantly, pointing toward the door.

Argument, entreaty were of no avail. He stamped crustily into the library, taking Bennett with him and leaving me with Elaine. Inside I could hear them talking, and managed to catch enough to piece together the story. I wanted to stay, but Elaine, smiling at my enthusiasm, shook her head and held out her hand in one of her frank, straight-arm hand shakes. There was nothing to do but go.

At least, I reflected, I had the greater part of the story—all except the one big thing, however,—the name of the criminal. But Dodge would know him tomorrow!

I hurried back to the Star to write my story in time to catch the last morning edition.

* * * * *

Meanwhile, if I may anticipate my story, I must tell of what we later learned had happened to Dodge so completely to upset him.

Ever since the Consolidated Mutual had been hit by the murders, he had had many lines out in the hope of enmeshing the perpetrator. That night, as I found out the next day, he had at last heard of a clue. One of the company's detectives had brought in a red-headed, lame, partly paralyzed crook who enjoyed the expressive monniker of "Limpy Red." "Limpy Red" was a gunman of some renown, evil faced and having nothing much to lose, desperate. Whoever the master criminal of the Clutching Hand might have been he had seen fit to employ Limpy but had not taken the precaution of getting rid of him soon enough when he was through.

Wherefore Limpy had a grievance and now descended under pressure to the low level of snitching to Dodge in his office.

"No, Governor," the trembling wretch had said as he handed over a grimy envelope, "I ain't never seen his face—but here is directions how to find his hang-out."

As Limpy ambled out, he turned to Dodge, quivering at the enormity of his unpardonable sin in gang-land, "For God's sake, Governor," he implored, "don't let on how you found out!"

Arthur B. Reeve

And yet Limpy Red had scarcely left with his promise not to tell, when Dodge, happening to turn over some papers came upon an envelope left on his own desk, bearing that mysterious Clutching Hand!

He tore it open, and read in amazement:

"Destroy Limpy Red's instructions within the next hour."

Dodge gazed about in wonder. This thing was getting on his nerves. He determined to go home and rest.

Outside the house, as he left his car, pasted over the monogram on the door, he had found another note, with the same weird mark and the single word:

"Remember!"

Much of this I had already gathered from what I overheard Dodge telling Bennett as they entered the library. Some, also, I have pieced together from the story of a servant who overheard.

At any rate, in spite of the pleadings of young Bennett, Dodge refused to take warning. In the safe in his beautifully fitted library he deposited Limpy's document in an envelope containing all the correspondence that had lead up to the final step in the discovery.

* * * * *

It was late in the evening when I returned to our apartment and, not finding Kennedy there, knew that I would discover him at the laboratory.

"Craig," I cried as I burst in on him, "I've got a case for

you—greater than any ever before!"

Kennedy looked up calmly from the rack of scientific instruments that surrounded him, test tubes, beakers, carefully labelled bottles.

He had been examining a piece of cloth and had laid it aside in disappointment near his magnifying glass. Just now he was watching a reaction in a series of test tubes standing on his table. He was looking dejectedly at the floor as I came in.

"Indeed?" he remarked coolly going back to the reaction.

"Yes," I cried. "It is a scientific criminal who seems to leave no clues."

Kennedy looked up gravely. "Every criminal leaves a trace," he said quietly. "If it hasn't been found, then it must be because no one has ever looked for it in the right way."

Still gazing at me keenly, he added, "Yes, I already knew there was such a man at large. I have been called in on that Fletcher case—he was a trustee of the University, you know."

"All right," I exclaimed, a little nettled that he should have anticipated me even so much in the case. "But you haven't heard the latest."

"What is it?" he asked with provoking calmness,

"Taylor Dodge," I blurted out, "has the clue. To-morrow he will track down the man!"

Kennedy fairly jumped as I repeated the news.

"How long has he known?" he demanded eagerly.

"Perhaps three or four hours," I hazarded.

Kennedy gazed at me fixedly.

"Then Taylor Dodge is dead!" he exclaimed, throwing off his acid- stained laboratory smock and hurrying into his street clothes.

"Impossible!" I ejaculated.

Kennedy paid no attention to the objection. "Come, Walter," he urged. "We must hurry, before the trail gets cold."

There was something positively uncanny about Kennedy's assurance. I doubted—yet I feared.

It was well past the middle of the night when we pulled up in a night-hawk taxicab before the Dodge house, mounted the steps and rang the bell.

Jennings answered sleepily, but not so much so that he did not recognize me. He was about to bang the door shut when Kennedy interposed his foot.

"Where is Mr. Dodge?" asked Kennedy. "Is he all right?"

"Of course he is—in bed," replied the butler.

Just then we heard a faint cry, like nothing exactly human. Or was it our heightened imaginations, under the spell of the darkness?

"Listen!" cautioned Kennedy.

We did, standing there now in the hall. Kennedy was the only one of us who was cool. Jennings' face blanched, then he turned tremblingly and went down to the library door whence the sounds had seemed to come.

He called but there was no answer. He turned the knob and opened the door. The Dodge library was a large room. In the center stood a big flat-topped desk of heavy mahogany. It was brilliantly lighted.

At one end of the desk was a telephone. Taylor Dodge was lying on the floor at that end of the desk—perfectly rigid—his face distorted—a ghastly figure. A pet dog ran over, sniffed frantically at his master's legs and suddenly began to howl dismally.

Dodge was dead!

"Help!" shouted Jennings.

Others of the servants came rushing in. There was for the moment the greatest excitement and confusion.

Suddenly a wild figure in flying garments flitted down the stairs and into the library, dropping beside the dead man, without seeming to notice us at all.

"Father!" shrieked a woman's voice, heart broken. "Father! Oh—my God—he—he is dead!"

It was Elaine Dodge.

With a mighty effort, the heroic girl seemed to pull herself together.

"Jennings," she cried, "Call Mr. Bennett—immediately!"

Arthur B. Reeve

From the one-sided, excited conversation of the butler over the telephone, I gathered that Bennett had been in the process of disrobing in his own apartment uptown and would be right down.

Together, Kennedy, Elaine and myself lifted Dodge to a sofa and Elaine's aunt, Josephine, with whom she lived, appeared on the scene, trying to quiet the sobbing girl.

Kennedy and I withdrew a little way and he looked about curiously.

"What was it?" I whispered. "Was it natural, an accident, or—or murder?"

The word seemed to stick in my throat. If it was a murder, what was the motive? Could it have been to get the evidence which Dodge had that would incriminate the master criminal?

Kennedy moved over quietly and examined the body of Dodge. When he rose, his face had a peculiar look.

"Terrible!" he whispered to me. "Apparently he had been working at his accustomed place at the desk when the telephone rang. He rose and crossed over to it. See! That brought his feet on this register let into the floor. As he took the telephone receiver down a flash of light must have shot from it to his ear. It shows the characteristic electric burn."

"The motive?" I queried.

"Evidently his pockets had been gone through, though none of the valuables were missing. Things on his desk show that a hasty search has been made."

Just then the door opened and Bennett burst in.

As he stood over the body, gazing down at it, repressing the emotions of a strong man, he turned to Elaine and in a low voice, exclaimed, "The Clutching Hand did this! I shall consecrate my life to bring this man to justice!"

He spoke tensely and Elaine, looking up into his face, as if imploring his help in her hour of need, unable to speak, merely grasped his hand.

Kennedy, who in the meantime had stood apart from the rest of us, was examining the telephone carefully.

"A clever crook," I heard him mutter between his teeth. "He must have worn gloves. Not a finger print—at least here."

* * * * *

Perhaps I can do no better than to reconstruct the crime as Kennedy later pieced these startling events together.

Long after I had left and even after Bennett left, Dodge continued working in his library, for he was known as a prodigious worker.

Had he taken the trouble, however, to pause and peer out into the moonlight that flooded the back of his house, he might have seen the figures of two stealthy crooks crouching in the half shadows of one of the cellar windows.

One crook was masked by a handkerchief drawn tightly about his lower face, leaving only his eyes visible beneath the cap with visor pulled down over his forehead. He had a peculiar stoop of the shoulders and wore his coat collar turned up. One hand, the right, seemed almost deformed. It

Arthur B. Reeve

was that which gave him his name in the underworld—the Clutching Hand.

The masked crook held carefully the ends of two wires attached to an electric feed, and sending his pal to keep watch outside, he entered the cellar of the Dodge house through a window whose pane they had carefully removed. As he came through the window he dragged the wires with him, and, alter a moment's reconnoitering attached them to the furnace pipe of the old-fashioned hot-air heater where the pipe ran up through the floor to the library above. The other wire was quickly attached to the telephone where its wires entered.

Upstairs, Dodge, evidently uneasy in his mind about the precious "Limpy Red" letter, took it from the safe along with most of the other correspondence and, pressing a hidden spring in the wall, opened a secret panel, placed most of the important documents in this hiding place. Then he put some blank sheets of paper in an envelope and returned it to the safe.

Downstairs the masked master criminal had already attached a voltmeter to the wires he had installed, waiting.

Just then could be heard the tinkle of Dodge's telephone and the old man rose to answer it. As he did so he placed his foot on the iron register, his hand taking the telephone and the receiver. At that instant came a powerful electric flash. Dodge sank on the floor grasping the instrument, electrocuted. Below, the master criminal could scarcely refrain from exclaiming with satisfaction as his voltmeter registered the powerful current that was passing.

A moment later the criminal slid silently into Dodge's room. Carefully putting on rubber gloves and avoiding touching the register, he wrenched the telephone from the grasp of the dead man, replacing it in its normal position. Only for a second did he pause to look at his victim as he destroyed the evidence of his work.

Minutes were precious. First Dodge's pockets, then his desk engaged his attention. There was left the safe.

As he approached the strong box, the master criminal took two vials from his pockets. Removing a bust of Shakespeare that stood on the safe, he poured the contents of the vials in two mixed masses of powder forming a heap on the safe, into which he inserted two magnesium wires.

He lighted them, sprang back, hiding his eyes from the light, and a blinding gush of flame, lasting perhaps ten seconds, poured out from the top of the safe.

It was not an explosion, but just a dazzling, intense flame that sizzled and crackled. It seemed impossible, but the glowing mass was literally sinking, sinking down into the cold steel. At last it burned through—as if the safe had been of tinder!

Without waiting a moment longer than necessary, the masked criminal advanced again and actually put his hand down through the top of the safe, pulling out a bunch of papers. Quickly he thrust them all, with just a glance, into his pocket.

Still working quickly, he took the bust of the great dramatist which he had removed and placed it under the light. Next from his pocket he drew two curious stencils, as it were, which he had apparently carefully prepared. With his hands, still carefully gloved, he rubbed the stencils on his hair, as if to cover them with a film of natural oils. Then he

Arthur B. Reeve

deliberately pressed them over the statue in several places. It was a peculiar action and he seemed to fairly gloat over it when it was done, and the bust returned to its place, covering the hole.

As noiselessly as he had come, he made his exit after one last malignant look at Dodge. It was now but the work of a moment to remove the wires he had placed, and climb out of the window, taking them and destroying the evidence down in the cellar.

A low whistle from the masked crook, now again in the shadow, brought his pal stealthily to his side.

"It's all right," he whispered hoarsely to the man. "Now, you attend to Limpy Red."

The villainous looking pal nodded and without another word the two made their getaway, safely, in opposite directions.

* * * * *

When Limpy Red, still trembling, left the office of Dodge earlier in the evening, he had repaired as fast as his shambling feet would take him to his favorite dive upon Park Row. There he might have been seen drinking with any one who came along, for Limpy had money—blood money,—and the recollection of his treachery and revenge must both be forgotten and celebrated.

Had the Bowery "sinkers" not got into his eyes, he might have noticed among the late revellers, a man who spoke to no one but took his place nearby at the bar.

Limpy had long since reached the point of saturation and, lurching forth from his new found cronies, he sought other fields of excitement. Likewise did the newcomer, who bore a strange resemblance to the look-out who had been stationed outside at the Dodge house a scant half hour before.

What happened later was only a matter of seconds. It came when the hated snitch—for gangdom hates the informer worse than anything else dead or alive—had turned a sufficiently dark and deserted corner.

A muffled thud, a stifled groan followed as a heavy section of lead pipe wrapped in a newspaper descended on the crass skull of Limpy. The wielder of the improvised but fatal weapon permitted himself the luxury of an instant's cruel smile—then vanished into the darkness leaving another complete job for the coroner and the morgue.

It was the vengeance of the Clutching Hand—swift, sure, remorseless.

And yet it had not been a night of complete success for the master criminal, as anyone might have seen who could have followed his sinuous route to a place of greater safety.

Unable to wait longer he pulled the papers he had taken from the safe from his pocket. His chagrin at finding them to be blank paper found only one expression of foiled fury—that menacing clutching hand!

* * * * *

Kennedy had turned from his futile examination for marks on the telephone. There stood the safe, a moderate sized strong box but of a modern type. He tried the door. It was locked. There was not a mark on it. The combination had not been tampered with. Nor had there been any attempt to "soup" the safe.

Arthur B. Reeve

With a quick motion he felt in his pocket as if looking for gloves. Finding none, he glanced about, and seized a pair of tongs from beside the grate. With them, in order not to confuse any possible finger prints on the bust, he lifted it off. I gave a gasp of surprise.

There, in the top of the safe, yawned a gaping hole through which one could have thrust his arm!

"What is it?" we asked, crowding about him.

"Thermit," he replied laconically.

"Thermit?" I repeated.

"Yes—a compound of iron oxide and powdered aluminum invented by a chemist at Essen, Germany. It gives a temperature of over five thousand degrees. It will eat its way through the strongest steel."

Jennings, his mouth wide open with wonder, advanced to take the bust from Kennedy.

"No—don't touch it," he waved him off, laying the bust on the desk. "I want no one to touch it—don't you see how careful I was to use the tongs that there might be no question about any clue this fellow may have left on the marble?"

As he spoke, Craig was dusting over the surface of the bust with some black powder.

"Look!" exclaimed Craig suddenly.

We bent over. The black powder had in fact brought out strongly some peculiar, more or less regular, black smudges.

"Finger prints!" I cried excitedly.

"Yes," nodded Kennedy, studying them closely. "A clue—perhaps."

"What—those little marks—a clue?" asked a voice behind us.

I turned and saw Elaine, looking over our shoulders, fascinated. It was evidently the first time she had realized that Kennedy was in the room.

"How can you tell anything by that?'" she asked.

"Why, easily," he answered picking up a brass blotting-pad which lay on the desk. "You see, I place my finger on this weight—so. I dust the powder over the mark—so. You could see it even without the powder on this glass. Do you see those lines? There are various types of markings—four general types—and each person's markings are different, even if of the same general type—loop, whorl, arch, or composite."

He continued working as he talked.

"Your thumb marks, for example, Miss Dodge, are different from mine. Mr. Jameson's are different from both of us. And this fellow's finger prints are still different. It is mathematically impossible to find two alike in every respect."

Kennedy was holding the brass blotter near the bust as he talked.

I shall never forget the look of blank amazement on his face as he bent over closer.

"My God!" he exclaimed excitedly, "this fellow is a master

criminal! He has actually made stencils or something of the sort on which by some mechanical process he has actually forged the hitherto infallible finger prints!"

I, too, bent over and studied the marks on the bust and those Kennedy had made on the blotter to show Elaine.

THE FINGER PRINTS ON THE BUST WERE KENNEDY'S OWN.

CHAPTER II

THE TWILIGHT SLEEP

Kennedy had thrown himself wholeheartedly into the solution of the mysterious Dodge case.

Far into the night, after the challenge of the forged finger print, he continued at work, endeavoring to extract a clue from the meagre evidence—the bit of cloth and trace of poison already obtained from other cases, and now added the strange succession of events that surrounded the tragedy we had just witnessed.

We dropped around at the Dodge house the next morning. Early though it was, we found Elaine, a trifle paler but more lovely than ever, and Perry Bennett themselves vainly endeavoring to solve the mystery of the Clutching Hand.

They were at Dodge's desk, she in the big desk chair, he standing beside her, looking over some papers.

"There's nothing there," Bennett was saying as we entered.

I could not help feeling that he was gazing down at Elaine a bit more tenderly than mere business warranted.

"Have you—found anything?" queried Elaine anxiously, turning eagerly to Kennedy.

"Nothing—yet," he answered shaking his head, but conveying a quiet idea of confidence in his tone.

Just then Jennings, the butler, entered, bringing the morning papers. Elaine seized the Star and hastily opened it. On the first page was the story I had telephone down very late in the hope of catching a last city edition.

We all bent over and Craig read aloud:

"CLUTCHING HAND" STILL AT LARGE

NEW YORK'S MASTER CRIMINAL REMAINS UNDETECTED—PERPETRATES NEW DARING MURDER AND ROBBERY OF MILLIONAIRE DODGE

He had scarcely finished reading the brief but alarming news story that followed and laid the paper on the desk, when a stone came smashing through the window from the street.

Startled, we all jumped to our feet. Craig hurried to the window. Not a soul was in sight!

He stooped and picked up the stone. To it was attached a piece of paper. Quickly he unfolded it and read:

"Craig Kennedy will give up his search for the "Clutching Hand"— or die!"

Later I recalled that there seemed to be a slight noise down-stairs, as if at the cellar window through which the masked man had entered the night before.

In point of fact, one who had been outside at the time might actually have seen a sinister face at that cellar window, but to us upstairs it was invisible. The face was that of the servant, Michael.

Without another word Kennedy passed into the drawing room and took his hat and coat. Both Elaine and Bennett followed.

"I'm afraid I must ask you to excuse me—for the present," Craig apologized.

Elaine looked at him anxiously.

"You—you will not let that letter intimidate you?" she pleaded, laying her soft white hand on his arm. "Oh, Mr. Kennedy," she added, bravely keeping back the tears, "avenge him! All the money in the world would be too little to pay—if only—"

At the mere mention of money Kennedy's face seemed to cloud, but only for a moment. He must have felt the confiding pressure of her hand, for as she paused, appealingly, he took her hand in his, bowing slightly over it to look closer into her upturned face.

"I'll try," he said simply.

Elaine did not withdraw her hand as she continued to look up at him. Craig looked at her, as I had never seen him look at a woman before in all our long acquaintance.

"Miss Dodge," he went on, his voice steady as though he were repressing something, "I will never take another case until the 'Clutching Hand' is captured."

The look of gratitude she gave him would have been a princely reward in itself.

I did not marvel that all the rest of that day and far into the night Kennedy was at work furiously in his laboratory, studying the notes, the texture of the paper, the character of the ink, everything that might perhaps suggest a new lead. It was all, apparently, however, without result.

* * * * *

It was some time after these events that Kennedy, reconstructing what had happened, ran across, in a strange way which I need not tire the reader by telling, a Dr. Haynes, head of the Hillside Sanitarium for Women, whose story I shall relate substantially as we received it from his own lips:

It must have been that same night that a distinguished visitor drove up in a cab to our Hillside Sanitarium, rang the bell and was admitted to my office. I might describe him as a moderately tall, well-built man with a pleasing way about him. Chiefly noticeable, it seems to me, were his mustache and bushy beard, quite medical and foreign.

I am, by the way, the superintending physician, and that night I was sitting with Dr. Thompson, my assistant, in the office discussing a rather interesting case, when an attendant came in with a card and handed it to me. It read simply, "Dr. Ludwig Reinstrom, Coblenz."

"Here's that Dr. Reinstrom, Thompson, about whom my friend in Germany wrote the other day," I remarked, nodding to the attendant to admit Dr. Reinstrom.

I might explain that while I was abroad some time ago, I made a particular study of the "Daemmerschlaf"—otherwise, the "twilight sleep," at Freiburg where it was developed and at other places in Germany where the subject had attracted great attention. I was much impressed and had imported the treatment to Hillside.

While we waited I reached into my desk and drew out the letter to which I referred, which ended, I recall:

"As Dr. Reinstrom is in America, he will probably call on you. I am sure you will be glad to know him.

"With kindest regards, I am,

"Fraternally yours,

"EMIL SCHWARZ, M. D.,

"Director, Leipsic Institute of Medicine."

"Most happy to meet you, Dr. Reinstrom," I greeted the new arrival, as he entered our office.

For several minutes we sat and chatted of things medical here and abroad.

"What is it, Doctor," I asked finally, "that interests you most in America?"

"Oh," he replied quickly with an expressive gesture, "it is the broadmindedness with which you adopt the best from all over the world, regardless of prejudice. For instance, I am very much interested in the new twilight sleep. Of course you have borrowed it largely from us, but it interests me to see whether you have modified it with practice. In fact I have come to the Hillside Sanitarium particularly to see it used. Perhaps we may learn something from you."

Arthur B. Reeve

It was most gracious and both Dr. Thompson and myself were charmed by our visitor. I reached over and touched a call-button and our head nurse entered from a rear room.

"Are there any operations going on now?" I asked.

She looked mechanically at her watch. "Yes, there are two cases, now, I think," she answered.

"Would you like to follow our technique, Doctor?" I asked, turning to Dr. Reinstorm.

"I should be delighted," he acquiesced.

A moment later we passed down the corridor of the Sanitarium, still chatting. At the door of a ward I spoke to the attendant who indicated that a patient was about to be anesthetized, and Reinstrom and I entered the room.

There, in perfect quiet, which is an essential part of the treatment, were several women patients lying in bed in the ward. Before us two nurses and a doctor were in attendance on one.

I spoke to the Doctor, Dr. Holmes, by the way, who bowed politely to the distinguished Dr. Reinstrom, then turned quickly to his work.

"Miss Sears," he asked of one of the nurses, "will you bring me that hypodermic needle? How are you getting on, Miss Stern?" to the other who was scrubbing the patient's arm with antiseptic soap and water, thoroughly sterilizing the skin.

"You will see, Dr. Reinstrom." I interposed in a low tone, "that we follow in the main your Freiburg treatment. We use scopolamin and narkophin."

I held up the bottle, as I said it, a rather peculiar shaped bottle, too.

"And the pain?" he asked.

"Practically the same as in your experience abroad. We do not render the patient unconscious, but prevent her from remembering anything that goes on."

Dr. Holmes, the attending physician, was just starting the treatment. Filling his hypodermic, he selected a spot on the patient's arm, where it had been scrubbed and sterilized, and injected the narcotic.

"How simply you do it all, here!" exclaimed Reinstrom in surprise and undisguised admiration. "You Americans are wonderful!"

"Come—see a patient who is just recovering," I added, much flattered by the praise, which, from a German physician, meant much.

Reinstrom followed me out of the door and we entered a private room of the hospital where another woman patient lay in bed carefully watched by a nurse.

"How do you do?" I nodded to the nurse in a modulated tone. "Everything progressing favorably?"

"Perfectly," she returned, as Reinstrom, Haynes and myself formed a little group about the bedside of the unconscious woman.

"And you say they have no recollection of anything that happens?" asked Reinstrom.

"Absolutely none—if the treatment is given properly," I replied confidently.

I picked up a piece of bandage which was the handiest thing about me and tied it quite tightly about the patient's arm.

As we waited, the patient, who was gradually coming from under the drug, roused herself.

"What is that—it hurts!" she said putting her hand on the bandage I had tied tightly.

"That is all right. Just a moment. I'll take it off. Don't you remember it?" I asked.

She shook her head. I smiled at Reinstrom.

"You see, she has no recollection of my tying the bandage on her arm," I pointed out.

"Wonderful!" ejaculated Reinstrom as we left the room.

All the way back to the office he was loud in his praises and thanked us most heartily, as he put on his hat and coat and shook hands a cordial good-bye.

Now comes the strange part of my story. After Reinstrom had gone, Dr. Holmes, the attending physician of the woman whom we had seen anesthetized, missed his syringe and the bottle of scopolamine.

"Miss Sears," he asked rather testily, "what have you done with the hypodermic and the scopolamine?"

"Nothing," she protested.

"You must have done something."

She repeated that she had not.

"Well, it is very strange then," he said, "I am positive I laid the syringe and the bottle right here on this tray on the table."

Holmes, Miss Sears and Miss Stern all hunted, but it could not be found. Others had to be procured.

I thought little of it at the time, but since then it has occurred to me that it might interest you, Professor Kennedy, and I give it to you for what it may be worth.

It was early the next morning that I awoke to find Kennedy already up and gone from our apartment. I knew he must be at the laboratory, and, gathering the mail, which the postman had just slipped through the letter slot, I went over to the University to see him. As I looked over the letters to cull out my own, one in a woman's handwriting on attractive notepaper addressed to him caught my eye.

As I came up the path to the Chemistry Building I saw through the window that, in spite of his getting there early, he was finding it difficult to keep his mind on his work. It was the first time I had ever known anything to interfere with science in his life.

I thought of the letter again.

Craig had lighted a Bunsen burner under a large glass retort. But he had no sooner done so than he sat down on a chair and, picking up a book which I surmised might be some work on toxicology, started to read.

He seemed not to be able, for the moment, to concentrate his mind and after a little while closed the book and gazed straight ahead of him. Again I thought of the letter, and the vision that, no doubt, he saw of Elaine making her pathetic appeal for his help.

As he heard my footstep in the hall, it must have recalled him for he snapped the book shut and moved over quickly to the retort.

"Well," I exclaimed as I entered, "you are the early bird. Did you have any breakfast?"

I tossed down the letters. He did not reply. So I became absorbed in the morning paper. Still, I did not neglect to watch him covertly out of the corner of my eye. Quickly he ran over the letters, instead of taking them, one by one, in his usual methodical way. I quite complimented my own superior acumen. He selected the dainty note.

A moment Craig looked at it in anticipation, then tore it open eagerly. I was still watching his face over the top of the paper and was surprised to see that it showed, first, amazement, then pain, as though something had hurt him.

He read it again—then looked straight ahead, as if in a daze.

"Strange, how much crime there is now," I commented, looking up from the paper I had pretended reading.

No answer.

"One would think that one master criminal was enough," I went on.

Still no answer.

He continued to gaze straight ahead at blankness.

"By George," I exclaimed finally, banging my fist on the table and raising my voice to catch his attention, "you would think we had nothing but criminals nowadays."

My voice must have startled him. The usually imperturbable old fellow actually jumped. Then, as my question did not evidently accord with what was in his mind, he answered at random, "Perhaps- -I wonder if—" and then he stopped, noncommittally.

Suddenly he jumped up, bringing his tightly clenched fist down with a loud clap into the palm of his hand.

"By heaven!" he exclaimed, "I—I will!"

Startled at his incomprehensible and unusual conduct I did not attempt to pursue the conversation but let him alone as he strode hastily to the telephone. Almost angrily he seized the receiver and asked for a number. It was not like Craig and I could not conceal my concern.

"Wh-what's the matter, Craig?" I blurted out eagerly.

As he waited for the number, he threw the letter over to me. I took it and read:

"Professor Craig Kennedy, "The University, The Heights, City.

"Dear Sir,—

"I have come to the conclusion that your work is a hindrance rather than an assistance in clearing up my father's death and I hereby beg to state that your services are no longer required. This is a final decision and I beg that you will not try to see me again regarding the matter.

"Very truly yours, ELAINE DODGE."

If it had been a bomb I could not have been more surprised. A moment before I think I had just a sneaking suspicion of jealousy that a woman—even Elaine—should interest my old chums. But now all that was swept away. How could any woman scorn him?

I could not make it out.

Kennedy impatiently worked the receiver up and down, repeating the number. "Hello—hello," he repeated, "Yes— hello. Is Miss—oh— good morning, Miss Dodge."

He was hurrying along as if to give her no chance to cut him off. "I have just received a letter, Miss Dodge, telling me that you don't want me to continue investigating your father's death, and not to try to see you again about—"

He stopped. I could hear the reply, as sometimes one can when the telephone wire conditions are a certain way and the quality of the voice of the speaker a certain kind.

"Why—no—Mr. Kennedy, I have written you no letter."

The look of mingled relief and surprise that crossed Craig's face spoke volumes.

"Miss Dodge," he almost shouted, "this is a new trick of the Clutching Hand. I—I'll be right over."

Craig hung up the receiver and turned from the telephone. Evidently he was thinking deeply. Suddenly his face seemed to light up. He made up his mind to something and a moment later he opened the cabinet—that inexhaustible storehouse from which he seemed to draw weird and curious instruments that met the ever new problems which his strange profession brought to him.

I watched curiously. He took out a bottle and what looked like a little hypodermic syringe, thrust them into his pocket and, for once, oblivious to my very existence, deliberately walked out of the laboratory.

I did not propose to be thus cavalierly dismissed. I suppose it would have looked ridiculous to a third party but I followed him as hastily as if he had tried to shut the door on his own shadow.

We arrived at the corner above the Dodge house just in time to see another visitor—Bennett—enter. Craig quickened his pace. Jennings had by this time become quite reconciled to our presence and a moment later we were entering the drawing room, too.

Elaine was there, looking lovelier than ever in the plain black dress, which set off the rosy freshness of her face.

"And, Perry," we heard her say, as we were ushered in, "someone has even forged my name—the handwriting and everything—telling Mr. Kennedy to drop the case—and I never knew."

She stopped as we entered. We bowed and shook hands with Bennett. Elaine's Aunt Josephine was in the room, a perfect duenna.

"That's the limit!" exclaimed Bennett. "Miss Dodge has just been telling me,—"

"Yes," interrupted Craig. "Look, Miss Dodge, this is it."

He handed her the letter. She almost seized it, examining it carefully, her large eyes opening wider in wonder.

"This is certainly my writing and my notepaper," she murmured, "but I never wrote the letter!"

Craig looked from the letter to her keenly. No one said a word. For a moment Kennedy hesitated, thinking.

"Might I—er—see your room, Miss Dodge?" he asked at length.

Aunt Josephine frowned. Bennett and I could not conceal our surprise.

"Why, certainly," nodded Elaine, as she led the way upstairs.

It was a dainty little room, breathing the spirit of its mistress. In fact it seemed a sort of profanation as we all followed in after her. For a moment Kennedy stood still, then he carefully looked about. At the side of the bed, near the head, he stooped and picked up something which he held in the palm of his hand. I bent over. Something gleamed in the morning sunshine—some little thin pieces of glass. As he tried deftly to fit the tiny little bits together, he seemed absorbed in thought. Quickly he raised it to his nose, as if to smell it.

"Ethyl chloride!" he muttered, wrapping the pieces carefully in a paper and putting them into his pocket.

An instant later he crossed the room to the window and examined it.

"Look!" he exclaimed.

There, plainly, were marks of a jimmy which had been inserted near the lock to pry it open.

"Miss Dodge," he asked, "might I—might I trouble you to let me see your arm?"

Wonderingly she did so and Kennedy bent almost reverently over her plump arm examining it.

On it was a small dark discoloration, around which was a slight redness and tenderness.

"That," he said slowly, "is the mark of a hypodermic needle."

As he finished examining Elaine's arm he drew the letter from his pocket. Still facing her he said in a low tone, "Miss Dodge—you did write this letter—but under the influence of the new 'twilight sleep.'"

We looked at one another amazed.

Outside, if we had been at the door in the hallway, we might have seen the sinister-faced Michael listening. He turned and slipped quietly away.

"Why, Craig," I exclaimed excitedly, "what do you mean?"

"Exactly what I say. With Miss Dodge's permission I shall show you. By a small administration of the drug which will injure you in no way, Miss Dodge, I think I can bring back the memory of all that occurred to you last night. Will you allow me?"

"Mercy, no!" protested Aunt Josephine.

Craig and Elaine faced each other as they had the day before when she had asked him whether the sudden warning of the Clutching Hand would intimidate him. She advanced a step nearer. Elaine trusted him.

"Elaine!" protested Aunt Josephine again.

"I want the experiment to be tried," she said quietly.

A moment later Kennedy had placed her in a wing chair in the corner of the room.

"Now, Mrs. Dodge," he said, "please bring me a basin and a towel."

Aunt Josephine, reconciled, brought them. Kennedy dropped an antiseptic tablet into the water and carefully sterilized Elaine's arm just above the spot where the red mark showed. Then he drew the hypodermic from his pocket—carefully sterilizing it, also, and filling it with scopolamine from the bottle.

"Just a moment, Miss Dodge," he encouraged as he jabbed the needle into her arm.

She did not wince.

"Please lie back on the couch," he directed. Then turning to us he added, "It takes some time for this to work. Our criminal got over that fact and prevented an outcry by using ethyl chloride first. Let me reconstruct the scene."

As we watched Elaine going under slowly, Craig talked.

"That night," he said, "warily, the masked criminal of the Clutching Hand might have been seen down below us in the alley. Up here, Miss Dodge, worn out by the strain of her father's death, let us say, was nervously trying to read, to do anything that would take her mind off the tragedy. Perhaps she fell asleep.

"Just then the Clutching Hand appeared. He came stealthily through that window which he had opened. A moment he hesitated, seeing Elaine asleep. Then he tiptoed over to the bed, let us say, and for a moment looked at her, sleeping.

"A second later he had thrust his hand into his pocket and had taken out a small glass bulb with a long thin neck. That was ethyl chloride, a drug which produces a quick anesthesia. But it lasts only a minute or two. That was enough, As he broke the glass neck of the bulb—letting the pieces fall on the floor near the bed—he shoved the thing under Elaine's face, turning his own head away and holding a handkerchief over his own nose. The mere heat of his hand was enough to cause the ethyl chloride to spray out and overcome her instantly. He stepped away from her a moment and replaced the now empty vial in his pocket.

"Then he took a box from his pocket, opened it. There must have been a syringe and a bottle of scopolamine. Where they came from I do not know, but perhaps from some hospital. I shall have to find that out later. He went to Elaine, quickly jabbing the needle, with no resistance from her now. Slowly he replaced the bottle and the needle in his pocket. He could not have been in any hurry now, for it takes time for the drug to work."

Kennedy paused. Had we known at the time, Michael—he of the sinister face—must have been in the hallway, careful that no one saw him. A tap at the door and the Clutching Hand, that night, must have beckoned him. A moment's parley and they separated— Clutching Hand going back to Elaine, who was now under the influence of the second drug.

"Our criminal," resumed Kennedy thoughtfully, "may have shaken Elaine. She did not answer. Then he may have partly revived her. She must have been startled. Clutching Hand, perhaps, was half crouching, with a big ugly blue steel revolver leveled full in her face.

"'One word and I shoot!' he probably cried. "Get up!'

"Trembling, she must have done so. 'Your slippers and a kimono,' he would naturally have ordered. She put them on mechanically. Then he must have ordered her to go out of the door and down the stairs. Clutching Hand must have followed and as he did so he would have cautiously put out the lights."

We were following, spell-bound, Kennedy's graphic reconstruction of what must have happened. Evidently he had struck close to the truth. Elaine's eyes were closed. Gently Kennedy led her along. "Now, Miss Dodge," he encouraged, "try—try hard to recollect just what it was that happened last night—everything."

As Kennedy paused after his quick recital, she seemed to tremble all over. Slowly she began to speak. We stood awestruck. Kennedy had been right!

The girl was now living over again those minutes that had been forgotten—blotted out by the drug.

And it was all real to her, too,—terribly real. She was speaking, plainly in terror.

"I see a man—oh, such a figure—with a mask. He holds a gun in my face—he threatens me. I put on my kimono and slippers, as he tells me. I am in a daze. I know what I am doing—and I don't know. I go out with him, downstairs, into the library."

Elaine shuddered again at the recollection. "Ugh! The room is dark, the room where he killed my father. Moonlight outside streams in. This masked man and I come in. He switches on the lights.

"'Go to the safe,' he says, and I do it, the new safe, you know. 'Do you know the combination?' he asks me. 'Yes,' I reply, too frightened to say no."

"'Open it then,' he says, waving that awful revolver closer. I do so. Hastily he rummages through it, throwing papers here and there. But he seems not to find what he is after and turns away, swearing fearfully."

"'Hang it!' he cries to me. 'Where else did your father keep papers?' I point in desperation at the desk. He takes one last look at the safe, shoves all the papers he has strewn on the floor back again and slams the safe shut."

"'Now, come on!' he says, indicating with the gun that he wants me to follow him away from the safe. At the desk he repeats the search. But he finds nothing. Almost I think he is about to kill me. 'Where else did your father keep papers?' he hisses fiercely, still threatening me with the gun."

"I am too frightened to speak. But at last I am able to say, 'I—I don't know!' Again he threatens me. 'As God is my judge,' I cry, 'I don't know.' It is fearful. Will he shoot me?"

"Thank heaven! At last he believes me. But such a look of foiled fury I have never seen on any human face before."

Arthur B. Reeve

"'Sit down!' he growls, adding, 'at the desk.' I do."

"'Take some of your notepaper—the best.' I do that, too."

"'And a pen,' he goes on. My fingers can hardly hold it."

"'Now—write!' he says, and as he dictates, I write—"

"This?" interjected Kennedy, eagerly holding up the letter that he had received from her.

Elaine looked it over with her drug-laden eyes. "Yes," she nodded, then lapsed again to the scene itself. "He reads it over and as he does so says, 'Now, address an envelope.' Himself he folds the letter, seals the envelope, stamps it, and drops it into his pocket, hastily straightening the desk.

"'Now, go ahead of me—again. Leave the room—no, by the hall door. We are going back upstairs.' I obey him, and at the door he switches off the lights. How I stand it, I don't know. I go upstairs, mechanically, into my own room—I and this masked man."

"'Take off the kimono and slippers!' he orders. I do that. 'Get into bed!' he growls. I crawl in fearfully. For a moment he looks about,—then goes out—with a look back as he goes. Oh! Oh! That hand—which he raises at me—THAT HAND!"

The poor girl was sitting bolt upright, staring straight at the hall door, as we watched and listened, fascinated.

Kennedy was bending over, soothing her. She gave evidences of coming out from the effect of the drug.

I noticed that Bennett had suddenly moved a step in the

direction of the door at which she stared.

"My God!" he muttered, staring, too. "Look!"

We did look. A letter was slowly being inserted under the door.

I took a quick step forward. That moment I felt a rough tug at my arm, and a voice whispered, "Wait—you chump!"

It was Kennedy. He had whipped out his automatic and had carefully leveled it at the door. Before he could fire, however, Bennett had rushed ahead.

I followed. We looked down the hall. Sure enough, the figure of a man could be seen disappearing around an angle. I followed Bennett out of the door and down the hall.

Words cannot keep pace with what followed. Together we rushed to the backstairs.

"Down there, while I go down the front!" cried Bennett.

I went down and he turned and went down the other flight. As he did so, Craig followed him.

Suddenly, in the drawing room, I bumped into a figure on the other side of the portieres. I seized him. We struggled. Rip! The portieres came down, covering me entirely. Over and over we went, smashing a lamp. It was vicious. Another man attacked me, too.

"I—I've got him—Kennedy!" I heard a voice pant over me.

A scream followed from Aunt Josephine. Suddenly the portieres were pulled off me.

"The deuce!" puffed Kennedy. "It's Jameson!"

Bennett had rushed plump into me, coming the other way, hidden by the portieres.

If we had known at the time, our Michael of the sinister face had gained the library and was standing in the center of the room. He had heard me coming and had fled to the drawing room. As we finished our struggle in the library, he rose hastily from behind the divan in the other room where he had dropped and had quietly and hastily disappeared through another door.

Laughing and breathing hard, they helped me to my feet. It was no joke to me. I was sore in every bone.

"Well, where DID he go?" insisted Bennett.

"I don't know—perhaps back there," I cried.

Bennett and I argued a moment, then started and stopped short. Aunt Josephine had run downstairs and now was shoving the letter into Craig's hands.

We gathered about him, curiously. He opened it. On it was that awesome Clutching Hand again.

Kennedy read it. For a moment he stood and studied it, then slowly crushed it in his hand.

Just then Elaine, pale and shaken from the ordeal she had voluntarily gone through, burst in upon us from upstairs. Without a word she advanced to Craig and took the letter from him.

Inside, as on the envelope, was that same signature of the

Clutching Hand.

Elaine gazed at it wild-eyed, then at Craig. Craig smilingly reached for the note, took it, folded it and unconcernedly thrust it into his pocket.

"My God!" she cried, clasping her hands convulsively and repeating the words of the letter. "YOUR LAST WARNING!"

Arthur B. Reeve

CHAPTER III

THE VANISHING JEWELS

Banging away at my typewriter, the next day, in Kennedy's laboratory, I was startled by the sudden, insistent ringing of the telephone near me.

"Hello," I answered, for Craig was at work at his table, trying still to extract some clue from the slender evidence thus far elicited in the Dodge mystery.

"Oh, Mr. Kennedy," I heard an excited voice over the wire reply, "my friend, Susie Martin is here. Her father has just received a message from that Clutching Hand and—"

"Just a moment, Miss Dodge," I interrupted. "This is Mr. Jameson."

"Oh!" came back the voice, breathless and disappointed. "Let me have Mr. Kennedy—quick."

I had already passed the telephone to Craig and was watching him keenly as he listened over it. The anticipation of a message from Elaine did not fade, yet his face grew grave as he listened.

He motioned to me for a pad and pencil that lay near me.

"Please read the letter again, slower, Miss Dodge," he asked, adding, "There isn't time for me to see it—just yet. But I want it exactly. You say it is made up of separate words and type cut from newspapers and pasted on note paper?"

I handed him paper and pencil.

"All right now, Miss Dodge, go ahead."

As he wrote, he indicated to me by his eyes that he wanted me to read. I did so:

"Sturtevant Martin, Jeweler, "739 1/2 Fifth Ave., "New York City.

"SIR:

"As you have failed to deliver the $10,000, I shall rob your main diamond case at exactly noon today."

"Thank you, Miss Dodge," continued Kennedy, laying down the pencil. "Yes, I understand perfectly—signed by that same Clutching Hand. Let me see," he pondered, looking at his watch. "It is now just about half past eleven. Very well. I shall meet you and Miss Martin at Mr. Martin's store directly."

It lacked five minutes of noon when Kennedy and I dashed up before Martin's and dismissed our taxi-cab.

A remarkable scene greeted us as we entered the famous jewelry shop. Involuntarily I drew back. Squarely in front of us a man had suddenly raised a revolver and leveled it at us.

"Don't!" cried a familiar voice. "That is Mr. Kennedy!"

Just then, from a little knot of people, Elaine Dodge sprang forward with a cry and seized the gun.

Kennedy turned to her, apparently not half so much concerned about the automatic that yawned at him as about the anxiety of the pretty girl who had intervened. The too eager plainclothesman lowered the gun sheepishly.

Sturtevant Martin was a typical society business man, quietly but richly dressed. He was inclined to be pompous and affected a pair of rather distinguished looking side whiskers.

In the excitement I glanced about hurriedly. There were two or three policemen in the shop and several plainclothesmen, some armed with formidable looking sawed-off shot guns.

Directly in front of me was a sign, tacked up on a pillar, which read, "This store will be closed at noon today. Martin & Co."

All the customers were gone. In fact the clerks had had some trouble in clearing the shop, as many of them expressed not only surprise but exasperation at the proceeding. Nevertheless the clerks had politely but insistently ushered them out.

Martin himself was evidently very nervous and very much alarmed. Indeed no one could blame him for that. Merely to have been singled out by this amazing master criminal was enough to cause panic. Already he had engaged detectives, prepared for whatever might happen, and they had advised him to leave the diamonds in the counter, clear the store, and let the crooks try anything, if they dared.

I fancied that he was somewhat exasperated at his daughter's presence, too, but could see that her explanation of Elaine's and Perry Bennett's interest in the Clutching Hand had considerably mollified him. He had been talking with Bennett as we came in and evidently had a high respect for the young lawyer.

Just back of us, and around the corner, as we came in, we had noticed a limousine which had driven up. Three faultlessly attired dandies had entered a doorway down the street, as we learned afterwards, apparently going to a fashionable tailor's which occupied the second floor of the old-fashioned building, the first floor having been renovated and made ready for renting. Had we been there a moment sooner we might have seen, I suppose, that one of them nodded to a taxicab driver who was standing at a public hack stand a few feet up the block. The driver nodded unostentatiously back to the men.

In spite of the excitement, Kennedy quietly examined the show case, which was, indeed, a veritable treasure store of brilliants. Then with a keen scrutinizing glance he looked over the police and detectives gathered around. There was nothing to do now but wait, as the detectives had advised.

I looked at a large antique grandfather's clock which was standing nearby. It now lacked scarcely a minute of twelve.

Slowly the hands of the clock came nearer together at noon.

We all gathered about the show case with its glittering hoard of wealth, forming a circle at a respectful distance.

Martin pointed nervously at the clock.

In deep-lunged tones the clock played the chords written, I

Arthur B. Reeve

believe, by Handel. Then it began striking.

As it did so, Martin involuntarily counted off the strokes, while one of the plainclothesmen waved his shotgun in unison.

Martin finished counting.

Nothing had happened.

We all breathed a sigh of relief.

"Well, it is still there!" exclaimed Martin, pointing at the show-case, with a forced laugh.

Suddenly came a rending and crashing sound. It seemed as if the very floor on which we stood was giving way.

The show-case, with all its priceless contents, went smashing down into the cellar below.

The flooring beneath the case had been cut through!

All crowded forward, gazing at the black yawning cavern. A moment we hesitated, then gingerly craned our necks over the edge.

Down below, three men, covered with linen dusters and their faces hidden by masks, had knocked the props away from the ceiling of the cellar, which they had sawed almost through at their leisure, and the show case had landed eight or ten feet below, shivered into a thousand bits.

A volley of shots whizzed past us, and another. While one crook was hastily stuffing the untold wealth of jewels into a burlap bag, the others had drawn revolvers and were firing up through the hole in the floor, desperately.

Martin, his detectives, and the rest of us fell back from the edge of the chasm hastily, to keep out of range of the hail of bullets.

"Look out!" cried someone behind us, before we could recover from our first surprise and return the fire.

One of the desperadoes had taken a bomb from under his duster, lighted it, and thrown it up through the hole in the floor.

It sailed up over our heads and landed near our little group on the floor, the fuse sputtering ominously.

Quickly we divided and backed away even further.

I heard an exclamation of fear from Elaine.

Kennedy had pushed his way past us and picked up the deadly infernal machine in his bare hands.

I watched him, fascinated. As near as he dared, he approached the hole in the floor, still holding the thing off at arm's length. Would he never throw it?

He was coolly holding it, allowing the fuse to burn down closer to the explosion point.

It was now within less than an inch sure death.

Suddenly he raised it and hurled the deadly thing down through the hole.

We could hear the imprecations of the crooks as it struck the

Arthur B. Reeve

cellar floor, near them. They had evidently been still cramming jewelry into the capacious maw of the bag. One of them, discovering the bomb, must have advanced toward it, then retreated when he saw how imminent was the explosion.

"Leave the store—quick!" rang out Kennedy's voice.

We backed away as fast as those behind us would permit. Kennedy and Bennett were the last to leave, in fact paused at the door.

Down below the crooks were beating a hasty retreat through a secret entrance which they had effected.

"The bag! The bag!" we could hear one of them bellow.

"The bomb—run!" cried another voice gruffly.

A second later came an ominous silence. The last of the three must have fled.

The explosion that followed lifted us fairly off our feet. A great puff of smoke came belching up through the hole, followed by the crashing of hundreds of dollars' worth of glass ware in the jewelry shop as fragments of stone, brick and mortar and huge splinters of wood were flung with tremendous force in every direction from the miniature volcano.

As the smoke from the explosion cleared away, Kennedy could be seen, the first to run forward.

Meanwhile Martin's detectives had rushed down a flight of back stairs that led into a coal cellar. With coal shovels and bars, anything they could lay hands on, they attacked the door that opened forward from the coal cellar into the front basement where the robbers had been.

A moment Kennedy and Bennett paused on the brink of the abyss which the bomb had made, waiting for the smoke to decrease. Then they began to climb down cautiously over the piled up wreckage.

The explosion had set the basement afire, but the fire had not gained much headway, by the time they reached the basement. Quickly Kennedy ran to the door into the coal cellar and opened it.

From the other side, Martin, followed by the police and the detectives, burst in.

"Fire!" cried one of the policemen, leaping back to turn in an alarm from the special apparatus upstairs.

All except Martin began beating out the flames, using such weapons as they already held in their hands to batter down the door.

To Martin there was one thing paramount—the jewels.

In the midst of the confusion, Elaine, closely followed by her friend Susie, made her way fearlessly into the stifle of smoke down the stairs.

"There are your jewels, Mr. Martin," cried Kennedy, kicking the precious burlap bag with his foot as if it had been so much ordinary merchandise, and turning toward what was in his mind the most important thing at stake—the direction taken by the agents of the Clutching Hand.

"Thank heaven!" ejaculated Martin, fairly pouncing on the

Arthur B. Reeve

bag and tearing it open. "They didn't get away with them—after all!" he exclaimed, examining the contents with satisfaction. "See—you must have frightened them off at just the right moment when you sent the bomb back at them."

Elaine and Susie pressed forward eagerly as he poured forth the sparkling stream of gems, intact.

"Wasn't he just simply wonderful!" I heard Susie whisper to Elaine.

Elaine did not answer. She had eyes or ears for nothing now in the melee but Kennedy.

* * * * *

Events were moving rapidly.

The limousine had been standing innocently enough at the curb near the corner, with the taxicab close behind it.

Less than ten minutes after they had entered, three well-dressed men came out of the vacant shop, apparently from the tailor's above, and climbed leisurely into their car.

As the last one entered, he half turned to the taxicab driver, hiding from passers-by the sign of the Clutching Hand which the taxicab driver returned, in the same manner. Then the big car whirled up the avenue.

All this we learned later from a street sweeper who was at work nearby.

Down below, while the police and detectives were putting out the fire, Kennedy was examining the wall of the cellar, looking for the spot where the crooks had escaped.

"A secret door!" he exclaimed, as he paused after tapping along the wall to determine its character. "You can see how the force of the explosion has loosened it."

Sure enough, when he pointed it out to us, it was plainly visible. One of the detectives picked up a crowbar and others, still with the hastily selected implements they had seized to fight the fire, started in to pry it open.

As it yielded, Kennedy pushed his way through. Elaine, always utterly fearless, followed. Then the rest of us went through.

There seemed to be nothing, however, that would help us in the cellar next door, and Kennedy mounted the steps of a stairway in the rear.

The stairway led to a sort of storeroom, full of barrels and boxes, but otherwise characterless. When I arrived Kennedy was gingerly holding up the dusters which the crooks had worn.

"We're on the right trail," commented Elaine as he showed them to her, "but where do you suppose the owners are?"

Craig shrugged his shoulders and gave a quick look about. "Evidently they came in from and went away by the street," he observed, hurrying to the door, followed by Elaine.

On the sidewalk, he gazed up the avenue, then catching sight of the street cleaner, called to him.

"Yes, sir," replied the man, stolidly looking up from his work. "I see three gentlemen come out and get into an auto-mobile."

"Which way did they go?" asked Kennedy.

For answer the man jerked his thumb over his shoulder in the general direction uptown.

"Did you notice the number of the car?" asked Craig eagerly.

The man shrugged his shoulders blankly.

With keen glance, Kennedy strained his eyes. Far up the avenue, he could descry the car threading its way in and out among the others, just about disappearing.

A moment later Craig caught sight of the vacant taxicab and crooked his finger at the driver, who answered promptly by cranking his engine.

"You saw that limousine standing there?" asked Craig.

"Yes," nodded the chauffeur with a show of alertness.

"Well, follow it," ordered Kennedy, jumping into the cab.

"Yes, sir."

Craig was just about to close the door when a slight figure flashed past us and a dainty foot was placed on the step.

"Please, Mr. Kennedy," pleaded Elaine, "let me go. They may lead to my father's slayer."

She said it so earnestly that Craig could scarcely have resisted if he had wanted to do so.

Just as Elaine and Kennedy were moving off, I came out of the vacant store, with Bennett and the detectives.

"Craig!" I called. "Where are you going?"

Kennedy stuck his head out of the window and I am quite sure that he was not altogether displeased that I was not with him.

"Chasing that limousine," he shouted back. "Follow us in another car."

A moment later he and Elaine were gone.

Bennett and I looked about.

"There are a couple of cabs—down there," I pointed out at the other end of the block. "I'll take one you take the other."

Followed by a couple of the detectives, I jumped into the first one I came to, excitedly telling the driver to follow Kennedy's taxi, directing him with my head out of the window.

"Mr. Jameson, please—can't I go with you?"

I turned. It was Susie Martin. "One of you fellows, go in the other car," I asked the detectives.

Before the man could move, Mr. Martin himself appeared.

"No, Susan, I—I won't allow it," he ordered.

"But Elaine went," she pouted.

"Well, Elaine is—ah—I won't have it," stormed Martin.

There was no time to waste. With a hasty apology, I drove off.

Arthur B. Reeve

Who, besides Bennett, went in the other car, I don't know, but it made no difference, for we soon lost them. Our driver, however, was a really clever fellow. Far ahead now we could see the limousine drive around a corner, making a dangerous swerve. Kennedy's cab followed, skidding dangerously near a pole.

But the taxicab was no match for the powerful limousine. On uptown they went, the only thing preventing the limousine from escaping being the fear of pursuit by traffic police if the driver let out speed. They were content to manage to keep just far enough ahead to be out of danger of having Kennedy overhaul them. As for us, we followed as best we could, on uptown, past the city line, and out into the country.

There Kennedy lost sight altogether of the car he was trailing. Worse than that, we lost sight of Kennedy. Still we kept on blindly, trusting to luck and common sense in picking the road.

I was peering ahead over the driver's shoulder, the window down, trying to direct him, when we approached a fork in the road. Here was a dilemma which must be decided at once rightly or wrongly.

As we neared the crossroad, I gave an involuntary exclamation. Beside the road, almost on it, lay the figure of a man. Our driver pulled up with a jerk and I was out of the car in an instant.

There lay Kennedy! Someone had blackjacked him. He was groaning and just beginning to show signs of consciousness as I bent over.

"What's the matter, old man?" I asked, helping him to his feet.

He looked about dazed a moment, then seeing me and comprehending, he pointed excitedly, but vaguely.

"Elaine!" he cried. "They've kidnapped Elaine!"

What had really happened, as we learned later from Elaine and others, was that when the cross roads was reached, the three crooks in the limousine had stopped long enough to speak to an accomplice stationed there, according to their plan for a getaway. He was a tough looking individual who might have been hoboing it to the city.

When, a few minutes later, Kennedy and Elaine had approached the fork, their driver had slowed up, as if in doubt which way to go. Craig had stuck his head out of the window, as I had done, and, seeing the crossroads, had told the chauffeur to stop. There stood the hobo.

"Did a car pass here, just now—a big car?" called Craig.

The man put his hand to his ear, as if only half comprehending.

"Which way did the big car go?" repeated Kennedy.

The hobo approached the taxicab sullenly, as if he had a grudge against cars in general.

One question after another elicited little that could be construed as intelligence. If Craig had only been able to see, he would have found out that, with his back toward the taxicab driver, the hobo held one hand behind him and made the sign of the Clutching Hand, glancing surreptitiously at the driver to catch the answering sign, while Craig gazed earnestly up the two roads.

Arthur B. Reeve

At last Craig gave him up as hopeless. "Well—go ahead—that way," he indicated, picking the most likely road.

As the chauffeur was about to start, he stalled his engine.

"Hurry!" urged Craig, exasperated at the delays.

The driver got out and tried to crank the engine. Again and again he turned it over, but, somehow, it refused to start. Then he lifted the hood and began to tinker.

"What's the matter?" asked Craig, impatiently jumping out and bending over the engine, too.

The driver shrugged his shoulders. "Must be something wrong with the ignition, I guess," he replied.

Kennedy looked the car over hastily. "I can't see anything wrong," he frowned.

"Well, there is," growled the driver.

Precious minutes were speeding away, as they argued. Finally with his characteristic energy, Kennedy put the taxi-cab driver aside.

"Let me try it," he said. "Miss Dodge, will you arrange that spark and throttle?"

Elaine, equal to anything, did so, and Craig bent down and cranked the engine. It started on the first spin.

"See!" he exclaimed. "There wasn't anything, after all."

He took a step toward the taxicab.

"Say," objected the driver, nastily, interposing himself between Craig and the wheel which he seemed disposed to take now, "who's running this boat, anyhow?"

Surprised, Kennedy tried to shoulder the fellow out of the way. The driver resisted sullenly.

"Mr. Kennedy—look out!" cried Elaine.

Craig turned. But it was too late. The rough looking fellow had wakened to life. Suddenly he stepped up behind Kennedy with a blackjack. As the heavy weight descended, Craig crumpled up on the ground, unconscious.

With a scream, Elaine turned and started to run. But the chauffeur seized her arm.

"Say, bo," he asked of the rough fellow, "what does Clutching Hand want with her? Quick! There's another cab likely to be along in a moment with that fellow Jameson in it."

The rough fellow, with an oath, seized her and dragged her into the taxicab. "Go ahead!" he growled, indicating the road.

And away they sped, leaving Kennedy unconscious on the side of the road where we found him.

* * * * *

"What are we to do?" I asked helplessly of Kennedy, when we had at last got him on his feet.

His head still ringing from the force of the blow of the blackjack, Craig stooped down, then knelt in the dust of the road, then ran ahead a bit where it was somewhat muddy.

"Which way—which way?" he muttered to himself.

I thought perhaps the blow had affected him and leaned over to see what he was doing. Instead, he was studying the marks made by the tire of the Clutching Hand cab. Very decidedly, there in the road, the little anti-skid marks on the tread of the tire showed—some worn, some cut—but with each revolution the same marks reappearing unmistakably. More than that, it was an unusual make of tire. Craig was actually studying the finger prints, so to speak, of an automobile!

More slowly now and carefully, we proceeded, for a mistake meant losing the trail of Elaine. Kennedy absolutely refused to get inside our cab, but clung tightly to a metal rod outside while he stood on the running board—now straining his eyes along the road to catch any faint glimpse of either taxi or limousine, or the dust from them, now gazing intently at the ground following the finger prints of the taxicab that was carrying off Elaine. All pain was forgotten by him now in the intensity of his anxiety for her.

We came to another crossroads and the driver glanced at Craig. "Stop!" he ordered.

In another instant he was down in the dirt, examining the road for marks.

"That way!" he indicated, leaping back to the running board.

We piled back into the car and proceeded under Kennedy's direction, as fast as he would permit. So it continued, perhaps for a couple of hours.

At last Kennedy stopped the cab and slowly directed the driver to veer into an open space that looked peculiarly lonesome. Near it stood a one story brick factory building, closed, but not abandoned.

As I looked about at the unattractive scene, Kennedy already was down on his knees in the dirt again, studying the tire tracks. They were all confused, showing that the taxicab we were following had evidently backed in and turned several times before going on.

"Crossed by another set of tire tracks!" he exclaimed excitedly, studying closer. "That must have been the limousine, waiting."

Laboriously he was following the course of the cars in the open space, when the one word escaped him, "Footprints!"

He was up and off in a moment, before we could imagine what he was after. We had got out of the cab, and followed him as, down to the very shore of a sort of cove or bay, he went. There lay a rusty, discarded boiler on the beach, half submerged in the rising tide. At this tank the footprints seemed to go right down the sand and into the waves which were slowly obliterating them. Kennedy gazed out as if to make out a possible boat on the horizon, where the cove widened out.

"Look!" he cried.

Farther down the shore, a few feet, I had discovered the same prints, going in the opposite direction, back toward the place from which we had just come. I started to follow them, but soon found myself alone. Kennedy had paused beside the old boiler.

"What is it?" I asked, retracing my steps.

He did not answer, but seemed to be listening. We listened

Arthur B. Reeve

also. There certainly was a most peculiar noise inside that tank.

Was it a muffled scream?

Kennedy reached down and picked up a rock, hitting the tank a resounding blow. As the echo died down, he listened again.

Yes, there was a sound—a scream perhaps—a woman's voice, faint, but unmistakable.

I looked at his face inquiringly. Without a word I read in it the confirmation of the thought that had flashed into my mind.

Elaine Dodge was inside!

* * * * *

First had come the limousine, with its three bandits, to the spot fixed on as a rendezvous. Later had come the taxicab. As it hove into sight, the three well-dressed crooks had drawn revolvers, thinking perhaps the plan for getting rid of Kennedy might possibly have miscarried. But the taxicab driver and the rough- faced fellow had reassured them with the sign of the Clutching Hand, and the revolvers were lowered.

As they parleyed hastily, the rough-neck and the fake chauffeur lifted Elaine out of the taxi. She was bound and gagged.

"Well, now we've got her, what shall we do with her?" asked one.

"It's got to be quick. There's another cab," put in the driver.

"The deuce with that."

"The deuce with nothing," he returned. "That fellow Kennedy's a clever one. He may come to. If he does, he won't miss us. Quick, now!"

"I wish I'd broken his skull," muttered the roughneck.

"We'd better leave her somewhere here," remarked one of the better-dressed three. "I don't think the chief wants us to kill her—yet," he added, with an ominous glance at Elaine, who in spite of threats was not cowed, but was vainly struggling at her bonds.

"Well, where shall it be?" asked another.

They looked about.

"See," cried the third. "See that old boiler down there at the edge of the water? Why not put her in there? No one'll ever think to look in such a place."

Down by the water's edge, where he pointed, lay a big boiler such as is used on stationary engines, with its end lapped by the waves. With a hasty expression of approval, the rough-neck picked Elaine up bodily, still struggling vainly, and together they carried her, bound and gagged, to the tank. The opening, which was toward the water, was small, but they managed, roughly, to thrust her in.

A moment later and they had rolled up a huge boulder against the small entrance, bracing it so that it would be impossible for her to get out from the inside. Then they drove off hastily.

Inside the old boiler lay Elaine, still bound and gagged. If she could only scream! Someone might hear. She must get help. There was water in the tank. She managed to lean up inside it, standing as high as the walls would allow her, trying to keep her head above the water.

Frantically, she managed to loosen the gag. She screamed. Her voice seemed to be bound around by the iron walls as was she herself. She shuddered, The water was rising—had reached her chest, and was still rising, slowly, inexorably.

What should she do? Would no one hear her? The water was up to her neck now. She held her head as high as she could and screamed again.

What was that? Silence? Or was someone outside?

* * * * *

Coolly, in spite of the emergency, Kennedy took in the perilous situation.

The lower end of the boiler, which was on a slant on the rapidly shelving beach, was now completely under water and impossible to get at. Besides, the opening was small, too small.

We pulled away the stone, but that did no good. No one could hope to get in and then out again that way alive— much less with a helpless girl. Yet something must be done. The tank was practically submerged inside, as I estimated quickly. Blows had no effect on the huge iron trap which had been built to resist many pounds of pressure.

Kennedy gazed about frantically and his eye caught the sign on the factory:

OXYACETYLENE WELDING CO.

"Come, Walter," he cried, running up the shore.

A moment later, breathless, we reached the doorway. It was, of course, locked. Kennedy whipped out his revolver and several well-directed shots through the keyhole smashed the lock. We put our shoulders to it and swung the door open, entering the factory.

There was not a soul about, not even a watchman. Hastily we took in the place, a forge and a number of odds and ends of metal sheets, rods, pipes and angles.

Beside a workbench stood two long cylinders, studded with bolts.

"That's what I'm looking for," exclaimed Craig. "Here, Walter, take one. I'll take the other—and the tubes—and—"

He did not pause to finish, but seized up a peculiar shaped instrument, like a huge hook, with a curved neck and sharp beak. Really it was composed of two metal tubes which ran into a cylinder or mixing chamber above the nozzle, while parallel to them ran another tube with a nozzle of its own.

We ran, for there was no time to lose. As nearly as I could estimate it, the water must now be slowly closing over Elaine.

"What is it?" I asked as he joined up the tubes from the tanks to the peculiar hook-like apparatus he carried.

"An oxyacetylene blowpipe," he muttered back feverishly working. "Used for welding and cutting, too," he added.

Arthur B. Reeve

With a light he touched the nozzle. Instantly a hissing, blinding flame-needle made the steel under it incandescent. The terrific heat from one nozzle made the steel glow. The stream of oxygen from the second completely consumed the hot metal. And the force of the blast carried a fine spray of disintegrated metal before it. It was a brilliant sight. But it was more than that. Through the very steel itself, the flame, thousands of degrees hot, seemed to eat its way in a fine line, as if it were a sharp knife cutting through ordinary cardboard.

With tense muscles Kennedy skillfully guided the terrible instrument that ate cold steel, wielding the torch as deftly as if it had been, as indeed it was, a magic wand of modern science.

He was actually cutting out a huge hole in the still exposed surface of the tank—all around, except for a few inches, to prevent the heavy piece from falling inward.

As Kennedy carefully bent outward the section of the tank which he had cut, he quickly reached down and lifted Elaine, unconscious, out of the water.

Gently he laid her on the sand. It was the work of only a moment to cut the cords that bound her hands.

There she lay, pale and still. Was she dead?

Kennedy worked frantically to revive her.

At last, slowly, the color seemed to return to her pale lips. Her eyelids fluttered. Then her great, deep eyes opened.

As she looked up and caught sight of Craig bending anxiously over her, she seemed to comprehend. For a moment both were silent. Then Elaine reached up and took his hand.

There was much in the look she gave him—admiration, confidence,— love itself.

Heroics, however, were never part of Kennedy's frank make-up. The fact was that her admiration, even though not spoken, plainly embarrassed him. Yet he forgot that as he looked at her lying there, frail and helpless.

He stroked her forehead gently, laying back the wet ringlets of her hair.

"Craig," she murmured, "you—you've saved my life!"

Her tone was eloquent.

"Elaine," he whispered, still gazing into her wonderful eyes, "the Clutching Hand shall pay for this! It is a fight to the finish between us!"

Arthur B. Reeve

CHAPTER IV

"THE FROZEN SAFE"

Kennedy swung open the door of our taxicab as we pulled up, safe at last, before the Dodge mansion, after the rescue of Elaine from the brutal machinations of the Clutching Hand.

Bennett was on the step of the cab in a moment and, together, one on each side of Elaine, they assisted her out of the car and up the steps to the house.

As they mounted the steps, Kennedy called back to me, "Pay the driver, Walter, please."

It was the first time I had thought of that. As it happened, I had quite a bankroll with me and, in my hurry, I peeled off a ten dollar bill and tossed it to the fellow, intending to be generous and tell him to keep the change.

"Say," he exclaimed, pointing to the clock, "come across—twenty- three, sixty."

Protesting, I peeled off some more bills.

Having satisfied this veritable anaconda and gorged his dilating appetite for banknotes, I turned to follow the others.

Jennings had opened the door immediately. Whether it was that he retained a grudge against me or whether he did not see me, he would have closed it before I could get up there. I called and took the steps two at a time.

Elaine's Aunt Josephine was waiting for us in the drawing room, very much worried. The dear old lady was quite scandalized as Elaine excitedly told of the thrilling events that had just taken place.

"And to think they—actually—carried you!" she exclaimed, horrified, adding, "And I not—"

"But Mr. Kennedy came along and saved me just in time," interrupted Elaine with a smile. "I was well chaperoned!"

Aunt Josephine turned to Craig gratefully. "How can I ever thank you enough, Mr. Kennedy," she said fervently.

Kennedy was quite embarrassed. With a smile, Elaine perceived his discomfiture, not at all displeased by it.

"Come into the library," she cried gaily, taking his arm. "I've something to show you."

Where the old safe which had been burnt through had stood was now a brand new safe of the very latest construction and design—one of those that look and are so formidable.

"Here is the new safe," she pointed out brightly. "It is not only proof against explosives, but between the plates is a lining that is proof against thermit and even that oxy-acety-lene blowpipe by which you rescued me from the old boiler. It has a time lock, too, that will prevent its being opened at night, even if anyone should learn the combination."

They stood before the safe a moment and Kennedy examined it closely with much interest.

"Wonderful!" he admired.

"I knew you'd approve of it," cried Elaine, much pleased. "Now I have something else to show you."

She paused at the desk and from a drawer took out a portfolio of large photographs. They were very handsome photographs of herself.

"Much more wonderful than the safe," remarked Craig earnestly. Then, hesitating and a trifle embarrassed, he added, "May I—may I have one?"

"If you care for it," she said, dropping her eyes, then glancing up at him quickly.

"Care for it?" he repeated. "It will be one of the greatest treasures."

She slipped the picture quickly into an envelope. "Come," she interrupted. "Aunt Josephine will be wondering where we are. She—she's a demon chaperone."

Bennett, Aunt Josephine and myself were talking earnestly as Elaine and Craig returned.

"Well," said Bennett, glancing at his watch and rising as he turned to Elaine, "I'm afraid I must go, now."

He crossed over to where she stood and shook hands. There was no doubt that Bennett was very much smitten by his fair client.

"Good-bye, Mr. Bennett," she murmured, "and thank you so much for what you have done for me today."

But there was something lifeless about the words. She turned quickly to Craig, who had remained standing.

"Must you go, too, Mr. Kennedy?" she asked, noticing his position.

"I'm afraid Mr. Jameson and I must be back on the job before this Clutching Hand gets busy again," he replied reluctantly.

"Oh, I hope you—we get him soon!" she exclaimed, and there was nothing lifeless about the way she gave Craig her hand, as Bennett, he and I left a moment later.

* * * * *

That morning I had noticed Kennedy fussing some time at the door of our apartment before we went over to the laboratory. As nearly as I could make out he had placed something under the rug at the door out into the hallway.

When we approached our door, now, Craig paused. By pressing a little concealed button he caused a panel in the wall outside to loosen, disclosing a small, boxlike plate in the wall underneath.

It was about a foot long and perhaps four inches wide. Through it ran a piece of paper which unrolled from one coil and wound up on another, actuated by clockwork. Across the blank white paper ran an ink line traced by a stylographic pen, such as I had seen in mechanical pencils used in offices, hotels, banks and such places.

Kennedy examined the thing with interest.

"What is it?" I asked.

"A new seismograph," he replied, still gazing carefully at the rolled up part of the paper. "I have installed it because it registers every footstep on the floor of our apartment. We can't be too careful with this Clutching Hand. I want to know whether we have any visitors or not in our absence. This straight line indicates that we have not. Wait a moment."

Craig hastily unlocked the door and entered. Inside, I could see him pacing up and down our modest quarters.

"Do you see anything, Walter?" he called.

I looked at the seismograph. The pen had started to trace its line, no longer even and straight, but zigzag, at different heights across the paper.

He came to the door. "What do you think of it?" he inquired.

"Splendid idea," I answered enthusiastically.

Our apartment was, as I have said, modest, consisting of a large living room, two bedrooms, and bath—an attractive but not ornate place, which we found very cosy and comfortable. On one side of the room was a big fire place, before which stood a fire screen. We had collected easy chairs and capacious tables and desks. Books were scattered about, literally overflowing from the crowded shelves. On the walls were our favorite pictures, while for ornament, I suppose I might mention my typewriter and now and then some of Craig's wonderful scientific apparatus as satisfying our limited desire for the purely aesthetic.

We entered and fell to work at the aforementioned type-writer, on a special Sunday story that I had been forced to neglect. I was not so busy, however, that I did not notice out of the corner of my eye that Kennedy had taken from its cover Elaine Dodge's picture and was gazing at it ravenously.

I put my hand surreptitiously over my mouth and coughed. Kennedy wheeled on me and I hastily banged a sentence out on the machine, making at least half a dozen mistakes.

I had finished as much of the article as I could do then and was smoking and reading it over. Kennedy was still gazing at the picture Miss Dodge had given him, then moving from place to place about the room, evidently wondering where it would look best. I doubt whether he had done another blessed thing since we returned.

He tried it on the mantel. That wouldn't do. At last he held it up beside a picture of Galton, I think, of finger print and eugenics fame, who hung on the wall directly opposite the fireplace. Hastily he compared the two. Elaine's picture was of precisely the same size.

Next he tore out the picture of the scientist and threw it carelessly into the fireplace. Then he placed Elaine's picture in its place and hung it up again, standing off to admire it.

I watched him gleefully. Was this Craig? Purposely I moved my elbow suddenly and pushed a book with a bang on the floor. Kennedy actually jumped. I picked up the book with a muttered apology. No, this was not the same old Craig.

Perhaps half an hour later, I was still reading. Kennedy was now pacing up and down the room, apparently unable to concentrate his mind on any but one subject.

He stopped a moment before the photograph, looked at it

Arthur B. Reeve

fixedly. Then he started his methodical walk again, hesitated, and went over to the telephone, calling a number which I recognized.

"She must have been pretty well done up by her experience," he said apologetically, catching my eye. "I was wondering if —Hello—oh, Miss Dodge—I—er—I—er—just called up to see if you were all right."

Craig was very much embarrassed, but also very much in earnest.

A musical laugh rippled over the telephone. "Yes, I'm all right, thank you, Mr. Kennedy—and I put the package you sent me into the safe, but—"

"Package?" frowned Craig. "Why, I sent you no package, Miss Dodge. In the safe?"

"Why, yes, and the safe is all covered with moisture—and so cold."

"Moisture—cold?" he repeated quickly.

"Yes, I have been wondering if it is all right. In fact, I was going to call you up, only I was afraid you'd think I was foolish."

"I shall be right over," he answered hastily, clapping the receiver back on its hook. "Walter," he added, seizing his hat and coat, "come on—hurry!"

A few minutes later we drove up in a taxi before the Dodge house and rang the bell.

Jennings admitted us sleepily.

It could not have been long after we left Miss Dodge late in the afternoon that Susie Martin, who had been quite worried over our long absence after the attempt to rob her father, dropped in on Elaine. Wide-eyed, she had listened to Elaine's story of what had happened.

"And you think this Clutching Hand has never recovered the incriminating papers that caused him to murder your father?" asked Susie.

Elaine shook her head. "No. Let me show you the new safe I've bought. Mr. Kennedy thinks it wonderful."

"I should think you'd be proud of it," admired Susie. "I must tell father to get one, too."

At that very moment, if they had known it, the Clutching Hand with his sinister, masked face, was peering at the two girls from the other side of the portieres.

Susie rose to go and Elaine followed her to the door. No sooner had she gone than the Clutching Hand came out from behind the curtains. He gazed about a moment, then moving over to the safe about which the two girls had been talking, stealthily examined it.

He must have heard someone coming, for, with a gesture of hate at the safe itself, as though he personified it, he slipped back of the curtains again.

Elaine had returned and as she sat down at the desk to go over some papers which Bennett had left relative to settling up the estate, the masked intruder stealthily and silently withdrew.

"A package for you, Miss Dodge," announced Michael later

in the evening as Elaine, in her dainty evening gown, was still engaged in going over the papers. He carried it in his hands rather gingerly.

"Mr. Kennedy sent it, ma'am. He says it contains clues and will you please put it in the new safe for him."

Elaine took the package eagerly and examined it. Then she pulled open the heavy door of the safe.

"It must be getting cold out, Michael," she remarked. "This package is as cold as ice."

"It is, ma'am," answered Michael, deferentially with a side-long glance that did not prevent his watching her intently.

She closed the safe and, with a glance at her watch, set the time lock and went upstairs to her room.

No sooner had Elaine disappeared than Michael appeared again, cat-like, through the curtains from the drawing room, and, after a glance about the dimly lighted library, discovering that the coast was clear, motioned to a figure hiding behind the portieres.

A moment, and Clutching Hand himself came out.

He moved over to the safe and looked it over. Then he put out his hand and touched it.

"Good, Michael," he exclaimed with satisfaction.

"Listen!" cautioned Michael.

Someone was coming and they hastily slunk behind the protecting portieres. It was Marie, Elaine's maid.

She turned up the lights and went over to the desk for a book for which Elaine had evidently sent her. She paused and appeared to be listening. Then she went to the door.

"Jennings!" she beckoned.

"What is it, Marie?" he replied.

She said nothing, but as he came up the hall led him to the center of the room.

"Listen! I heard sighs and groans!"

Jennings looked at her a moment, puzzled, then laughed. "You girls!" he exclaimed. "I suppose you'll always think the library haunted, now."

"But, Jennings, listen," she persisted.

Jennings did listen. Sure enough, there were sounds, weird, uncanny. He gazed about the room. It was eerie. Then he took a few steps toward the safe. Marie put out her hand to it, and started back.

"Why, that safe is all covered with cold sweat!" she cried with bated breath.

Sure enough the face of the safe was beaded with dampness. Jennings put his hand on it and quickly drew it away, leaving a mark on the dampness.

"Wh-what do you think of that?" he gasped.

"I'm going to tell Miss Dodge," cried Marie, genuinely frightened.

A moment later she burst into Elaine's room.

"What is the matter, Marie?" asked Elaine, laying down her book. "You look as if you had seen a ghost."

"Ah, but, mademoiselle—it ees just like that. The safe—if mademoiselle will come downstairs, I will show it you."

Puzzled but interested, Elaine followed her. In the library Jennings pointed mutely at the new safe. Elaine approached it. As they stood about new beads of perspiration, as it were, formed on it. Elaine touched it, and also quickly withdrew her hand.

"I can't imagine what's the matter," she said. "But—well—Jennings, you may go—and Marie, also."

When the servants had gone she still regarded the safe with the same wondering look, then turning out the light, she followed.

She had scarcely disappeared when, from the portiered doorway nearby, the Clutching Hand appeared, and, after gazing out at them, took a quick look at the safe.

"Good!" he muttered.

Noiselessly Michael of the sinister face moved in and took a position in the center of the room, as if on guard, while Clutching Hand sat before the safe watching it intently.

"Someone at the door—Jennings is answering the bell," Michael whispered hoarsely.

"Confound it!" muttered Clutching Hand, as both moved again behind the heavy velour curtains.

"I'm so glad to see you, Mr. Kennedy," greeted Elaine unaffectedly as Jennings admitted us.

She had heard the bell and was coming downstairs as we entered. We three moved toward the library and someone switched on the lights.

Craig strode over to the safe. The cold sweat on it had now turned to icicles. Craig's face clouded with thought as he examined it more closely. There was actually a groaning sound from within.

"It can't be opened," he said to himself. "The time lock is set for tomorrow morning."

Outside, if we had not been so absorbed in the present mystery, we might have seen Michael and the Clutching Hand listening to us. Clutching Hand looked hastily at his watch.

"The deuce!" he muttered under his breath, stifling his suppressed fury.

We stood looking at the safe. Kennedy was deeply interested, Elaine standing close beside him. Suddenly he seemed to make up his mind.

"Quick—Elaine!" he cried, taking her arm. "Stand back!"

We all retreated. The safe door, powerful as it was, had actually begun to warp and bend. The plates were bulging. A moment later, with a loud report and concussion the door blew off.

A blast of cold air and flakes like snow flew out. Papers were scattered on every side.

Arthur B. Reeve

We stood gazing, aghast, a second, then ran forward. Kennedy quickly examined the safe. He bent down and from the wreck took up a package, now covered with white.

As quickly he dropped it.

"That is the package that was sent," cried Elaine.

Taking it in a table cover, he laid it on the table and opened it. Inside was a peculiar shaped flask, open at the top, but like a vacuum bottle.

"A Dewar flask!" ejaculated Craig.

"What is it?" asked Elaine, appealing to him.

"Liquid air!" he answered. "As it evaporated, the terrific pressure of expanding air in the safe increased until it blew out the door. That is what caused the cold sweating and the groans."

We watched him, startled.

On the other side of the portieres Michael and Clutching Hand waited. Then, in the general confusion, Clutching Hand slowly disappeared, foiled.

"Where did this package come from?" asked Kennedy of Jennings suspiciously.

Jennings looked blank.

"Why," put in Elaine, "Michael brought it to me."

"Get Michael," ordered Kennedy.

"Yes, sir," nodded Jennings.

A moment later he returned. "I found him, going upstairs," reported Jennings, leading Michael in.

"Where did you get this package?" shot out Kennedy.

"It was left at the door, sir, by a boy, sir."

Question after question could not shake that simple, stolid sentence. Kennedy frowned.

"You may go," he said finally, as if reserving something for Michael later.

A sudden exclamation followed from Elaine as Michael passed down the hall again. She had moved over to the desk, during the questioning, and was leaning against it.

Inadvertently she had touched an envelope. It was addressed, "Craig Kennedy."

Craig tore it open, Elaine bending anxiously over his shoulder, frightened.

We read:

"YOU HAVE INTERFERED FOR THE LAST TIME. IT IS THE END."

Beneath it stood the fearsome sign of the Clutching Hand!

* * * * *

The warning of the Clutching Hand had no other effect on Kennedy than the redoubling of his precautions for safety.

Arthur B. Reeve

Nothing further happened that night, however, and the next morning found us early at the laboratory.

It was the late forenoon, when after a hurried trip down to the office, I rejoined Kennedy at his scientific workshop.

We walked down the street when a big limousine shot past. Kennedy stopped in the middle of a remark. He had recognized the car, with a sort of instinct.

At the same moment I saw a smiling face at the window of the car. It was Elaine Dodge.

The car stopped in something less than twice its length and then backed toward us.

Kennedy, hat off, was at the window in a moment. There were Aunt Josephine, and Susie Martin, also.

"Where are you boys going?" asked Elaine, with interest, then added with a gaiety that ill concealed her real anxiety, "I'm so glad to see you—to see that—er—nothing has happened from that dreadful Clutching Hand."

"Why, we were just going up to our rooms," replied Kennedy.

"Can't we drive you around?"

We climbed in and a moment later were off. The ride was only too short for Kennedy. We stepped out in front of our apartment and stood chatting for a moment.

"Some day I want to show you the laboratory," Craig was saying.

"It must be so—interesting!" exclaimed Elaine enthusiastically. "Think of all the bad men you must have caught!"

"I have quite a collection of stuff here at our rooms," remarked Craig, "almost a museum. Still," he ventured, "I can't promise that the place is in order," he laughed.

Elaine hesitated. "Would you like to see it?" she wheedled of Aunt Josephine.

Aunt Josephine nodded acquiescence, and a moment later we all entered the building.

"You—you are very careful since that last warning?" asked Elaine as we approached our door.

"More than ever—now," replied Craig. "I have made up my mind to win."

She seemed to catch at the words as though they had a hidden meaning, looking first at him and then away, not displeased.

Kennedy had started to unlock the door, when he stopped short.

"See," he said, "this is a precaution I have just installed. I almost forgot in the excitement."

He pressed a panel and disclosed the box-like apparatus.

"This is my seismograph which tells me whether I have had any visitors in my absence. If the pen traces a straight line, it is, all right; but if—hello—Walter, the line is wavy."

We exchanged a significant glance.

Arthur B. Reeve

"Would you mind—er—standing down the hall just a bit while I enter?" asked Craig.

"Be careful," cautioned Elaine.

He unlocked the door, standing off to one side. Then he extended his hand across the doorway. Still nothing happened. There was not a sound. He looked cautiously into the room. Apparently there was nothing.

* * * * *

It had been about the middle of the morning that an express wagon had pulled up sharply before our apartment.

"Mr. Kennedy live here?" asked one of the expressmen, descending with his helper and approaching our janitor, Jens Jensen, a typical Swede, who was coming up out of the basement.

Jens growled a surly, "Yes—but Mr. Kannady, he bane out."

"Too bad—we've got this large cabinet he ordered from Grand Rapids. We can't cart it around all day. Can't you let us in so we can leave it?"

Jensen muttered. "Wall—I guess it bane all right."

They took the cabinet off the wagon and carried it upstairs. Jensen opened our door, still grumbling, and they placed the heavy cabinet in the living room.

"Sign here."

"You fallers bane a nuisance," protested Jens, signing nevertheless.

Scarcely had the sound ox their footfalls died away in the outside hallway when the door of the cabinet slowly opened and a masked face protruded, gazing about the room.

It was the Clutching Hand!

From the cabinet he took a large package wrapped in newspapers. As he held it, looking keenly about, his eye rested on Elaine's picture. A moment he looked at it, then quickly at the fireplace opposite.

An idea seemed to occur to him. He took the package to the fireplace, removed the screen, and laid the package over the andirons with one end pointing out into the room.

Next he took from the cabinet a couple of storage batteries and a coil of wire. Deftly and quickly he fixed them on the package.

Meanwhile, before an alleyway across the street and further down the long block the express wagon had stopped. The driver and his helper clambered out and for a moment stood talking in low tones, with covert glances at our apartment. They moved into the alley and the driver drew out a battered pair of opera glasses, levelling them at our windows.

Having completed fixing the batteries and wires, Clutching Hand ran the wires along the moulding on the wall overhead, from the fireplace until he was directly over Elaine's picture. Skillfully, he managed to fix the wires, using them in place of the picture wires to support the framed photograph. Then he carefully moved the photograph until it hung very noticeably askew on the wall.

The last wire joined, he looked about the room, then noise-lessly moved to the window and raised the shade.

Arthur B. Reeve

Quickly he raised his hand and brought the fingers slowly together. It was the sign.

Off in the alley, the express driver and his helper were still gazing up through the opera glass.

"What d'ye see, Bill?" he asked, handing over the glass.

The other took it and looked. "It's him—the Hand, Jack," whispered the helper, handing the glasses back.

They jumped into the wagon and away it rattled.

Jensen was smoking placidly as the wagon pulled up the second time.

"Sorry," said the driver sheepishly, "but we delivered the cabinet to the wrong Mr. Kennedy."

He pulled out the inevitable book to prove it.

"Wall, you bane fine fallers," growled Jensen, puffing like a furnace, in his fury. "You cannot go up agane."

"We'll get fired for the mistake," pleaded the helper.

"Just this once," urged the driver, as he rattled some loose change in his pocket. "Here—there goes a whole day's tips."

He handed Jens a dollar in small change.

Still grumpy but mollified by the silver Jens let them go up and opened the door to our rooms again. There stood the cabinet, as outwardly innocent as when it came in.

Lugging and tugging they managed to get the heavy piece of

furniture out and downstairs again, loading it on the wagon. Then they drove off with it, accompanied by a parting volley from Jensen.

In an unfrequented street, perhaps half a mile away, the wagon stopped. With a keen glance around, the driver and his helper made sure that no one was about.

"Such a shaking up as you've given me!" growled a voice as the cabinet door opened. "But I've got him this time!"

It was the Clutching Hand.

"There, men, you can leave me here," he ordered.

He motioned to them to drive off and, as they did so, pulled off his masking handkerchief and dived into a narrow street leading up to a thoroughfare.

* * * * *

Craig gazed into our living room cautiously.

"I can't see anything wrong," he said to me as I stood just beside him. "Miss Dodge," he added, "will you and the rest excuse me if I ask you to wait just a moment longer?"

Elaine watched him, fascinated. He crossed the room, then went into each of our other rooms. Apparently nothing was wrong and a minute later he reappeared at the doorway.

"I guess it's all right," he said. "Perhaps it was only Jensen, the janitor."

Elaine, Aunt Josephine and Susie Martin entered. Craig placed chairs for them, but still I could see that he was uneasy. From time to time, while they were admiring one of our treasures after another, he glanced about suspiciously. Finally he moved over to a closet and flung the door open, ready for anything. No one was in the closet and he closed it hastily.

"What is the trouble, do you think?" asked Elaine wonderingly, noticing his manner.

"I—I can't just say," answered Craig, trying to appear easy.

She had risen and with keen interest was looking at the books, the pictures, the queer collection of weapons and odds and ends from the underworld that Craig had amassed in his adventures.

At last her eye wandered across the room. She caught sight of her own picture, occupying a place of honor—but hanging askew.

"Isn't that just like a man!" she exclaimed laughingly. "Such housekeepers as you are—such carelessness!"

She had taken a step or two across the room to straighten the picture.

"Miss Dodge!" almost shouted Kennedy, his face fairly blanched, "Stop!"

She turned, her stunning eyes filled with amazement at his suddenness. Nevertheless she moved quickly to one side, as he waved his arms, unable to speak quickly enough.

Kennedy stood quite still, gazing at the picture, askew, with suspicion.

"That wasn't that way when we left, was it, Walter?" he asked.

"It certainly was not," I answered positively, "There was more time spent in getting that picture just right than I ever saw you spend on all the rest of the room."

Craig frowned.

As for myself, I did not know what to make of it.

"I'm afraid I shall have to ask you to step into this back room," said Craig at length to the ladies. "I'm sorry—but we can't be too careful with this intruder, whoever he was."

They rose, surprised, but, as he continued to urge them, they moved into my room.

Elaine, however, stopped at the door.

For a moment Kennedy appeared to be considering. Then his eye fell on a fishing rod that stood in a corner. He took it and moved toward the picture.

On his hands and knees, to one side, down as close as he could get to the floor, with the rod extended at arm's length, he motioned to me to do the same, behind him.

Elaine, unable to repress her interest took a half step forward, breathless, from the doorway, while Susie Martin and Aunt Josephine stood close behind her.

Carefully Kennedy reached out with the pole and straightened the picture.

As he did so there was a flash, a loud, deafening report, and a great puff of smoke from the fireplace.

The fire screen was riddled and overturned. A charge of buckshot shattered the precious photograph of Elaine.

We had dropped flat on the floor at the report. I looked about. Kennedy was unharmed, and so were the rest.

With a bound he was at the fireplace, followed by Elaine and the rest of us. There, in what remained of a package done up roughly in newspaper, was a shot gun with its barrel sawed off about six inches from the lock, fastened to a block of wood, and connected to a series of springs on the trigger, released by a little electromagnetic arrangement actuated by two batteries and leading by wires up along the moulding to the picture where the slightest touch would complete the circuit.

The newspapers which were wrapped about the deadly thing were burning, and Kennedy quickly tore them off, throwing them into the fireplace.

A startled cry from Elaine caused us to turn.

She was standing directly before her shattered picture where it hung awry on the wall. The heavy charges of buckshot had knocked away large pieces of paper and plaster under it.

"Craig!" she gasped.

He was at her side in a second.

She laid one hand on his arm, as she faced him. With the other she traced an imaginary line in the air from the level of the buckshot to his head and then straight to the infernal thing that had lain in the fireplace.

"And to think," she shuddered, "that it was through ME that he tried to kill you!"

"Never mind," laughed Craig easily, as they gazed into each other's eyes, drawn together by their mutual peril, "Clutching Hand will have to be cleverer than this to get either of us— Elaine!"

Arthur B. Reeve

CHAPTER V

THE POISONED ROOM

Elaine and Craig were much together during the next few days.

Somehow or other, it seemed that the chase of the Clutching Hand involved long conferences in the Dodge library and even, in fact, extended to excursions into that notoriously crime-infested neighborhood of Riverside Drive with its fashionable processions of automobiles and go-carts—as far north, indeed, as that desperate haunt known as Grant's Tomb.

More than that, these delvings into the underworld involved Kennedy in the necessity of wearing a frock coat and silk hat in the afternoon, and I found that he was selecting his neckwear with a care that had been utterly foreign to him during all the years previous that I had known him.

It all looked very suspicious to me.

But, to return to the more serious side of the affair.

Kennedy and Elaine had scarcely come out of the house and descended the steps, one afternoon, when a sinister face appeared in a basement areaway nearby.

The figure was crouched over, with his back humped up almost as if deformed, and his left hand had an unmistakable twist.

It was the Clutching Hand.

He wore a telephone inspector's hat and coat and carried a bag slung by a strap over his shoulder. For once he had left off his mask, but, in place of it, his face was covered by a scraggly black beard. In fact, he seemed to avoid turning his face full, three-quarters or even profile to anyone, unless he had to do so. As much as possible he averted it, but he did so in a clever way that made it seem quite natural. The disguise was effective.

He saw Kennedy and Miss Dodge and slunk unobtrusively against a railing, with his head turned away. Laughing and chatting, they passed. As they walked down the street, Clutching Hand turned and gazed after them. Involuntarily the menacing hand clutched in open hatred.

Then he turned in the other direction and, going up the steps of the Dodge house, rang the bell.

"Telephone inspector," he said in a loud tone as Michael, in Jennings' place for the afternoon, opened the door.

He accompanied the words with the sign and Michael, taking care that the words be heard, in case anyone was listening, admitted him.

As it happened, Aunt Josephine was upstairs in Elaine's room. She was fixing flowers in a vase on the dressing table of her idolized niece. Meanwhile, Rusty, the collie, lay, half

Arthur B. Reeve

blinking, on the floor.

"Who is this?" she asked, as Michael led the bogus telephone inspector into the room.

"A man from the telephone company," he answered deferentially.

Aunt Josephine, unsophisticated, allowed them to enter without a further question.

Quickly, like a good workman, Clutching Hand went to the telephone instrument and by dint of keeping his finger on the hook and his back to Aunt Josephine succeeded in conveying the illusion that he was examining it.

Aunt Josephine moved to the door. Not so, Rusty. He did not like the looks of the stranger and he had no scruples against letting it be known.

As she put her hand on the knob to go out into the hall, Rusty uttered a low growl which grew into a full-lunged snarl at the Clutching Hand. Clutching Hand kicked at him vigorously, if surreptitiously. Rusty barked.

"Lady," he disguised his voice, "will yer please ter call off the dog? Me and him don't seem to cotton to each other."

"Here, Rusty," she commanded, "down!"

Together Aunt Josephine and Michael removed the still protesting Rusty.

No sooner was the door shut than the Clutching Hand moved over swiftly to it. For a few seconds, he stood gazing at them as they disappeared down-stairs. Then he came back into the center of the room.

Hastily he opened his bag and from it drew a small powder-spraying outfit such as I have seen used for spraying bug-powder. He then took out a sort of muzzle with an elastic band on it and slipped it over his head so that the muzzle protected his nose and mouth.

He seemed to work a sort of pumping attachment and from the nozzle of the spraying instrument blew out a cloud of powder which he directed at the wall.

The wall paper was one of those rich, fuzzy varieties and it seemed to catch the powder. Clutching Hand appeared to be more than satisfied with the effect.

Meanwhile, Michael, in the hallway, on guard to see that no one bothered the Clutching Hand at his work, was overcome by curiosity to see what his master was doing. He opened the door a little bit and gazed stealthily through the crack into the room.

Clutching Hand was now spraying the rug close to the dressing table of Elaine and was standing near the mirror. He stooped down to examine the rug. Then, as he raised his head, he happened to look into the mirror. In it he could see the full reflection of Michael behind him, gazing into the room.

"The scoundrel!" muttered Clutching Hand, with repressed fury at the discovery.

He rose quickly and shut off the spraying instrument, stuffing it into the bag. He took a step or two toward the door. Michael drew back, fearfully, pretending now to be on guard.

Clutching Hand opened the door and, still wearing the muzzle, beckoned to Michael. Michael could scarcely control his fears. But he obeyed, entering Elaine's room after the Clutching Hand, who locked the door.

"Were you watching me?" demanded the master criminal, with rage.

Michael, trembling all over, shook his head. For a moment Clutching Hand looked him over disdainfully at the clumsy lie.

Then he brutally struck Michael in the face, knocking him down. An ungovernable, almost insane fury seemed to possess the man as he stood over the prostrate footman, cursing.

"Get up!" he ordered.

Michael obeyed, thoroughly cowed.

"Take me to the cellar, now," he demanded.

Michael led the way from the room without a protest, the master criminal following him closely.

Down into the cellar, by a back way, they went, Clutching Hand still wearing his muzzle and Michael saying not a word.

Suddenly Clutching Hand turned on him and seized him by the collar.

"Now, go upstairs, you," he muttered, shaking him until his teeth fairly chattered, "and if you watch me again—I'll kill you!"

He thrust Michael away and the footman, overcome by fear, hurried upstairs. Still trembling and fearful, Michael paused In the hallway, looking back resentfully, for even one who is in the power of a super-criminal is still human and has feelings that may be injured.

Michael put his hand on his face where the Clutching Hand had struck him. There he waited, muttering to himself. As he thought it over, anger took the place of fear. He slowly turned in the direction of the cellar. Closing both his fists, Michael made a threatening gesture at his master in crime.

Meanwhile, Clutching Hand was standing by the electric meter. He examined it carefully, feeling where the wires entered and left it starting to trace them out. At last he came to a point where it seemed suitable to make a connection for some purpose he had in mind.

Quickly he took some wire from his bag and connected it with the electric light wires. Next, he led these wires, concealed of course, along the cellar floor, in the direction of the furnace.

The furnace was one of the old hot air heaters and he paused before it as though seeking something. Then he bent down beside it and uncovered a little tank. He took off the top on which were cast in the iron the words:

"This tank must be kept full of water."

He thrust his hand gingerly into it, bringing it out quickly. The tank was nearly full of water and he brought his hand out wet. It was also hot. But he did not seem to mind that, for he shook his head with a smile of satisfaction.

Next, from his capacious bag he took two metal poles, or

Arthur B. Reeve

electrodes, and fastened them carefully to the ends of the wires, placing them at opposite ends of the tank in the water.

For several moments he watched. The water inside the tank seemed the same as before, only on each electrode there appeared bubbles, on one bubbles of oxygen, on the other of hydrogen. The water was decomposing under the current by electrolysis.

Another moment he surveyed his work to see that he had left no loose ends. Then he picked up his bag and moved toward the cellar steps. As he did so, he removed the muzzle from his nose and quietly let himself out of the house.

* * * * *

The next morning, Rusty, who had been Elaine's constant companion since the trouble had begun, awakened his mistress by licking her hand as it hung limply over the side of her bed.

She awakened with a start and put her hand to her head. She felt ill.

"Poor old fellow," she murmured, half dazedly, for the moment endowing her pet with her own feelings, as she patted his faithful shaggy head.

Rusty moved away again, wagging his tail listlessly. The collie, too, felt ill. Elaine watched him as he walked, dejected, across the room and then lay down.

"Why, Miss Elaine—what ees ze mattair? You are so pale!" exclaimed the maid, Marie, as she entered the room a moment later with the morning's mail on a salver.

"I don't feel well, Marie," she replied, trying with her slender white hand to brush the cobwebs from her brain. "I—I wish you'd tell Aunt Josephine to telephone Dr. Hayward."

"Yes, mademoiselle," answered Marie, deftly and sympathetically straightening out the pillows.

Languidly Elaine took the letters one by one off the salver. She looked at them, but seemed not to have energy enough to open them.

Finally she selected one and slowly tore it open. It had no superscription, but it at once arrested her attention and transfixed her with terror.

It read:

"YOU ARE SICK THIS MORNING. TOMORROW YOU WILL BE WORSE. THE NEXT DAY YOU WILL DIE UNLESS YOU DISCHARGE CRAIG KENNEDY."

It was signed by the mystic trademark of the fearsome Clutching Hand!

Elaine drew back into the pillows, horror stricken.

Quickly she called to Marie. "Go—get Aunt Josephine— right away!"

As Marie almost flew down the hall, Elaine still holding the letter convulsively, pulled herself together and got up, trembling. She almost seized the telephone as she called Kennedy's number.

* * * * *

Kennedy, in his stained laboratory apron, was at work before his table, while I was watching him with intense interest, when the telephone rang.

Without a word he answered the call and I could see a look of perturbation cross his face. I knew it was from Elaine, but could tell nothing about the nature of the message.

An instant later he almost tore off the apron and threw on his hat and coat. I followed him as he dashed out of the laboratory.

"This is terrible—terrible," he muttered, as we hurried across the campus of the University to a taxi-cab stand.

A few minutes later, when we arrived at the Dodge mansion, we found Aunt Josephine and Marie doing all they could under the circumstances. Aunt Josephine had just given her a glass of water which she drank eagerly. Rusty had, meanwhile, crawled under the bed, caring only to be alone and undisturbed.

Dr. Hayward had arrived and had just finished taking her pulse and temperature as our cab pulled up.

Jennings who had evidently been expecting us let us in without a word and conducted us up to Elaine's room. We knocked.

"Mr. Kennedy and Mr. Jameson," we could hear Marie whisper in a subdued voice.

"Tell them to come in," answered Elaine eagerly.

We entered. There she lay, beautiful as ever, but with a whiteness of her fresh cheek that was too etherially unnatural.

Elaine was quite ill indeed.

"Oh—I'm so glad to see you," she breathed, with an air of relief as Kennedy advanced.

"Why—what is the matter?" asked Craig, anxiously.

Dr. Hayward shook his head dubiously, but Kennedy did not notice him, for, as he approached Elaine, she drew from the covers where she had concealed it a letter and handed it to him.

Craig took it and read:

"YOU ARE SICK THIS MORNING. TOMORROW YOU WILL BE WORSE. THE NEXT DAY YOU WILL DIE UNLESS YOU DISCHARGE CRAIG KENNEDY."

At the signature of the Clutching Hand he frowned, then, noticing Dr. Hayward, turned to him and repeated his question, "What is the matter?"

Dr. Hayward continued shaking his head. "I cannot diagnose her symptoms," he shrugged.

As I watched Kennedy's face, I saw his nostrils dilating, almost as if he were a hound and had scented his quarry. I sniffed, too. There seemed to be a faint odor, almost as if of garlic, in the room. It was unmistakable and Craig looked about him curiously but said nothing.

As he sniffed, he moved impatiently and his foot touched Rusty, under the bed. Rusty whined and moved back lazily. Craig bent over and looked at him.

"What's the matter with Rusty?" he asked. "Is he sick, too?"

"Why—yes," answered Elaine, following Craig with her deep eyes. "Poor Rusty. He woke me up this morning. He feels as badly as I do, poor old fellow."

Craig reached down and gently pulled the collie out into the room. Rusty crouched down close to the floor. His nose was hot and dry and feverish. He was plainly ill.

"How long has Rusty been in the room?" asked Craig.

"All night," answered Elaine. "I wouldn't think of being without him now."

Kennedy lifted the dog by his front paws. Rusty submitted patiently, but without any spirit.

"May I take Rusty along with me?" he asked finally.

Elaine hesitated. "Surely," she said at length, "only, be gentle with him."

Craig looked at her as though it would be impossible to be otherwise with anything belonging to Elaine.

"Of course," he said simply. "I thought that I might be able to discover the trouble from studying him."

We stayed only a few minutes longer, for Kennedy seemed to realize the necessity of doing something immediately and even Dr. Hayward was fighting in the dark. As for me, I gave it up, too. I could find no answer to the mystery of what was the peculiar malady of Elaine.

Back in the laboratory, Kennedy set to work immediately, brushing everything else aside. He began by drawing off a little of Rusty's blood in a tube, very carefully.

"Here, Walter," he said pointing to the little incision he had made. "Will you take care of him?"

I bound up the wounded leg and gave the poor beast a drink of water. Rusty looked at me gratefully from his big sad brown eyes. He seemed to appreciate our gentleness and to realize that we were trying to help him.

In the meantime, Craig had taken a flask with a rubber stopper. Through one hole in it was fitted a long funnel; through another ran a glass tube. The tube connected with a large U-shaped drying tube filled with calcium chloride, which, in turn, connected with a long open tube with an upturned end.

Into the flask, Craig dropped some pure granulated zinc. Then he covered it with dilute sulphuric acid, poured in through the funnel tube.

"That forms hydrogen gas," he explained to me, "which passes through the drying tube and the ignition tube. Wait a moment until all the air is expelled from the tubes."

He lighted a match and touched it to the open, upturned end. The hydrogen, now escaping freely, was ignited with a pale blue flame.

A few moments later, having extracted something like a serum from the blood he had drawn off from Rusty. He added the extract to the mixture in the flask, pouring it in, also through the funnel tube.

Almost immediately the pale, bluish flame turned to bluish white, and white fumes were formed. In the ignition tube a sort of metallic deposit appeared.

Quickly Craig made one test after another.

As he did so, I sniffed. There was an unmistakable odor of garlic in the air which made me think of what I had already noticed in Elaine's room.

"What is it?" I asked, mystified.

"Arseniuretted hydrogen," he answered, still engaged in verifying his tests. "This is the Marsh test for arsenic."

I gazed from Kennedy to the apparatus, then to Rusty and a picture of Elaine, pale and listless, flashed before me.

"Arsenic!" I repeated in horror.

* * * * *

I had scarcely recovered from the surprise of Kennedy's startling revelation when the telephone rang again. Kennedy seized the receiver, thinking evidently that the message might be from or about Elaine.

But from the look on his face and from his manner, I could gather that, although it was not from Elaine herself, it was about something that interested him greatly. As he talked, he took his little notebook and hastily jotted down something in it. Still, I could not make out what the conversation was about.

"Good!" I heard him say finally. "I shall keep the appointment—absolutely."

His face wore a peculiar puzzled look as he hung up the receiver.

"What was it?" I asked eagerly.

"It was Elaine's footman, Michael," he replied thoughtfully. "As I suspected, he says that he is a confederate of the Clutching Hand and if we will protect him he will tell us the trouble with Elaine."

I considered a moment. "How's that?" I queried.

"Well," added Craig, "you see, Michael has become infuriated by the treatment he received from the Clutching Hand. I believe he cuffed him in the face yesterday. Anyway, he says he has determined to get even and betray him. So, after hearing how Elaine was, he slipped out of the servant's door and looking about carefully to see that he wasn't followed, he went straight to a drug store and called me up. He seemed extremely nervous and fearful."

I did not like the looks of the thing, and said so. "Craig," I objected vehemently, "don't go to meet him. It is a trap."

Kennedy had evidently considered my objection already.

"It may be a trap," he replied slowly, "but Elaine is dying and we've got to see this thing through."

As he spoke, he took an automatic from a drawer of a cabinet and thrust it into his pocket. Then he went to another drawer and took out several sections of thin tubing which seemed to be made to fasten together as a fishing pole is fastened, but were now separate, as if ready for travelling.

"Well—are you coming, Walter?" he asked finally—the only answer to my flood of caution.

Then he went out. I followed, still arguing.

"If YOU go, *I* go," I capitulated. "That's all there is to it."

Following the directions that Michael had given over the telephone Craig led me into one of the toughest parts of the lower West Side.

"Here's the place," he announced, stopping across the street from a dingy Raines Law Hotel.

"Pretty tough," I objected. "Are you sure?"

"Quite," replied Kennedy, consulting his note book again.

"Well, I'll be hanged if I'll go in that joint," I persisted.

It had no effect on Kennedy. "Nonsense, Walter," he replied, crossing the street.

Reluctantly I followed and we entered the place.

"I want a room," asked Craig as we were accosted by the proprietor, comfortably clad in a loud checked suit and striped shirt sleeves. "I had one here once before—forty-nine, I think."

"Fifty—" I began to correct.

Kennedy trod hard on my toes.

"Yes, forty-nine," he repeated.

The proprietor called a stout negro porter, waiter, and bell-hop all combined in one, who led us upstairs.

"Fohty-nine, sah," he pointed out, as Kennedy dropped a dime into his ready palm.

The negro left us and as Craig started to enter, I objected, "But, Craig, it was fifty-nine, not forty-nine. This is the wrong room."

"I know it," he replied. "I had it written in the book. But I want forty-nine—now. Just follow me, Walter."

Nervously I followed him into the room.

"Don't you understand?" he went on. "Room forty-nine is probably just the same as fifty-nine, except perhaps the pictures and furniture, only it is on the floor below."

He gazed about keenly. Then he took a few steps to the window and threw it open. As he stood there he took the parts of the rods he had been carrying and fitted them together until he had a pole some eight or ten feet long. At one end was a curious arrangement that seemed to contain lenses and a mirror. At the other end was an eye-piece, as nearly as I could make out.

"What is that?" I asked as he completed his work.

"That? That is an instrument something on the order of a miniature submarine periscope," Craig replied, still at work.

I watched him, fascinated at his resourcefulness. He stealthily thrust the mirror end of the periscope out of the window and up toward the corresponding window up stairs. Then he gazed eagerly through the eye-piece.

"Walter—look!" he exclaimed to me.

I did. There, sure enough, was Michael, pacing up and down the room. He had already preceded us. In his scared and stealthy manner, he had entered the Raines Law hotel which announced "Furnished Rooms for Gentlemen Only." There he had sought a room, fifty-nine, as he had said.

As he came into the room, he had looked about, overcome by the enormity of what he was about to do. He locked the door. Still, he had not been able to avoid gazing about fearfully, as he was doing now that we saw him.

Nothing had happened. Yet he brushed his hand over his forehead and breathed a sigh of relief. The air seemed to be stifling him and already he had gone to the window and thrown it open. Then he had gazed out as though there might be some unknown peril in the very air. He had now drawn back from the window and was considering. He was actually trembling. Should he flee? He whistled softly to himself to keep his shaking fears under control. Then he started to pace up and down the room in nervous impatience and irresolution.

As I looked at him nervously walking to and fro, I could not help admitting that things looked safe enough and all right to me. Kennedy folded the periscope up and we left our room, mounting the remaining flight of stairs.

In fifty-nine we could hear the measured step of the footman. Craig knocked. The footsteps ceased. Then the door opened slowly and I could see a cold blue automatic.

"Look out!" I cried.

Michael in his fear had drawn a gun.

"It's all right, Michael," reassured Craig calmly. "All right, Walter," he added to me.

The gun dropped back into the footman's pocket. We entered

and Michael again locked the door. Not a word had been spoken by him so far.

Next Michael moved to the center of the room and, as I realized later, brought himself in direct lines with the open window. He seemed to be overcome with fear at his betrayal and stood there breathing heavily.

"Professor Kennedy," he began, "I have been so mistreated that I have made up my mind to tell you all I know about this Clutching— "

Suddenly he drew a sharp breath and both his hands clutched at his own breast. He did not stagger and fall in the ordinary manner, but seemed to bend at the knees and waist and literally crumple down on his face.

We ran to him. Craig turned him over gently on his back and examined him. He called. No answer. Michael was almost pulseless.

Quickly Craig tore off his collar and bared his breast, for the man seemed to be struggling for breath. As he did so, he drew from Michael's chest a small, sharp-pointed dart.

"What's that?" I ejaculated, horror stricken.

"A poisoned blow gun dart such as is used by the South American Indians on the upper Orinoco," he said slowly.

He examined it carefully.

"What is the poison?" I asked.

"Curari," he replied simply. "It acts on the respiratory muscles, paralyzing them, and causing asphyxiation."

Arthur B. Reeve

The dart seemed to have been made of a quill with a very sharp point, hollow, and containing the deadly poison in the sharpened end.

"Look out!" I cautioned as he handled it.

"Oh, that's all right," he answered casually. "If I don't scratch myself, I am safe enough. I could swallow the stuff and it wouldn't hurt me—unless I had an abrasion of the lips or some internal cut."

Kennedy continued to examine the dart until suddenly I heard a low exclamation of surprise from him. Inside the hollow quill was a thin sheet of tissue paper, tightly rolled. He drew it out and read:

"To know me is DEATH Kennedy—Take Warning!"

Underneath was the inevitable Clutching Hand sign.

We jumped to our feet. Kennedy rushed to the window and slammed it shut, while I seized the key from Michael's pocket, opened the door and called for help.

A moment before, on the roof of a building across the street, one might have seen a bent, skulking figure. His face was copper colored and on his head was a thick thatch of matted hair. He looked like a South American Indian, in a very dilapidated suit of castoff American clothes.

He had slipped out through a doorway leading to a flight of steps from the roof to the hallway of the tenement. His fatal dart sent on its unerring mission with a precision born of long years in the South American jungle, he concealed the deadly blow-gun in his breast pocket, with a cruel smile, and, like one of his native venomous serpents, wormed his way down the stairs again.

*   *   *   *   *

My outcry brought a veritable battalion of aid. The hotel proprietor, the negro waiter, and several others dashed upstairs, followed shortly by a portly policeman, puffing at the exertion.

"What's the matter, here?" he panted. "Ye're all under arrest!"

Kennedy quietly pulled out his card case and taking the policeman aside showed it to him.

"We had an appointment to meet this man—in that Clutching Hand case, you know. He is Miss Dodge's footman," Craig explained.

Then he took the policeman into his confidence, showing him the dart and explaining about the poison. The officer stared blankly.

"I must get away, too," hurried on Craig. "Officer, I will leave you to take charge here. You can depend on me for the inquest."

The officer nodded.

"Come on, Walter," whispered Craig, eager to get away, then adding the one word, "Elaine!"

I followed hastily, not slow to understand his fear for her.

Nor were Craig's fears groundless. In spite of all that could be done for her, Elaine was still in bed, much weaker now than before. While we had been gone, Dr. Hayward, Aunt Josephine and Marie were distracted.

More than that, the Clutching Hand had not neglected the opportunity, either.

Suddenly, just before our return, a stone had come hurtling through the window, without warning of any kind, and had landed on Elaine's bed.

Below, as we learned some time afterwards, a car had drawn up hastily and the evil-faced crook whom the Clutching Hand had used to rid himself of the informer, "Limpy Red," had leaped out and hurled the stone through the window, as quickly leaping back into the car and whisking away.

Elaine had screamed. All had reached for the stone. But she had been the first to seize it and discover that around it was wrapped a piece of paper on which was the ominous warning, signed as usual by the Hand:

"Michael is dead. Tomorrow, you. Then Kennedy. Stop before it is too late."

Elaine had sunk back into her pillows, paler than ever from this second shock, while the others, as they read the note, were overcome by alarm and despair, at the suddenness of the thing.

It was just then that Kennedy and I arrived and were admitted.

"Oh, Mr. Kennedy," cried Elaine, handing him the note.

Craig took it and read. "Miss Dodge," he said, as he held the note out to me, "you are suffering from arsenic poisoning—

but I don't know yet how it is being administered."

He gazed about keenly. Meanwhile, I had taken the crumpled note from him and was reading it. Somehow, I had leaned against the wall. As I turned, Craig happened to glance at me.

"For heaven's sake, Walter," I heard him exclaim. "What have you been up against?"

He fairly leaped at me and I felt him examining my shoulder where I had been leaning on the wall. Something on the paper had come off and had left a white mark on my shoulder. Craig looked puzzled from me to the wall.

"Arsenic!" he cried.

He whipped out a pocket lens and looked at the paper. "This heavy fuzzy paper is fairly loaded with it, powdered," he reported.

I looked, too. The powdered arsenic was plainly discernible. "Yes, here it is," he continued, standing absorbed in thought. "But why did it work so effectively?"

He sniffed as he had before. So did I. There was still the faint smell of garlic. Kennedy paced the room. Suddenly, pausing by the register, an idea seemed to strike him.

"Walter," he whispered, "come down cellar with me."

"Oh—be careful," cried Elaine, anxious for him.

"I will," he called back.

As he flashed his pocket electric bull's-eye about, his gaze

Arthur B. Reeve

fell on the electric meter. He paused before it. In spite of the fact that it was broad daylight, it was running. His face puckered.

"They are using no current at present in the house," he ruminated. "Yet the meter is running."

He continued to examine the meter. Then he began to follow the electric wires along. At last he discovered a place where they had been tampered with and tapped by other wires.

"The work of the Clutching Hand!" he muttered.

Eagerly he followed the wires to the furnace and around to the back. There they led right into a little water tank. Kennedy yanked them out. As he did so he pulled something with them.

"Two electrodes—the villain placed there," he exclaimed, holding them up triumphantly for me to see.

"Y-yes," I replied dubiously, "but what does it all mean?"

"Why, don't you see? Under the influence of the electric current the water was decomposed and gave off oxygen and hydrogen. The free hydrogen passed up the furnace pipe and combining with the arsenic in the wall paper formed the deadly arseniuretted hydrogen."

He cast the whole improvised electrolysis apparatus on the floor and dashed up the cellar steps.

"I've found it!" he cried, hurrying into Elaine's room. "It's in this room—a deadly gas—arseniuretted hydrogen."

He tore open the windows and threw them all open. "Have

her moved," he cried to Aunt Josephine. "Then have a vacuum cleaner go over every inch of wall, carpet and upholstery."

Standing beside her, he breathlessly explained his discovery. "That wall paper has been loaded down with arsenic, probably Paris green or Schweinfurth green, which is aceto-arsenite of copper. Every minute you are here, you are breathing arseniuretted hydrogen. The Clutching Hand has cleverly contrived to introduce the nascent gas into the room. That acts on the arsenic compounds in the wall paper and hangings and sets free the gas. I thought I knew the smell the moment I got a whiff of it. You are slowly being poisoned by minute quantities of the deadly gas. This Clutching Hand is a diabolical genius. Think of it—poisoned wall paper!"

No one said a word. Kennedy reached down and took the two Clutching Hand messages Elaine had received. "I shall want to study these notes, more, too," he said, holding them up to the wall at the head of the bed as he flashed his pocket lens at them. "You see, Elaine, I may be able to get something from studying the ink, the paper, the handwriting—"

Suddenly both leaped back, with a cry.

Their faces had been several inches apart. Something had whizzed between them and literally impaled the two notes on the wall.

Down the street, on the roof of a carriage house, back of a neighbor's, might have been seen the uncouth figure of the dilapidated South American Indian crouching behind a chimney and gazing intently at the Dodge house.

As Craig had thrown open Elaine's window and turned to Elaine, the figure had crouched closer to his chimney.

Then with an uncanny determination he slowly raised the blow-gun to his lips.

I jumped forward, followed by Dr. Hayward, Aunt Josephine, and Marie. Kennedy had a peculiar look as he pulled out from the wall a blow-gun dart similar in every way to that which had killed Michael.

"Craig!" gasped Elaine, reaching up and laying her soft white hand on his arm in undisguised fear for him, "you—you must give up this chase for the Clutching Hand!"

"Give up the chase for the Clutching Hand?" he repeated in surprise. "Never! Not until either he or I is dead!"

There was both fear and admiration mingled in her look, as he reached down and patted her dainty shoulder encouragingly.

CHAPTER VI

THE VAMPIRE

Kennedy went the next day to the Dodge house, and, as usual, Perry Bennett was there in the library with Elaine, still going over the Clutching Hand case, in their endeavor to track down the mysterious master criminal.

Bennett seemed as deeply as ever in love with Elaine. Still, as Jennings admitted Craig, it was sufficiently evident by the manner in which Elaine left Bennett and ran to meet Craig that she had the highest regard for him.

"I've brought you a little document that may interest you," remarked Kennedy, reaching into his pocket and pulling out an envelope.

Elaine tore it open and looked at the paper within.

"Oh, how thoughtful of you!" she exclaimed in surprise.

It was a permit from the police made out in her name allowing her to carry a revolver.

A moment later, Kennedy reached into his coat pocket and produced a little automatic which he handed to her.

"Thank you," she cried eagerly.

Elaine examined the gun with interest, then, raising it, pointed it playfully at Bennett.

"Oh—no—no!" exclaimed Kennedy, taking her arm quickly, and gently deflecting the weapon away. "You mustn't think it is a toy. It explodes at a mere touch of the trigger—when that safety ratchet is turned."

Bennett had realized the danger and had jumped back, almost mechanically. As he did so, he bumped into a suit of medieval armor standing by the wall, knocking it over with a resounding crash.

"I beg pardon," he ejaculated, "I'm very sorry. That was very awkward of me."

Jennings, who had been busy about the portieres at the doorway, started to pick up the fallen knight. Some of the pieces were broken, and the three gathered about as the butler tried to fit them together again as best he could.

"Too bad, too bad," apologized Bennett profusely. "I really forgot how close I was to the thing."

"Oh, never mind," returned Elaine, a little crestfallen, "It is smashed all right—but it was my fault. Jennings, send for someone to repair it."

She turned to Kennedy. "But I do wish you would teach me how to use this thing," she added, touching the automatic gingerly.

"Gladly," he returned.

"Won't you join us, Mr. Bennett?" asked Elaine.

"No," the young lawyer smiled, "I'm afraid I can't. You see, I had an engagement with another client and I'm already late."

He took his hat and coat and, with a reluctant farewell, moved toward the hallway.

A moment later Elaine and Craig followed, while Jennings finished restoring the armor as nearly as possible as it had been.

* * * * *

It was late that night that a masked figure succeeded in raising itself to the narrow ornamental ledge under Elaine's bedroom window.

Elaine was a light sleeper and, besides, Rusty, her faithful collie, now fully recovered from the poison, was in her room.

Rusty growled and the sudden noise wakened her.

Startled, Elaine instantly thought of the automatic. She reached under her pillow, keeping very quiet, and drew forth the gun that Craig had given her. Stealthily concealing her actions under the covers, she levelled the automatic at the figure silhouetted in her window and fired three times.

The figure fell back.

Down in the street, below, the assistant of the Clutching Hand who had waited while Taylor Dodge was electrocuted, was waiting now as his confederate, "Pitts Slim"—which indicated that he was both wiry in stature and libellous in delegating his nativity—made the attempt.

As Slim came tumbling down, having fallen back from the window above, mortally wounded, the confederate lifted him up and carried him out of sight hurriedly.

Elaine, by this time, had turned on the lights and had run to the window to look out. Rusty was barking loudly.

In a side street, nearby, stood a waiting automobile, at the wheel of which sat another of the emissaries of the Clutching Hand. The driver looked up, startled, as he saw his fellow hurry around the corner carrying the wounded Pitts Slim. It was the work of just a moment to drop the wounded man, as comfortably as possible under the circumstances, in the rear seat, while his pals started the car off with a jerk in the hurry of escape.

Jennings, having hastily slipped his trousers on over his pajamas came running down the hall, while Marie, frightened, came in the other direction. Aunt Josephine appeared a few seconds later, adding to the general excitement.

"What's the matter?" she asked, anxiously.

"A burglar, I think," exclaimed Elaine, still holding the gun in her hand. "Someone tried to get into my window."

"My gracious," cried Aunt Josephine, in alarm, "where will this thing end?"

Elaine was doing her best now to quiet the fears of her aunt and the rest of the household.

"Well," she laughed, a little nervously, now that it was all over, "I want you all to go to bed and stop worrying about me. Don't you see, I'm perfectly able to take care of myself? Besides, there isn't a chance, now, of the burglar coming back. Why, I shot him."

"Yes," put in Aunt Josephine, "but—"

Elaine laughingly interrupted her and playfully made as though she were driving them out of her room, although they were all very much concerned over the affair. However, they went finally, and she locked the door.

"Rusty!" she called, "Down there!"

The intelligent collie seemed to understand. He lay down by the doorway, his nose close to the bottom of the door and his ears alert.

Finally Elaine, too, retired again.

* * * * *

Meanwhile the wounded man was being hurried to one of the hangouts of the mysterious Clutching Hand, an old-fashioned house in the Westchester suburbs. It was a carefully hidden place, back from the main road, surrounded by trees, with a driveway leading up to it.

The car containing the wounded Pitts Slim drew up and the other two men leaped out of it. With a hurried glance about, they unlocked the front door with a pass-key and entered, carrying the man.

Indoors was another emissary of the Clutching Hand, a rather studious looking chap.

"Why, what's the matter?" he exclaimed, as the crooks entered his room, supporting their half-fainting, wounded pal.

"Slim got a couple of pills," they panted, as they laid him on a couch.

"How?" demanded the other.

"Trying to get into the Dodge house. Elaine did it."

Slim was, quite evidently, badly wounded and was bleeding profusely. A glance at him was enough for the studious-looking chap. He went to a secret panel and, pressing it down, took out what was apparently a house telephone.

In another part of this mysterious house was the secret room of the Clutching Hand himself where he hid his identity from even his most trusted followers. It was a small room, lined with books on every conceivable branch of science that might aid him and containing innumerable little odds and ends of paraphernalia that might help in his nefarious criminal career.

His telephone rang and he took down the receiver.

"Pitts Slim's been wounded—badly—Chief," was all he waited to hear.

With scarcely a word, he hung up the receiver, then opened a table drawer and took out his masking handkerchief. Next he went to a nearby bookcase, pressed another secret spring, and a panel opened. He passed through, the handkerchief adjusted.

Across, in the larger, outside study, another panel opened and the Clutching Hand, all crouched up, transformed, appeared. Without a word he advanced to the couch on which the wounded crook lay and examined him.

"How did it happen?" he asked at length.

"Miss Dodge shot him," answered the others, "with an automatic."

"That Craig Kennedy must have given it to her!" he exclaimed with suppressed fury.

For a moment the Clutching Hand stopped to consider. Then he seized the regular telephone.

"Dr. Morton?" he asked as he got the number he called.

Late as it was the doctor, who was a well-known surgeon in that part of the country, answered, apparently from an extension of his telephone near his bed.

The call was urgent and apparently from a family which he did not feel that he could neglect.

"Yes, I'll be there—in a few moments," he yawned, hanging up the receiver and getting out of bed.

Dr. Morton was a middle-aged man, one of those medical men in whose judgment one instinctively relies. From the brief description of the "hemorrhage" which the Clutching Hand had cleverly made over the wire, he knew that a life was at stake. Quickly he dressed and went out to his garage, back of the house to get his little runabout.

It was only a matter of minutes before the doctor was speeding over the now deserted suburban roads, apparently on his errand of mercy.

At the address that had been given him, he drew up to the side of the road, got out and ran up the steps to the door. A ring at the bell brought a sleepy man to the door, in his trousers and nightshirt.

"How's the patient?" asked Dr. Morton, eagerly.

"Patient?" repeated the man, rubbing his eyes. "There's no one sick here."

"Then what did you telephone for?" asked the doctor peevishly,

"Telephone? I didn't call up anyone, I was asleep."

Slowly it dawned on the doctor that it was a false alarm and that he must be the victim of some practical joke.

"Well, that's a great note," he growled, as the man shut the door.

He descended the steps, muttering harsh language at some unknown trickster. As he climbed back into his machine and made ready to start, two men seemed to rise before him, as if from nowhere.

As a matter of fact, they had been sent there by the Clutching Hand and were hiding in a nearby cellar way until their chance came.

One man stood on the running board, on either side of him, and two guns yawned menacingly at him.

"Drive ahead—that way!" muttered one man, seating himself in the runabout with his gun close to the doctor's ribs.

The other kept his place on the running board, and on they drove in the direction of the mysterious, dark house. Half a mile, perhaps, down the road, they halted and left the car beside the walk.

Dr. Morton was too surprised to marvel at anything now and he realized that he was in the power of two desperate men. Quickly, they blindfolded him.

It seemed an interminable walk, as they led him about to confuse him, but at last he could feel that they had taken him into a house and along passageways, which they were making unnecessarily long in order to destroy all recollection that they could. Finally he knew that he was in a room in which others were present. He suppressed a shudder at the low, menacing voices.

A moment later he felt them remove the bandage from his eyes, and, blinking at the light, he could see a hard-faced fellow, pale and weak, on a blood-stained couch. Over him bent a masked man and another man stood nearby, endeavoring by improvised bandages to stop the flow of blood.

"What can you do for this fellow?" asked the masked man.

Dr. Morton, seeing nothing else to do, for he was more than outnumbered now, bent down and examined him.

As he rose, he said, "He will be dead from loss of blood by morning, no matter if he is properly bandaged."

"Is there nothing that can save him?" whispered the Clutching Hand hoarsely.

"Blood transfusion might save him," replied the Doctor. "But so much blood would be needed that whoever gives it would be liable to die himself."

Arthur B. Reeve

Clutching Hand stood silent a moment, thinking, as he gazed at the man who had been one of his chief reliances. Then, with a menacing gesture, he spoke in a low, bitter tone.

"SHE WHO SHOT HIM SHALL SUPPLY THE BLOOD."

* * * * *

A few quick directions followed to his subordinates, and as he made ready to go, he muttered, "Keep the doctor here. Don't let him stir from the room."

Then, with the man who had aided him in the murder of Taylor Dodge, he sallied out into the blackness that precedes dawn.

It was just before early daybreak when the Clutching Hand and his confederate reached the Dodge House in the city and came up to the back door, over the fences. As they stood there, the Clutching Hand produced a master key and started to open the door. But before he did so, he took out his watch.

"Let me see," he ruminated. "Twenty minutes past four. At exactly half past, I want you to do as I told you—see?"

The other crook nodded.

"You may go," ordered the Clutching Hand.

As the crook slunk away, Clutching Hand stealthily let himself into the house. Noiselessly he prowled through the halls until he came to Elaine's doorway.

He gave a hasty look up and down the hall. There was no sound. Quickly he took a syringe from his pocket and bent down by the door. Inserting the end under it, he squirted some liquid through which vaporized rapidly in a wide, fine stream of spray. Before he could give an alarm, Rusty was overcome by the noxious fumes, rolled over on his back and lay still.

Outside, the other crook was waiting, looking at his watch. As the hand slowly turned the half hour, he snapped the watch shut. With a quick glance up and down the deserted street, he deftly started up the rain pipe that passed near Elaine's window.

This time there was no faithful Rusty to give warning and the second intruder, after a glance at Elaine, still sleeping, went quickly to the door, dragged the insensible dog out of the way, turned the key and admitted the Clutching Hand. As he did so he closed the door.

Evidently the fumes had not reached Elaine, or if they had, the inrush of fresh air revived her, for she waked and quickly reached for the gun. In an instant the other crook had leaped at her. Holding his hand over her mouth to prevent her screaming he snatched the revolver away before she could fire it.

In the meantime the Clutching Hand had taken out some chloroform and, rolling a towel in the form of a cone, placed it over her face. She struggled, gasping and gagging, but the struggles grew weaker and weaker and finally ceased altogether.

When Elaine was completely under the influence of the drug, they lifted her out of bed, the chloroform cone still over her face, and quietly carried her to the door which they opened stealthily.

Downstairs they carried her until they came to the library

Arthur B. Reeve

with its new safe and there they placed her on a couch.

* * * * *

At an early hour an express wagon stopped before the Dodge house and Jennings, half dressed, answered the bell.

"We've come for that broken suit of armor to be repaired," said a workman.

Jennings let the men in. The armor was still on the stand and the repairers took armor, stand, and all, laying it on the couch where they wrapped it in the covers they had brought for the purpose. They lifted it up and started to carry it out.

"Be careful," cautioned the thrifty Jennings.

Rusty, now recovered, was barking and sniffing at the armor.

"Kick the mutt off," growled one man.

The other did so and Rusty snarled and snapped at him. Jennings took him by the collar and held him as the repairers went out, loaded the armor on the wagon, and drove off.

Scarcely had they gone, while Jennings straightened out the disarranged library, when Rusty began jumping about, barking furiously. Jennings looked at him in amazement, as the dog ran to the window and leaped out.

He had no time to look after the dog, though, for at that very instant he heard a voice calling, "Jennings! Jennings!"

It was Marie, almost speechless. He followed her as she led the way to Miss Elaine's room. There Marie pointed mutely at the bed.

Elaine was not there.

There, too, were her clothes, neatly folded, as Marie had hung them for her.

"Something must have happened to her!" wailed Marie.

Jennings was now thoroughly alarmed.

Meanwhile the express wagon outside was driving off, with Rusty tearing after it.

"What's the matter?" cried Aunt Josephine coming in where the footman and the maid were arguing what was to be done.

She gave one look at the bed, the clothes, and the servants.

"Call Mr. Kennedy!" she cried in alarm.

* * * * *

"Elaine is gone—no one knows how or where," announced Craig as he leaped out of bed that morning to answer the furious ringing of our telephone bell.

It was very early, but Craig dressed hurriedly and I followed as best I could, for he had the start of me, tieless and collarless.

When we arrived at the Dodge house, Aunt Josephine and Marie were fully dressed. Jennings let us in.

"What has happened?" demanded Kennedy breathlessly.

While Aunt Josephine tried to tell him, Craig was busy examining the room.

Arthur B. Reeve

"Let us see the library," he said at length.

Accordingly down to the library we went. Kennedy looked about. He seemed to miss something.

"Where is the armor?" he demanded.

"Why, the men came for it and took it away to repair," answered Jennings.

Kennedy's brow clouded in deep thought.

Outside we had left our taxi, waiting. The door was open and a new footman, James, was sweeping the rug, when past him flashed a dishevelled hairy streak.

We were all standing there still as Craig questioned Jennings about the armor. With a yelp Rusty tore frantically into the room. A moment he stopped and barked. We all looked at him in surprise. Then, as no one moved, he seemed to single out Kennedy. He seized Craig's coat in his teeth and tried to drag him out.

"Here, Rusty—down, sir, down!" called Jennings.

"No, Jennings, no," interposed Craig. "What's the matter, old fellow?"

Craig patted Rusty whose big brown eyes seemed mutely appealing. Out of the doorway he went, barking still. Craig and I followed while the rest stood in the vestibule.

Rusty was trying to lead Kennedy down the street!

"Wait here," called Kennedy to Aunt Josephine, as he stepped with me on the running board of the cab. "Go on,

Rusty, good dog!"

Rusty needed no urging. With an eager yelp he started off, still barking, ahead of us, our car following. On we went, much to the astonishment of those who were on the street at such an early hour.

It seemed miles that we went, but at last we came to a peculiarly deserted looking house. Here Rusty turned in and began scratching at the door. We jumped off the cab and followed.

The door was locked when we tried and from inside we could get no answer. We put our shoulders to it and burst it in. Rusty gave a leap forward with a joyous bark.

We followed, more cautiously. There were pieces of armor strewn all over the floor. Rusty sniffed at them and looked about, disappointed, then howled.

I looked from the armor to Kennedy, in blank amazement.

"Elaine was kidnapped—in the armor," he cried.

* * * * *

He was right. Meanwhile, the armor repairers had stopped at last at this apparently deserted house, a strange sort of repair shop. Still keeping it wrapped in blankets, they had taken the armor out of the wagon and now laid it down on an old broken bed. Then they had unwrapped it and taken off the helmet.

There was Elaine!

She had been stupefied, bound and gagged. Piece after piece

Arthur B. Reeve

of the armor they removed, finding her still only half conscious.

"Sh! What's that?" cautioned one of the men. They paused and listened. Sure enough, there was a sound outside. They opened the window cautiously. A dog was scratching on the door, endeavoring to get in. It was Rusty.

"I think it's her dog," said the man, turning. "We'd better let him in. Someone might see him."

The other nodded and a moment later the door opened and in ran Rusty. Straight to Elaine he went, starting to lick her hand.

"Right—her dog," exclaimed the other man, drawing a gun and hastily levelling it at Rusty.

"Don't!" cautioned the first. "It would make too much noise. You'd better choke him!"

The fellow grabbed for Rusty. Rusty was too quick. He jumped. Around the room they ran. Rusty saw the wide open window—and his chance. Out he went and disappeared, leaving the man cussing at him.

A moment's argument followed, then they wrapped Elaine in the blankets alone, still bound and gagged, and carried her out.

* * * * *

In the secret den, the Clutching Hand was waiting, gazing now and then at his watch, and then at the wounded man before him. In a chair his first assistant sat, watching Dr. Morton.

A knock at the door caused them to turn their heads. The crook opened it and in walked the other crooks who had carried off Elaine in the suit of armor.

Elaine was now almost conscious, as they sat her down in a chair and partly loosed her bonds and the gag. She gazed about, frightened.

"Oh—help! help!" she screamed as she caught sight of the now familiar mask of the Clutching Hand.

"Call all you want—here, young lady," he laughed un-naturally. "No one can hear. These walls are soundproof!"

Elaine shrank back.

"Now, doc.," he added harshly to Dr. Morton. "It was she who shot him. Her blood must save him."

Dr. Morton recoiled at the thought of torturing the beautiful young girl before him.

"Are—you willing—to have your blood transfused?" he parleyed.

"No—no—no!" she cried in horror,

Dr. Morton turned to the desperate criminal. "I cannot do it."

"The deuce you can't!" A cold steel revolver pressed down on Dr. Morton's stomach. In the other hand the master crook held his watch.

"You have just one minute to make up your mind."

Dr. Morton shrank back. The revolver followed. The

pressure of a fly's foot meant eternity for him.

"I—I'll try!"

The other crooks next carried Elaine, struggling, and threw her down beside the wounded man. Together they arranged another couch beside him.

Dr. Morton, still covered by the gun, bent over the two, the hardened criminal and the delicate, beautiful girl. Clutching Hand glared fiendishly, insanely.

From his bag he took a little piece of something that shone like silver. It was in the form of a minute, hollow cylinder, with two grooves on it, a cylinder so tiny that it would scarcely have slipped over the point of a pencil.

"A cannulla," he explained, as he prepared to make an incision in Elaine's arm and in the arm of the wounded rogue.

He cuffed it over the severed end of the artery, so cleverly that the inner linings of the vein and artery, the endothelium as it is called, were in complete contact with each other.

Clutching Hand watched eagerly, as though he had found some new, scientific engine of death in the little hollow cylinder.

A moment and the blood that was, perhaps, to save the life of the wounded felon was coursing into his veins from Elaine.

A moment later, Dr. Morton looked up at the Clutching Hand and nodded, "Well, it's working!"

At Elaine's head, Clutching Hand himself was administering

just enough ether to keep her under and prevent a struggle that would wreck all. The wounded man had not been anesthetized and seemed feebly conscious of what was being done to save him.

All were now bending over the two.

Dr. Morton bent closest over Elaine. He looked at her anxiously, felt her pulse, watched her breathing, then pursed up his lips.

"This is—dangerous," he ventured, gazing askance at the grim Clutching Hand.

"Can't help it," came back laconically and relentlessly.

The doctor shuddered.

The man was a veritable vampire!

* * * * *

Outside the deserted house, Kennedy and I were looking helplessly about.

Suddenly Kennedy dashed back and reappeared a minute later with a couple of pieces of armor. He held them down to Rusty and the dog sniffed at them.

But Rusty stood still.

Kennedy pointed to the ground.

Nothing doing. In leading us where he had been before, Rusty had reached the end of his canine ability.

Everything we could do to make Rusty understand that we wanted him to follow a trail was unavailing. He simply could not do it. Kennedy coaxed and scolded. Rusty merely sat up on his hind legs and begged with those irresistible brown eyes.

"You can't make a bloodhound out of a collie," despaired Craig, looking about again helplessly.

Then he reached into his pocket and pulled out a police whistle. He blew three sharp blasts.

Would it bring help?

* * * * *

While we were thus despairing, the continued absence of Dr. Morton from home had alarmed his family and had set in motion another train of events.

When he did not return, and could not be located at the place to which he was supposed to have gone, several policemen had been summoned to his house, and they had come, finally, with real bloodhounds from a suburban station.

There were the tracks of his car. That the police themselves could follow, while two men came along holding in leash the pack, leaders of which were "Searchlight" and "Bob."

It had not been long before the party came across the deserted runabout beside the road. There they had stopped, for a moment.

It was just then that they heard Kennedy's call, and one of them had been detailed to answer it.

"Well, what do YOU want?" asked the officer, eyeing Kennedy suspiciously as he stood there with the armor. "What's them pieces of tin—hey?"

Kennedy quickly flashed his own special badge. "I want to trail a girl," he exclaimed hurriedly. "Can I find a bloodhound about here?"

"A hound? Why, we have a pack—over there."

"Bring them—quick!" ordered Craig.

The policeman, who was an intelligent fellow, saw at once that, as Kennedy said, the two trails probably crossed. He shouted and in a few seconds the others, with the pack, came.

A brief parley resulted in our joining forces.

Kennedy held the armor down to the dogs. "Searchlight" gave a low whine, then, followed by "Bob" and the others, was off, all with noses close to the ground. We followed.

The armor was, after all, the missing link.

Through woods and fields the dogs led us.

Would we be in time to rescue Elaine?

* * * * *

In the mysterious haunt of the Clutching Hand, all were still standing around Elaine and the wounded Pitts Slim.

Just then a cry from one of the group startled the rest. One of them, less hardened than the Clutching Hand, had turned

Arthur B. Reeve

away from the sight, had gone to the window, and had been attracted by something outside.

"Look!" he cried.

From the absolute stillness of death, there was now wild excitement among the crooks.

"Police! Police!" they shouted to each other as they fled by a doorway to a secret passage.

Clutching Hand turned to his first assistant.

"You—go—too," he ordered.

* * * * *

The dogs had led us to a strange looking house, and were now baying and leaping up against the door. We did not stop to knock, but began to break through, for inside we could hear faintly sounds of excitement and cries of "Police— police!"

The door yielded and we rushed into a long hallway. Up the passage we went until we came to another door.

An instant and we were all against it. It was stout, but it shook before us. The panels began to yield.

* * * * *

On the other side of that door from us, the master crook stood for a moment. Dr. Morton hesitated, not knowing quite what to do.

Just then the wounded Pitts Slim lifted his hand feebly. He

seemed vaguely to understand that the game was up. He touched the Clutching Hand.

"You did your best, Chief," he murmured thickly. "Beat it, if you can. I'm a goner, anyway."

Clutching Hand hesitated by the wounded crook. This was the loyalty of gangland, worthy a better cause. He could not bring himself to desert his pal. He was undecided, still.

But there was the door, bulging, and a panel bursting.

He moved over to a panel in the wall and pushed a spring. It slid open and he stepped through. Then it closed—not a second too soon.

Back in his private room, he quickly stepped to a curtained iron door. Pushing back the curtains, he went through it and disappeared, the curtains falling back.

At the end of the passageway, he stopped, in a sort of grotto or cave. As he came out, he looked back. All was still. No one was about. He was safe here, at least!

Off came the mask and he turned down the road a few rods distant beyond some bushes, as little concerned about the wild happenings as any other passer-by might have been.

* * * * *

At the very moment when we burst in, Dr. Morton, seeing his chance, stopped the blood transfusion, working frantically to stop the flow of blood.

Kennedy sprang to Elaine's side, horrified by the blood that had spattered over everything.

Arthur B. Reeve

With a mighty effort he checked a blow that he had aimed at Dr. Morton, as it flashed over him that the surgeon, now free again, was doing his best to save the terribly imperilled life of Elaine.

Just then the police burst through the secret panel and rushed on, leaving us alone, with the unconscious, scarcely breathing Elaine. From the sounds we could tell that they had come to the private room of the Clutching Hand. It was empty and they were non- plussed.

"Not a window!" called one.

"What are those curtains?"

They pulled them back, disclosing an iron door. They tried it but it was bolted on the other side. Blows had no effect. They had to give it up for the instant.

A policeman now stood beside Elaine and the wounded burglar who was muttering deliriously to himself.

He was pretty far gone, as the policeman knelt down and tried to get a statement out of him.

"Who was that man who left you—last—the Clutching Hand?"

Not a word came from the crook.

The policeman repeated his question.

With his last strength, he looked disdainfully at the officer's pad and pencil. "The gangster never squeals," he snarled, as he fell back.

Dr. Morton had paid no attention whatever to him, but was working desperately now over Elaine, trying to bring her back to life.

"Is she—going to—die?" gasped Craig, frantically.

Every eye was riveted on Dr. Morton.

"She is all right," he muttered. "But the man is going to die."

At the sound of Craig's voice Elaine had feebly opened her eyes.

"Thank heaven," breathed Craig, with a sigh of relief, as his hand gently stroked Elaine's unnaturally cold forehead.

Arthur B. Reeve

CHAPTER VII

THE DOUBLE TRAP

Mindful of the sage advice that a time of peace is best employed in preparing for war, I was busily engaged in cleaning my automatic gun one morning as Kennedy and I were seated in our living room.

Our door buzzer sounded and Kennedy, always alert, jumped up, pushing aside a great pile of papers which had accumulated in the Dodge case.

Two steps took him to the wall where the day before he had installed a peculiar box about four by six inches long connected in some way with a lens-like box of similar size above our bell and speaking tube in the hallway below. He opened it, disclosing an oblong plate of ground glass.

"I thought the seismograph arrangement was not quite enough after that spring-gun affair," he remarked, "so I have put in a sort of teleview of my own invention—so that I can see down into the vestibule downstairs. Well—just look who's here!"

"Some new fandangled periscope arrangement, I suppose?" I queried moving slowly over toward it.

However, one look was enough to interest me. I can express it only in slang. There, framed in the little thing, was a vision of as swell a "chicken" as I have ever seen.

I whistled under my breath.

"Um!" I exclaimed shamelessly, "A peach! Who's your friend?"

I had never said a truer word than in my description of her, though I did not know it at the time. She was indeed known as "Gertie the Peach" in the select circle to which she belonged.

Gertie was very attractive, though frightfully over-dressed. But, then, no one thinks anything of that now, in New York.

Kennedy had opened the lower door and our fair visitor was coming upstairs. Meanwhile he was deeply in thought before the "teleview." He made up his mind quickly, however.

"Go in there, Walter," he said, seizing me quickly and pushing me into my room. "I want you to wait there and watch her carefully."

I slipped the gun into my pocket and went, just as a knock at the door told me she was outside.

Kennedy opened the door, disclosing a very excited young woman.

"Oh, Professor Kennedy," she cried, all in one breath, with much emotion, "I'm so glad I found you in. I can't tell you. Oh—my jewels! They have been stolen—and my husband must not know of it. Help me to recover them—please!"

Arthur B. Reeve

She had not paused, but had gone on in a wild, voluble explanation.

"Just a moment, my dear young lady," interrupted Craig, finding at last a chance to get a word in edgewise. "Do you see that table—and all those papers? Really, I can't take your case. I am too busy as it is even to take the cases of many of my own clients."

"But, please, Professor Kennedy—please!" she begged. "Help me. It means—oh, I can't tell you how much it means to me!"

She had come close to him and had laid her warm, little soft hand on his, in ardent entreaty.

From my hiding place in my room, I could not help seeing that she was using every charm of her sex and personality to lure him on, as she clung confidingly to him. Craig was very much embarrassed, and I could not help a smile at his discomfiture. Seriously, I should have hated to have been in his position.

Gertie had thrown her arms about Kennedy, as if in wildest devotion. I wondered what Elaine would have thought, if she had a picture of that!

"Oh," she begged him, "please—please, help me!"

Still Kennedy seemed utterly unaffected by her passionate embrace. Carefully he loosened her fingers from about his neck and removed the plump, enticing arms.

Gertie sank into a chair, weeping, while Kennedy stood before her a moment in deep abstraction.

Finally he seemed to make up his mind to something. His manner toward her changed. He took a step to her side.

"I WILL help you," he said, laying his hand on her shoulder. "If it is possible I will recover your jewels. Where do you live?"

"At Hazlehurst," she replied, gratefully. "Oh, Mr. Kennedy, how can I ever thank you?"

She seemed overcome with gratitude and took his hand, pressed it, even kissed it.

"Just a minute," he added, carefully extricating his hand. "I'll be ready in just a minute."

Kennedy entered the room where I was listening.

"What's it all about, Craig?" I whispered, mystified.

For a moment he stood thinking, apparently reconsidering what he had just done. Then his second thought seemed to approve it.

"This is a trap of the Clutching Hand, Walter," he whispered, adding tensely, "and we're going to walk right into it."

I looked at him in amazement.

"But, Craig," I demurred, "that's foolhardy. Have her trailed —anything—but—-"

He shook his head and with a mere motion of his hand brushed aside my objections as he went to a cabinet across the room.

From one shelf he took out a small metal box and from another a test tube, placing the test tube in his waistcoat pocket, and the small box in his coatpocket, with excessive care.

Then he turned and motioned to me to follow him out into the other room. I did so, stuffing my "gatt" into my pocket.

"Let me introduce my friend, Mr. Jameson," said Craig, presenting me to the pretty crook.

The introduction quickly over, we three went out to get Craig's car which he kept at a nearby garage.

* * * * *

That forenoon, Perry Bennett was reading up a case. In the outer office Milton Schofield, his office boy, was Industriously chewing gum and admiring his feet cocked up on the desk before him.

The door to the waiting room opened and an attractive woman of perhaps thirty, dressed in extreme mourning, entered with a boy.

Milton cast a glance of scorn at the "little dude." He was in reality about fourteen years old but was dressed to look much younger.

Milton took his feet down in deference to the lady, but snickered openly at the boy. A fight seemed imminent.

"Did you wish to see Mr. Bennett?" asked the precocious Milton politely on one hand while on the other he made a wry grimace.

"Yes—here is my card," replied the woman.

It was deeply bordered in black. Even Milton was startled at reading it: "Mrs. Taylor Dodge."

He looked at the woman in open-mouthed astonishment. Even he knew that Elaine's mother had been dead for years.

The woman, however, true to her name in the artistic coterie in which she was leader, had sunk into a chair and was sobbing convulsively, as only "Weepy Mary" could.

It was so effective that even Milton was visibly moved. He took the card in, excitedly, to Bennett.

"There's a woman outside—says she is Mrs. Dodge!" he cried.

If Milton had had an X-ray eye he could have seen her take a cigarette from her handbag and light it nonchalantly the moment he was gone.

As for Bennett, Milton, who was watching him closely, thought he was about to discharge him on the spot for bothering him. He took the card, and his face expressed the most extreme surprise, then anger. He thought a moment.

"Tell that woman to state her business in writing," he thundered curtly at Milton.

As the boy turned to go back to the waiting room, Weepy Mary, hearing him coming, hastily shoved the cigarette into her "son's" hand.

"Mr. Bennett says for you to write out what it is you want to see him about," reported Milton, indicating the table before which she was sitting.

Mary had automatically taken up sobbing, with the release of the cigarette. She looked at the table on which were letter paper, pens and ink.

"I may write here?" she asked.

"Surely, ma'am," replied Milton, still very much overwhelmed by her sorrow.

Weepy Mary sat there, writing and sobbing.

In the midst of his sympathy, however, Milton sniffed. There was an unmistakable odor of tobacco smoke about the room. He looked sharply at the "son" and discovered the still smoking cigarette.

It was too much for Milton's outraged dignity. Bennett did not allow him that coveted privilege. This upstart could not usurp it.

He reached over and seized the boy by the arm and swung him around till he faced a sign in the corner on the wall.

"See?" he demanded.

The sign read courteously:

"No Smoking in This Office—Please.
"PERRY BENNETT."

"Leggo my arm," snarled the "son," putting the offending cigarette defiantly into his mouth.

Milton coolly and deliberately reached over and, with an

exaggerated politeness swiftly and effectively removed it, dropping it on the floor and stamping defiantly on it.

"Son" raised his fists pugnaciously, for he didn't care much for the role he was playing, anyhow.

Milton did the same.

There was every element of a gaudy mix-up, when the outer door of the office suddenly swung open and Elaine Dodge entered.

Gallantry was Milton's middle name and he sprang forward to hold the door, and then opened Bennett's door, as he ushered in Elaine.

As she passed "Weepy Mary," who was still writing at the table and crying bitterly, Elaine hesitated and looked at her curiously. Even after Milton had opened Bennett's door, she could not resist another glance. Instinctively Elaine seemed to scent trouble.

Bennett was still studying the black-bordered card, when she greeted him.

"Who is that woman?" she asked, still wondering about the identity of the Niobe outside.

At first he said nothing. But finally, seeing that she had noticed it, he handed Elaine the card, reluctantly.

Elaine read it with a gasp. The look of surprise that crossed her face was terrible.

Before she could say anything, however, Milton had returned with the sheet of paper on which "Weepy Mary" had written and handed it to Bennett.

Bennett read it with uncontrolled astonishment.

"What is it?" demanded Elaine.

He handed it to her and she read:

"As the lawful wife and widow of Taylor Dodge, I demand my son's rights and my own.

"MRS. TAYLOR DODGE."

Elaine gasped at it.

"She—my father's wife!" she exclaimed, "What effrontery! What does she mean?"

Bennett hesitated.

"Tell me," Elaine cried, "Is there—can there be anything in it? No—no—there isn't!"

Bennett spoke in a low tone. "I have heard a whisper of some scandal or other connected with your father—but—" He paused.

Elaine was first shocked, then indignant.

"Why—such a thing is absurd. Show the woman in!"

"No—please—Miss Dodge. Let me deal with her."

By this time Elaine was furious.

"Yes—I WILL see her."

She pressed the button on Bennett's desk and Milton responded.

"Milton, show the—the woman in," she ordered, "and that boy, too."

As Milton turned to crook his finger at "Weepy Mary," she nodded surreptitiously and dug her fingers sharply into "son's" ribs.

"Yell—you little fool,—yell," she whispered.

Obedient to his "mother's" commands, and much to Milton's disgust, the boy started to cry in close imitation of his elder.

Elaine was still holding the paper in her hands when they entered.

"What does all this mean?" she demanded.

"Weepy Mary," between sobs, managed to blurt out, "You are Miss Elaine Dodge, aren't you? Well, it means that your father married me when I was only seventeen and this boy is his son—your half brother."

"No—never," cried Elaine vehemently, unable to restrain her disgust. "He never married again. He was too devoted to the memory of my mother."

"Weepy Mary" smiled cynically. "Come with me and I will show you the church records and the minister who married us."

"You will?" repeated Elaine defiantly. "Well, I'll just do as you ask. Mr. Bennett shall go with me."

Arthur B. Reeve

"No, no, Miss Dodge—don't go. Leave the matter to me," urged Bennett. "I will take care of HER. Besides, I must be in court in twenty minutes."

Elaine paused, but she was thoroughly aroused.

"Then I will go with her myself," she cried defiantly.

In spite of every objection that Bennett made, "Weepy Mary," her son, and Elaine went out to call a taxicab to take them to the railroad station where they could catch a train to the little town where the woman asserted she had been married.

* * * * *

Meanwhile, before a little country church in the town, a closed automobile had drawn up.

As the door opened, a figure, humped up and masked, alighted.

It was the Clutching Hand.

The car had scarcely pulled away, when he gave a long rap, followed by two short taps, at the door of the vestry, a secret code, evidently.

Inside the vestry room a well-dressed man but with a very sinister face heard the knock and a second later opened the door.

"What—not ready yet?" growled the Clutching Hand. "Quick—now—get on those clothes. I heard the train whistle as I came in the car. In which closet does the minister keep them?"

The crook, without a word, went to a closet and took out a suit of clothes of ministerial cut. Then he hastily put them on, adding some side-whiskers, which he had brought with him.

At about the same time, Elaine, acompanied by "Weepy Mary" and her "son," had arrived at the little tumble-down station and had taken the only vehicle in sight, a very ancient carriage.

It ambled along until, at last, it pulled up before the vestry room door of the church, just as the bogus minister was finishing his transformation from a frank crook. Clutching Hand was giving him final instructions.

Elaine and the others alighted and approached the church, while the ancient vehicle rattled away.

"They're coming," whispered the crook, peering cautiously out of the window.

Clutching Hand moved silently and snake-like into the closet and shut the door.

"How do you do, Dr. Carton?" greeted "Weepy Mary." "I guess you don't remember me."

The clerical gentleman looked at her fixedly a moment.

"Remember you?" he repeated. "Of course, my dear. I remember everyone I marry."

"And you remember to whom you married me?"

"Perfectly. To an older man—a Taylor Dodge."

Arthur B. Reeve

Elaine was overcome.

"Won't you step in?" he asked suavely. "Your friend here doesn't seem well."

They all entered.

"And you—you say—you married this—this woman to Taylor Dodge?" queried Elaine, tensely.

The bogus minister seemed to be very fatherly. "Yes," he assented, "I certainly did so."

"Have you the record?" asked Elaine, fighting to the last.

"Why, yes. I can show you the record."

He moved over to the closet. "Come over here," he asked.

He opened the door. Elaine screamed and drew back. There stood her arch enemy, the Clutching Hand himself.

As he stepped forth, she turned, wildly, to run—anywhere. But strong arms seized her and forced her into a chair.

She looked at the woman and the minister. It was a plot!

A moment Clutching Hand looked Elaine over. "Put the others out," he ordered the other crook.

Quickly the man obeyed, leading "Weepy Mary" and her "son" to the door, and waving them away as he locked it. They left, quite as much in the dark about the master criminal's identity as Elaine.

"Now, my pretty dear," began the Clutching Hand as the lock

turned in the vestry door, "we shall be joined shortly by your friend, Craig Kennedy, and," he added with a leer, "I think your rather insistent search for a certain person will cease."

Elaine drew back in the chair, horrified, at the implied threat.

Clutching Hand laughed, diabolically.

* * * * *

While these astounding events were transpiring in the little church, Kennedy and I had been tearing across the country in his big car, following the directions of our fair friend.

We stopped at last before a prosperous, attractive-looking house and entered a very prettily furnished but small parlor. Heavy portieres hung over the doorway into the hall, over another into a back room and over the bay windows.

"Won't you sit down a moment?" coaxed Gertie. "I'm quite blown to pieces after that ride. My, how you drive!"

As she pulled aside the hall portieres, three men with guns thrust their hands out. I turned. Two others had stepped from the back room and two more from the bay window. We were surrounded. Seven guns were aimed at us with deadly precision.

"No—no—Walter—it's no use," shouted Kennedy calmly restraining my hand which I had clapped on my own gun.

At the same time, with his other hand, he took from his pocket the small can which I had seen him place there, and held it aloft.

"Gentlemen," he said quietly. "I suspected some such thing. I have here a small box of fulminate of mercury. If I drop it, this building and the entire vicinity will be blown to atoms. Go ahead- -shoot!" he added, nonchalantly.

The seven of them drew back, rather hurriedly.

Kennedy was a dangerous prisoner.

He calmly sat down in an arm chair, leaning back as he carefully balanced the deadly little box of fulminate of mercury on his knee. He placed his finger tips together and smiled at the seven crooks, who had gathered together, staring breathlessly at this man who toyed with death.

Gertie ran from the room.

For a moment they looked at each other, undecided, then one by one, they stepped away from Kennedy toward the door.

The leader was the last to go. He had scarcely taken a step.

"Stop!" ordered Kennedy.

The crook did so. As Craig moved toward him, he waited, cold sweat breaking out on his face.

"Say," he whined, "you let me be!"

It was ineffectual. Kennedy, still smiling confidently, came closer, still holding the deadly little box, balanced between two fingers.

He took the crook's gun and dropped it into his pocket.

"Sit down!" ordered Craig.

Outside, the other six parleyed in hoarse whispers. One raised a gun, but the woman and the others restrained him and fled.

"Take me to your master!" demanded Kennedy.

The crook remained silent.

"Where is he?" repeated Craig. "Tell me!"

Still the man remained silent. Craig looked the fellow over again. Then, still with that confident smile, he reached into his inside pocket and drew forth the tube I had seen him place there.

"No matter how much YOU accuse me," added Craig casually, "no one will ever take the word of a crook that a reputable scientist like me would do what I am about to do."

He had taken out his penknife and opened it. Then he beckoned to me.

"Bare his arm and hold his wrist, Walter," he said.

Craig bent down with the knife and the tube, then paused a moment and turned the tube so that we could see it.

On the label were the ominous words:

Germ culture 6248A Bacillus Leprae (Leprosy)

Calmly he took the knife and proceeded to make an incision in the man's arm. The crook's feelings underwent a terrific struggle.

"No—no—no—don't," he implored. "I will take you to the

Clutching Hand—even if it kills me!"

Kennedy stepped back, replacing the tube in his pocket.

"Very well, go ahead!" he agreed.

We followed the crook, Craig still holding the deadly box of fulminate of mercury carefully balanced so that if anyone shot him from a hiding place it would drop.

* * * * *

No sooner had we gone than Gertie hurried to the nearest telephone to inform the Clutching Hand of our escape.

Elaine had sunk back into the chair, as the telephone rang. Clutching Hand answered it.

A moment later, in uncontrollable fury he hurled the instrument to the floor.

"Here—we've got to act quickly—that devil has escaped again," he hissed. "We must get her away. You keep her here. I'll be back—right away—with a car."

He dashed madly from the church, pulling off his mask as he gained the street.

* * * * *

Kennedy had forced the crook ahead of us into the car which was waiting and I followed, taking the wheel this time.

"Which way, now—quick!" demanded Craig, "And if you get me in wrong—I've got that tube yet—you remember."

Our crook started off with a whole burst of directions that rivalled the motor guide—"through the town, following trolley tracks, jog right, jog left under the R. R. bridge, leaving trolley tracks; at cemetery turn left, stopping at the old stone church."

"Is this it?" asked Craig incredulously.

"Yes—as I live," swore the crook in a cowed voice.

He had gone to pieces. Kennedy jumped from the machine.

"Here, take this gun, Walter," he said to me. "Don't take your eyes off the fellow—keep him covered."

Craig walked around the church, out of sight, until he came to a small vestry window and looked in.

There was Elaine, sitting in a chair, and near her stood an elderly looking man in clerical garb, which to Craig's trained eye was quite evidently a disguise.

Elaine happened just then to glance at the window and her eyes grew wide with astonishment at the sight of Craig.

He made a hasty motion to her to make a dash for the door. She nodded quietly.

With a glance at her guardian, she suddenly made a rush.

He was at her in a moment, pouncing on her, cat-like.

Kennedy had seized an iron bar that lay beside the window where some workmen had been repairing the stone pavement, and, with a blow shattered the glass and the sash.

Arthur B. Reeve

At the sound of the smashing glass the crook turned and with a mighty effort threw Elaine aside, drawing his revolver. As he raised it, Elaine sprang at him and frantically seized his wrist.

Utterly merciless, the man brought the butt of the gun down with full force on Elaine's head. Only her hat and hair saved her, but she sank unconscious.

Then he turned at Craig and fired twice.

One shot grazed Craig's hat, but the other struck him in the shoulder and Kennedy reeled.

With a desperate effort he pulled himself together and leaped forward again, closing with the fellow and wrenching the gun from him before he could fire again.

It fell to the floor with a clang.

Just then the man broke away and made a dash for the door leading back into the church itself, with Kennedy after him. At the foot of a flight of stairs, he turned long enough to pick up a chair. As Kennedy came on, he deliberately smashed it over Craig's head.

Kennedy warded off the blow as best he could, then, still undaunted, started up the stairs after the fellow.

Up they went, into the choir loft and then into the belfry itself. There they came to sheer hand to hand struggle. Kennedy tripped on a loose board and would have fallen backwards, if he had not been able to recover himself just in time. The crook, desperate, leaped for the ladder leading further up into the steeple. Kennedy followed.

Elaine had recovered consciousness almost immediately and, hearing the commotion, stirred and started to rise and look about.

From the church she could hear sounds of the struggle. She paused just long enough to seize the crook's revolver lying on the floor.

She hurried into the church and up into the belfry, thence up the ladder, whence the sounds came.

The crook by this time had gained the outside of the steeple through an opening. Kennedy was in close pursuit.

On the top of the steeple was a great gilded cross, considerably larger than a man. As the crook clambered outside, he scaled the steeple, using a lightning rod and some projecting points to pull himself up, desperately.

Kennedy followed unhesitatingly.

There they were, struggling in deadly combat, clinging to the gilded cross.

The first I knew of it was a horrified gasp from my own crook. I looked up carefully, fearing it was a stall to get me off my guard. There were Kennedy and the other crook, struggling, swaying back and forth, between life and death.

I looked at my man. What should I do? Should I leave him and go to Craig? If I did, might he not pick us both off, from a safe vantage point, by some sharp-shooting skill?

There was nothing I could do.

Kennedy was clinging to a lightning rod on the cross.

It broke.

I gasped as Craig reeled back. But he managed to catch hold of the rod further down and cling to it.

The crook seemed to exult diabolically. Holding with both hands to the cross, he let himself out to his full length and stamped on Kennedy's fingers, trying every way to dislodge him. It was all Kennedy could do to keep his hold.

I cried out in agony at the sight, for he had dislodged one of Craig's hands. The other could not hold on much longer. He was about to fall.

Just then I saw a face at the little window opening out from the ladder to the outside of the steeple—a woman's face, tense with horror.

It was Elaine!

Quickly a hand followed and in it was a revolver.

Just as the crook was about to dislodge Kennedy's other hand, I saw a flash and a puff of smoke and a second later, heard a report—and another—and another.

Horrors!

The crook who had taken refuge seemed to stagger back, wildly, taking a couple of steps in the thin air.

Kennedy regained his hold.

With a sickening thud, the body of the crook landed on the ground around the corner of the church from me.

"Come—you!" I ground out, covering my own crook with the pistol, "and if you attempt a getaway, I'll kill you, too!"

He followed, trembling, unnerved.

We bent over the man. It seemed that every bone in his body must be broken. He groaned, and before I could even attempt anything for him, he was dead.

As Kennedy let himself slowly and painfully down the lightning rod, Elaine seized him and, with all her strength, pulled him in through the window.

He was quite weak now from loss of blood.

"Are you—all right?" she gasped, as they reached the foot of the ladder in the belfry.

Craig looked down at his torn and soiled clothes. Then, in spite of the smarting pain of his wounds, he smiled, "Yes—all right!" "Thank heaven!" she murmured fervently, trying to staunch the flow of blood.

Craig gazed at her eagerly. The great look of relief in her face seemed to take away all the pain from his own face. In its place came a look of wonder—and hope.

He could not resist.

"This time—it was you—saved me!" he cried, "Elaine!"

Involuntarily his arms sought hers—and he held her a moment, looking deep into her wonderful eyes.

Then their faces came slowly together in their first kiss.

Arthur B. Reeve

CHAPTER VIII

THE HIDDEN VOICE

"Jameson—wake up!"

The strain of the Dodge case was beginning to tell on me, for it was keeping us at work at all kinds of hours to circumvent the Clutching Hand, by far the cleverest criminal with whom Kennedy had ever had anything to do.

I had slept later than usual that morning and, in a half doze, I heard a voice calling me, strangely like Kennedy's and yet unlike it.

I leaped out of bed, still in my pajamas, and stood for a moment staring about. Then I ran into the living room. I looked about, rubbing my eyes, startled. No one was there.

"Hey—Jameson—wake up!"

It was spooky.

I ran back into Craig's room. He was gone. There was no one in any of our rooms. The surprise had now thoroughly awakened me.

"Where—the deuce—are you?" I demanded.

Suddenly I heard the voice again—no doubt about it, either.

"Here I am—over on the couch!"

I scratched my head, puzzled. There was certainly no one on that couch.

A laugh greeted me. Plainly, though, it came from the couch. I went over to it and, ridiculous as it seemed, began to throw aside the pillows.

There lay nothing but a little oblong oaken box, perhaps eight or ten inches long and three or four inches square at the ends. In the face were two peculiar square holes and from the top projected a black disc, about the size of a watch, fastened on a swinging metal arm. In the face of the disc were several perforated holes.

I picked up the strange looking thing in wonder and from that magic oak box actually came a burst of laughter.

"Come over to the laboratory, right away," pealed forth a merry voice. "I've something to show you."

"Well," I gasped, "what do you know about that?"

Very early that morning Craig had got up, leaving me snoring. Cases never wearied him. He thrived on excitement.

He had gone over to the laboratory and set to work in a corner over another of those peculiar boxes, exactly like that which he had already left in our rooms.

In the face of each of these boxes, as I have said, were two

Arthur B. Reeve

square holes. The sides of these holes converged inward into the box, in the manner of a four sided pyramid, ending at the apex in a little circle of black, perhaps half an inch across.

Satisfied at last with his work, Craig had stood back from the weird apparatus and shouted my name. He had enjoyed my surprise to the fullest extent, then had asked me to join him.

Half an hour afterward I walked into the laboratory, feeling a little sheepish over the practical joke, but none the less curious to find out all about it.

"What is it?" I asked indicating the apparatus.

"A vocaphone," he replied, still laughing, "the loud speaking telephone, the little box that hears and talks. It talks right out in meeting, too—no transmitter to hold to the mouth, no receiver to hold to the ear. You see, this transmitter is so sensitive that it picks up even a whisper, and the receiver is placed back of those two megaphone-like pyramids."

He was standing at a table, carefully packing up one of the vocaphones and a lot of wire.

"I believe the Clutching Hand has been shadowing the Dodge house," he continued thoughtfully. "As long as we watch the place, too, he will do nothing. But if we should seem, ostentatiously, not to be watching, perhaps he may try something, and we may be able to get a clue to his identity over this vocaphone. See?"

I nodded. "We've got to run him down somehow," I agreed.

"Yes," he said, taking his coat and hat. "I am going to connect up one of these things in Miss Dodge's library and arrange with the telephone company for a clear wire so that we can listen in here, where that fellow will never suspect."

* * * * *

At about the same time that Craig and I sallied forth on this new mission, Elaine was arranging some flowers on a stand near the corner of the Dodge library where the secret panel was in which her father had hidden the papers for the possession of which the Clutching Hand had murdered him. They did not disclose his identity, we knew, but they did give directions to at least one of his hang-outs and were therefore very important.

She had moved away from the table, but, as she did so, her dress caught in something in the woodwork. She tried to loosen it and in so doing touched the little metallic spring on which her dress had caught.

Instantly, to her utter surprise, the panel moved. It slid open, disclosing a strong box.

Elaine took it amazed, looked at it a moment, then carried it to a table and started to pry it open.

It was one of those tin dispatch boxes which, as far as I have ever been able to determine, are chiefly valuable for allowing one to place a lot of stuff in a receptacle which is very convenient for a criminal. She had no trouble in opening it.

Inside were some papers, sealed in an envelope and marked "Limpy Red Correspondence."

"They must be the Clutching Hand papers!" she exclaimed to herself, hesitating a moment in doubt what to do. The fatal documents seemed almost uncanny. Their very presence frightened her. What should she do?

Arthur B. Reeve

She seized the telephone and eagerly called Kennedy's number.

"Hello," answered a voice.

"Is that you, Craig?" she asked excitedly.

"No, this is Mr. Jameson."

"Oh, Mr. Jameson, I've discovered the Clutching Hand papers," she began, more and more excited.

"Have you read them?" came back the voice quickly.

"No—shall I?"

"Then don't unseal them," cautioned the voice. "Put them back exactly as you found them and I'll tell Mr. Kennedy the moment I can get hold of him."

"All right," nodded Elaine. "I'll do that. And please get him —as soon as you possibly can."

"I will."

"I'm going out shopping now," she returned, suddenly. "But, tell him I'll be back—right away."

"Very well."

Hanging up the receiver, Elaine dutifully replaced the papers in the box and returned the box to its secret hiding place, pressing the spring and sliding the panel shut.

A few minutes later she left the house in the Dodge car.

Outside our laboratory, leaning up against a railing, Dan the Dude, an emissary of the Clutching Hand, whose dress now greatly belied his underworld "monniker," had been shadowing us, watching to see when we left.

The moment we disappeared, he raised his hand carefully above his head and made the sign of the Clutching Hand. Far down the street, in a closed car, the Clutching Hand himself, his face masked, gave an answering sign.

A moment later he left the car, gazing about stealthily. Not a soul was in sight and he managed to make his way to the door of our laboratory without being observed. Then he opened it with a pass key which he must have obtained in some way by working the janitor or the university officials.

Probably he thought that the papers might be at the laboratory, for he had repeatedly failed to locate them at the Dodge house. At any rate he was busily engaged in ransacking drawers and cabinets in the laboratory, when the telephone suddenly rang. He did not want to answer it, but if it kept on ringing someone outside might come in.

An instant he hesitated. Then, disguising his voice as much as he could to imitate mine, he took off the receiver.

"Hello!" he answered.

His face was a study in all that was dark as he realized that it was Elaine calling. He clenched his crooked hand even more viciously.

"Have you read them?" he asked, curbing his impatience as she unsuspectingly poured forth her story, supposedly to me.

"Then don't unseal them," he hastened to reply. "Put them back. Then there can be no question about them. You can open them before witnesses."

For a moment he paused, then added, "Put them back and tell no one of their discovery. I will tell Mr. Kennedy the moment I can get him."

A smile spread over his sinister face as Elaine confided in him her intention to go shopping.

"A rather expensive expedition for you, young lady," he muttered to himself as he returned the receiver to the hook.

Clutching Hand lost no further time at the laboratory. He had thus, luckily for him, found out what he wanted. The papers were not there after all, but at the Dodge house.

Suppose she should really be gone on only a short shopping trip and should return to find that she had been fooled over the wire? Quickly, he went to the telephone again.

"Hello, Dan," he called when he got his number.

"Miss Dodge is going shopping. I want you and the other Falsers to follow her—delay her all you can. Use your own judgment."

It was what had come to be known in his organization as the "Brotherhood of Falsers." There, in the back room of a low dive, were Dan the Dude, the emissary who had been loitering about the laboratory, a gunman, Dago Mike, a couple of women, slatterns, one known as Kitty the Hawk, and a boy of eight or ten, whom they called Billy. Before them stood large schooners of beer, while the precocious youngster grumbled over milk.

"All right, Chief," shouted back Dan, their leader as he hung up the telephone after noting carefully the hasty instructions. "We'll do it—trust us."

The others, knowing that a job was to lighten the monotony of existence, gathered about him.

They listened intently as he detailed to them the orders of the Clutching Hand, hastily planning out the campaign like a division commander disposing his forces in battle and assigning each his part.

With alacrity the Brotherhood went their separate ways.

* * * * *

Elaine had not been gone long from the house when Craig and I arrived there. She had followed the telephone instructions of the Clutching Hand and had told no one.

"Too bad," greeted Jennings, "but Miss Elaine has just gone shopping and I don't know when she'll be back."

Shopping being an uncertain element as far as time was concerned, Kennedy asked if anyone else was at home.

"Mrs. Dodge is in the library reading, sir," replied Jennings, taking it for granted that we would see her.

Aunt Josephine greeted us cordially and Craig set down the vocaphone package he was carrying.

She nodded to Jennings to leave us and he withdrew.

"I'm not going to let anything happen here to Miss Elaine again if I can help it," remarked Craig in a low tone, a moment later, gazing about the library.

"What are you thinking of doing?" asked Aunt Josephine keenly.

"I'm going to put in a vocaphone," he returned unwrapping it.

"What's that?" she asked.

"A loud speaking telephone—connected with my laboratory," he explained, repeating what he had already told me, while she listened almost awe-struck at the latest scientific wonder.

He was looking about, trying to figure out just where it could be placed to best advantage, when he approached the suit of armor.

"I see you have brought it back and had it repaired," he remarked to Aunt Josephine. Suddenly his face lighted up. "Ah—an idea!" he exclaimed. "No one will ever think to look INSIDE that."

It was indeed an inspiration. Kennedy worked quickly now, placing the little box inside the breast plate of the ancient armourer with the top of the instrument projecting right up into the helmet. It was a strange combination—the medieval and the ultra- modern.

"Now, Mrs. Dodge," he said finally, as he had completed installing the thing and hiding the wire under carpets and rugs until it ran out to the connection which he made with the telephone, "don't breathe a word of it—to anyone. We don't know who to trust or suspect."

"I shall not," she answered, by this time thoroughly educated in the value of silence.

Kennedy looked at his watch.

"I've got an engagement with the telephone company, now," he said rather briskly, although I knew that if Elaine had been there the company and everything could have gone hang for the present. "Sorry not to have seen Miss Elaine," he added as we bowed ourselves out, "but I think we've got her protected now."

"I hope so," sighed her aunt.

* * * * *

Elaine's car had stopped finally at a shop on Fifth Avenue. She stepped out and entered, leaving her chauffeur to wait.

As she did so, Dan and Billy sidled along the crowded sidewalk.

"There she is, Billy," pointed out Dan as Elaine disappeared through the swinging doors of the shop. "Now, you wait right here," he instructed stealthily, "and when she comes out—you know what to do. Only, be careful."

Dan the Dude left Billy, and Billy surreptitiously drew from under his coat a dirty half loaf of bread. With a glance about, he dropped it into the gutter close to the entrance to Elaine's car. Then he withdrew a little distance.

When Elaine came out and approached her car, Billy, looking as cold and forlorn as could be, shot forward. Pretending to spy the dirty piece of bread in the gutter, he made a dive for it, just as Elaine was about to step into the car.

Arthur B. Reeve

Elaine, surprised, drew back. Billy picked up the piece of bread and, with all the actions of having discovered a treasure, began to gnaw at it voraciously.

Shocked at the disgusting sight, she tried to take the bread away from him.

"I know it's dirty, Miss," whimpered Billy, "but it's the first food I've seen for four days."

Instantly Elaine was full of sympathy. She had taken the food away. That would not suffice.

"What's your name, little boy?" she asked.

"Billy," he replied, blubbering.

"Where do you live?"

"With me mother and father—they're sick—nothing to eat—"

He was whimpering an address far over on the East Side.

"Get into the car," Elaine directed.

"Gee—but this is swell," he cried, with no fake, this time.

On they went, through the tenement canyons, dodging children and pushcarts, stopping first at a grocer's, then at a butcher's and a delicatessen. Finally the car stopped where Billy directed. Billy hobbled out, followed by Elaine and her chauffeur, his arms piled high with provisions. She was indeed a lovely Lady Bountiful as a crowd of kids quickly surrounded the car.

In the meantime Dago Mike and Kitty the Hawk had gone to

a wretched flat, before which Billy stopped. Kitty sat on the bed, putting dark circles under her eyes with a blackened cork. She was very thin and emaciated, but it was dissipation that had done it. Dago Mike was correspondingly poorly dressed.

He had paused beside the window to look out. "She's coming," he announced finally.

Kitty hastily jumped into the rickety bed, while Mike took up a crutch that was standing idly in a corner. She coughed resignedly and he limped about, forlorn. They had assumed their parts which were almost to the burlesque of poverty, when the door was pushed open and Billy burst in followed by Elaine and the chauffeur.

"Oh, ma—oh, pa," he cried running forward and kissing his pseudo-parents, as Elaine, overcome with sympathy, directed the chauffeur to lay the things on a shaky table.

"God bless you, lady, for a benevolent angel!" muttered the pair, to which Elaine responded by moving over to the wretched bed and bending down to stroke the forehead of the sick woman.

Billy and Mike exchanged a sly wink.

Just then the door opened again. All were genuinely surprised this time, for a prim, spick and span, middle-aged woman entered.

"I am Miss Statistix, of the organized charities," she announced, looking around sharply. "I saw your car standing outside, Miss, and the children below told me you were up here. I came up to see whether you were aiding really DESERVING poor."

She laid a marked emphasis on the word, pursing up her lips. There was no mistaking the apprehension that these fine birds of prey had of her, either.

Miss Statistix took a step forward, looking in a very superior manner from Elaine to the packages of food and then at these prize members of the Brotherhood. She snorted contemptuously.

"Why—wh-what's the matter?" asked Elaine, fidgeting uncomfortably, as if she were herself guilty, in the icy atmosphere that now seemed to envelope all things.

"This man is a gunman, that woman is a bad woman, the boy is Billy the Bread-Snatcher," she answered precisely, drawing out a card on which to record something, "and you, Miss, are a fool!"

"Ya!" snarled the two precious falsers, "get out o' here!"

There was no combating Miss Statistix. She overwhelmed all arguments by the very exactness of her personality.

"YOU get out!" she countered.

Kitty and Mike, accompanied by Billy, sneaked out. Elaine, now very much embarrassed, looked about, wondering at the rapid-fire change. Miss Statistix smiled pityingly.

"Such innocence!" she murmured sadly shaking her head as she lead Elaine to the door. "Don't you know better than to try to help anybody without INVESTIGATING?"

Elaine departed, speechless, properly squelched, followed by her chauffeur.

Meanwhile, a closed car, such as had stood across from the laboratory, had drawn up not far from the Dodge house. Near it was a man in rather shabby clothes and a visored cap on which were the words in dull gold lettering, "Metropolitan Window Cleaning Co." He carried a bucket and a small extension ladder.

In the darkened recesses of the car was the Clutching Hand himself, masked as usual. He had his watch in his hand and was giving most minute instructions to the window cleaner about something. As the latter turned to go, a sharp observer would have noted that it was Dan the Dude, still further disguised.

A few moments later, Dan appeared at the servants' entrance of the Dodge house and rang the bell. Jennings, who happened to be down there, came to the door.

"Man to clean the windows," saluted the bogus cleaner, touching his hat in a way quietly to call attention to the words on it and drawing from his pocket a faked written order.

"All right," nodded Jennings examining the order and finding it apparently all right.

Dan followed him in, taking the ladder and bucket upstairs, where Aunt Josephine was still reading.

"The man to clean the windows, ma'am," apologized Jennings.

"Oh, very well," she nodded, taking up her book, to go. Then, recalling the frequent injunctions of Kennedy, she paused long enough to speak quietly to Jennings.

"Stay here and watch him," she whispered as she went out.

Jennings nodded, while Dan opened a window and set to work.

* * * * *

Elaine had scarcely started again in her car down the crowded narrow street. From her position she could not possibly have seen Johnnie, another of the Brotherhood, watching her eagerly up the street.

But as her car approached, Johnnie, with great determination, pulled himself together and ran forward across the street. She saw that.

"Oh!" she screamed, her heart almost stopping.

He had fallen directly in front of the wheels of the car, apparently, and although the chauffeur stopped with a jolt, it seemed that the boy had been run over.

They jumped out. There he was, sure enough, under the very wheels. People came running now in all directions and lifted him up, groaning piteously. He seemed literally twisted into a knot which looked as if every bone in his body was broken or dislocated.

Elaine was overcome. For, following their natural instincts the crowd began pushing in with cries of "Lynch the driver!" It would have gone hard with him, too, if she had not interfered.

"Here!" cried Elaine, stepping in. "It wasn't his fault. The boy ran across the street right in front of the car. Now—we're just going to rush this boy to the hospital—right away!"

She lifted Johnnie gently into the car herself and they drove off, to a very vigorous blowing of the horn.

A few moments later they pulled up before the ambulance entrance to the hospital.

"Quick!" beckoned Elaine to the attendants, who ran out and carried Johnnie, still a complicated knot of broken bones, inside.

In the reception room were a couple of nurses and a young medical student, when Johnnie was carried in and laid on the bed. The student, more interested in Elaine than the boy, examined him. His face wore a puzzled look and there was every reason to believe that Johnnie was seriously injured.

At that moment the door opened and an elderly, gray-bearded house physician entered. The others stepped back from the bed respectfully. He advanced and examined Johnnie.

The doctor looked at the boy a moment, then at Elaine.

"I will now effect a miraculous cure by the laying on of hands," he announced, adding quickly, "—and of feet!"

To the utter surprise of all he seized the boy by the coat collar, lifting him up and actually bouncing him on the floor. Then he picked him up, shook him and ran him out of the room, delivering one last kick as he went through the door. By the way Johnnie went, it was quite evident that he was no more injured than the chauffeur. Elaine did not know whether to be angry or to laugh, but finally joined in the general laugh.

"That was Double-Jointed Johnnie," puffed the doctor, as he

Arthur B. Reeve

returned to them, "one of the greatest accident fakers in the city."

Elaine, having had two unfortunate experiences during the day, now decided to go home and the doctor politely escorted her to her car.

* * * * *

From his closed car, the Clutching Hand gazed intently at the Dodge house. He could see Dan on the ladder, now washing the library window, his back toward him.

Dan turned slowly and made the sign of the hand. Turning to his chauffeur, the master criminal spoke a few words in a low tone and the driver hurried off.

A few minutes later the driver might have been seen entering a near-by drug store and going into the telephone booth. Without a moment's hesitation he called up the Dodge house and Marie, Elaine's maid, answered.

"Is Jennings there?" he asked. "Tell him a friend wants to speak to him."

"Wait a minute," she answered. "I'll get him."

Marie went toward the library, leaving the telephone off the hook. Dan was washing the windows, half inside, half outside the house, while Jennings was trying to be very busy, although it was apparent that he was watching Dan closely.

"A friend of yours wants to speak to you over the telephone, Jennings," said Marie, as she came into the library.

The butler responded slowly, with a covert glance at Dan.

No sooner had they gone, however, than Dan climbed all the way into the room, ran to the door and looked after them. Then he ran to the window. Across and down the street, the Clutching Hand was gazing at the house. He had seen Dan disappear and suspected that the time had come.

Sure enough, there was the sign of the hand. He hastily got out of the car and hurried up the street. All this time the chauffeur was keeping Jennings busy over the telephone with some trumped-up story.

As the master criminal came in by the ladder through the open window, Dan was on guard, listening down the hallway. A signal from Dan, and Clutching Hand slid back of the portieres. Jennings was returning.

"I've finished these windows," announced Dan as the butler reappeared. "Now, I'll clean the hall windows."

Jennings followed like a shadow, taking the bucket.

No sooner had they gone than Clutching Hand stealthily came from behind the portieres.

One of the maids was sweeping in the hall as Dan went toward the window, about to wash it.

"I wonder whether I locked these windows?" muttered Jennings, pausing in the hallway. "I guess I'd better make sure."

He had taken only a step toward the library again, when Dan watchfully caught sight of him. It would never do to have Jennings snooping around there now. Quick action was necessary. Dan knocked over a costly Sevres vase.

"There—clumsy—see what you've done!" berated Jennings, starting to pick up the pieces.

Dan had acted his part well and promptly. In the library, Clutching Hand was busily engaged at that moment beside the secret panel searching for the spring that released it. He ran his finger along the woodwork, pausing here and there without succeeding.

"Confound it!" he muttered, searching feverishly.

* * * * *

Kennedy, having made the arrangements with the telephone company by which he had a clear wire from the Dodge house to his laboratory, had rejoined me there and was putting on the finishing touches to his installation of the vocaphone.

Every now and then he would switch it on, and we would listen in as he demonstrated the wonderful little instrument to me. He had heard the window cleaner and Jennings, but thought nothing of it at the time.

Once, however, Craig paused and I saw him listening more intently than usual.

"They've gone out," he muttered, "but surely there is someone in the Dodge library."

I listened; too. The thing was so sensitive that even a whisper could be magnified and I certainly did hear something.

Kennedy frowned. What was that scratching noise? Could it be Jennings? Perhaps it was Rusty.

Just then we could distinguish a sound as though someone

had moved about.

"No—that's not Jennings," cried Craig. "He went out."

He looked at me a moment. The same stealthy noise was repeated.

"It's the Clutching Hand!" he exclaimed excitedly.

* * * * *

A moment later, Dan hurried into the Dodge library.

"For heaven's sake, Chief, hurry!" he whispered hoarsely. "The falsers must have fallen down. The girl herself is coming!"

Dan himself had no time to waste. He retreated into the hallway just as Jennings was opening the door for Elaine.

Marie took her wraps and left her, while Elaine handed her numerous packages to Jennings. Dan watched every motion.

"Put them away, Jennings," she said softly.

Jennings had obeyed and gone upstairs. Elaine moved toward the library. Dan took a quiet step or two behind her, in the same direction.

In the library, Clutching Hand was now frantically searching for the spring. He heard Elaine coming and dodged behind the curtains again just as she entered.

With a hasty look about, she saw no one. Then she went quickly to the panel, found the spring, and pressed it. So many queer things had happened to her since she went out that she had begun to worry over the safety of the papers.

The panel opened. They were there, all right. She opened the box and took them out, hesitating to break the seal before Kennedy arrived.

Stealthy and tiger-like the Clutching Hand crept up behind her. As he did so, Dan gazed in through the portieres from the hall.

With a spring, Clutching Hand leaped at Elaine, snatching at the papers. Elaine clung to them tenaciously in spite of the surprise, and they struggled for them, Clutching Hand holding one hand over her mouth to prevent her screaming. Instantly Dan was there, aiding his chief.

"Choke her! Strangle her! Don't let her scream!" he ground out.

They fought viciously. Would they succeed? It was two desperate, unscrupulous men against one frail girl.

Suddenly, from the man in armor in the corner, as if by a miracle came a deep, loud voice.

"Help! Help! Murder! Police! They are strangling me!"

The effect was terrific.

Clutching Hand and Dan, hardened in crime as they were, fell back, dazed, overcome for the moment at the startling effect.

They looked about. Not a soul.

Then to their utter consternation, from the vizor of the

helmet again came the deep, vibrating warning.

"Help! Murder! Police!"

* * * * *

Kennedy and I had been listening over the vocaphone, for the moment non-plussed at the fellow's daring.

Then we heard from the uncanny instrument, "For Heaven's sake, Chief, hurry! The falsers have fallen down. The girl herself is coming!"

What it meant we did not know. But Craig was almost beside himself, as he ordered me to try to get the police by telephone, if there was any way to block them. Only instant action would count, however. What to do?

He could hear the master criminal plainly fumbling, now.

"Yes, that's the Clutching Hand," he repeated.

"Wait," I cautioned, "someone else is coming!"

By a sort of instinct he seemed to recognize the sounds.

"Elaine!" he exclaimed, paling.

Instantly followed, in less time than I can tell it, the sounds of a suppressed scuffle.

"He has seized her—gagged her," I cried in an agony of suspense.

We could now hear everything that was going on in the library. Craig was wildly excited. As for me, I was speechless.

Arthur B. Reeve

Here was the vocaphone we had installed. It had warned us. But what could we do?

I looked blankly at Kennedy. He was equal to the emergency.

He calmly turned a switch.

Then, at the top of his lungs, he shouted, "Help! Help! Police! They are strangling me!"

I looked at him in amazement. What did he think he could do—blocks away?

"It works both ways," he muttered. "Help! Murder! Police!"

We could hear the astounded cursing of the two men. Also, down the hall, now, we could hear footsteps approaching in answer to his call for help—Aunt Josephine, Jennings, Marie, and others, all shouting out that there were cries in the library.

"The deuce! What is it?" muttered a gruff voice.

"The man in armor!" hissed Clutching Hand.

"Here they come, too, Chief!"

There was a parting scuffle.

"There—take that!"

A loud metallic ringing came from the vocaphone.

Then, silence!

What had happened

In the library, recovered from their first shock of surprise, Dan cried out to the Clutching Hand, "The deuce. What is it?"

Then, looking about, Clutching Hand quickly took in the situation.

"The man in armor!" he pointed out.

Dan was almost dead with fright at the weird thing.

"Here they come, too, Chief," he gasped, as, down the hall he could hear the family shouting out that someone was in the library.

With a parting thrust, Clutching Hand sent Elaine reeling.

She held on to only a corner of the papers. He had the greater part of them. They were torn and destroyed, anyway.

Finally, with all the venomousness of which he was capable, Clutching Hand rushed at the armor suit, drew back his gloved fist, and let it shoot out squarely in a vicious solar plexus blow.

"There—take that!" he roared.

The suit rattled, furiously. Out of it spilled the vocaphone with a bang on the floor.

An instant later those in the hall rushed in. But the Clutching Hand and Dan were gone out of the window, the criminal carrying the greater part of the precious papers.

Some ran to Elaine, others to the window. The ladder had been kicked away and the criminals were gone. Leaping into the waiting car, they had been whisked away.

"Hello! Hello! Hello!" called a voice, apparently from nowhere.

"What is that?" cried Elaine, still blankly wondering.

She had risen by this time and was gazing about, wondering at the strange voice. Suddenly her eye fell on the armor scattered all over the floor. She spied the little oak box.

"Elaine!"

Apparently the voice came from that. Besides, it had a familiar ring to her ears.

"Yes—Craig!" she cried.

"This is my vocaphone—the little box that hears and talks," came back to her. "Are you all right?"

"Yes—all right,—thanks to the vocaphone."

She had understood in an instant. She seized the helmet and breastplate to which the vocaphone still was attached and was holding them close to herself.

* * * * *

Kennedy had been calling and listening intently over the machine, wondering whether it had been put out of business in some way.

"It works—yet!" he cried excitedly to me. "Elaine!"

"Yes, Craig," came back over the faithful little instrument.

"Are you all right?"

"Yes—all right."

"Thank heaven!" breathed Craig, pushing me aside.

Literally he kissed that vocaphone as if it had been human!

CHAPTER IX

THE DEATH RAY

Kennedy was reading a scientific treatise one morning, while I was banging on the typewriter, when a knock at the laboratory door disturbed us.

By some intuition, Craig seemed to know who it was. He sprang to open the door, and there stood Elaine Dodge and her lawyer, Perry Bennett.

Instantly, Craig read from the startled look on Elaine's face that something dreadful had happened.

"Why—what's the matter?" he asked, solicitously.

"A—another letter—from the Clutching Hand!" she exclaimed breathlessly. "Mr. Bennett was calling on me, when this note was brought in. We both thought we'd better see you at once about it and he was kind enough to drive me here right away in his car."

Craig took the letter and we both read, with amazement:

"Are you an enemy of society? If not, order Craig Kennedy to leave the country by nine o'clock to-morrow morning.

Otherwise, a pedestrian will drop dead outside his laboratory every hour until he leaves."

The note was signed by the now familiar sinister hand, and had, added, a postcript, which read:

"As a token of his leaving, have him place a vase of flowers on his laboratory window to-day."

"What shall we do?" queried Bennett, evidently very much alarmed at the threat.

"Do?" replied Kennedy, laughing contemptuously at the apparently futile threat, "why, nothing. Just wait."

* * * * *

The day proved uneventful and I paid no further attention to the warning letter. It seemed too preposterous to amount to anything.

Kennedy, however, with his characteristic foresight, as I learned afterwards, had not been entirely unprepared, though he had affected to treat the thing with contempt.

His laboratory, I may say, was at the very edge of the University buildings, with the campus back of it, but opening on the other side on a street that was ordinarily not overcrowded.

We got up as usual the next day and, quite early, went over to the laboratory. Kennedy, as was his custom, plunged straightway into his work and appeared absorbed by it, while I wrote.

"There IS something queer going on, Walter," he remarked.

Arthur B. Reeve

"This thing registers some kind of wireless rays—infra-red, I think,—something like those that they say that Italian scientist, Ulivi, claims he has discovered and called the 'F-rays.'"

"How do you know?" I asked, looking up from my work. "What's that instrument you are using?"

"A bolometer, invented by the late Professor Langley," he replied, his attention riveted on it.

Some time previously, Kennedy had had installed on the window ledge one of those mirror-like arrangements, known as a "busybody," which show those in a room what is going on on the street.

As I moved over to look at the bolometer, I happened to glance into the busybody and saw that a crowd was rapidly collecting on the sidewalk.

"Look, Craig!" I called hastily.

He hurried over to me and looked. We could both see in the busybody mirror a group of excited passersby bending over a man lying prostrate on the sidewalk.

He had evidently been standing on the curbstone outside the laboratory and had suddenly put his hand to his forehead. Then he had literally crumpled up into a heap, as he sank to the ground.

The excited crowd lifted him up and bore him away, and I turned in surprise to Craig. He was looking at his watch.

It was now only a few moments past nine o'clock!

Not quarter of an hour later, our door was excitedly flung open and Elaine and Perry Bennett arrived.

"I've just heard of the accident," she cried, fearfully. "Isn't it terrible. What had we better do?"

For a few moments no one said a word. Then Kennedy began carefully examining the bolometer and some other recording instruments he had, while the rest of us watched, fascinated.

Somehow that "busybody" seemed to attract me. I could not resist looking into it from time to time as Kennedy worked.

I was scarcely able to control my excitement when, again, I saw the same scene enacted on the sidewalk before the laboratory. Hurriedly I looked at my watch. It was ten o'clock!

"Craig!" I cried. "Another!"

Instantly he was at my side, gazing eagerly. There was a second innocent pedestrian lying on the sidewalk while a crowd, almost panic-stricken, gathered about him.

We watched, almost stunned by the suddenness of the thing, until finally, without a word, Kennedy turned away, his face set in tense lines.

"It's no use," he muttered, as we gathered about him. "We're beaten. I can't stand this sort of thing. I will leave to-morrow for South America."

I thought Elaine Dodge would faint at the shock of his words coming so soon after the terrible occurrence outside. She looked at him, speechless.

Arthur B. Reeve

It happened that Kennedy had some artificial flowers on a stand, which he had been using long before in the study of synthetic coloring materials. Before Elaine could recover her tongue, he seized them and stuck them into a tall beaker, like a vase. Then he deliberately walked to the window and placed the beaker on the ledge in a most prominent position.

Elaine and Bennett, to say nothing of myself, gazed at him, awe- struck.

"Is—is there no other way but to surrender?" she asked.

Kennedy mournfully shook his head.

"I'm afraid not," he answered slowly. "There's no telling how far a fellow who has this marvellous power might go. I think I'd better leave to save you. He may not content himself with innocent outsiders always."

Nothing that any of us could say, not even the pleadings of Elaine herself could move him. The thought that at eleven o'clock a third innocent passerby might lie stricken on the street seemed to move him powerfully.

When, at eleven, nothing happened as it had at the other two hours, he was even more confirmed in his purpose. Entreaties had no effect, and late in the morning, he succeeded in convincing us all that his purpose was irrevocable.

As we stood at the door, mournfully bidding our visitors farewell until the morrow, when he had decided to sail, I could see that he was eager to be alone. He had been looking now and then at the peculiar instrument which he had been studying earlier in the day and I could see on his face a sort of subtle intentness.

"I'm so sorry—Craig," murmured Elaine, choking back her emotion, and finding it impossible to go on.

"So am I, Elaine," he answered, tensely. "But—perhaps—when this trouble blows over—"

He paused, unable to speak, turned, and shook his head. Then with a forced gaiety he bade Elaine and Perry Bennett adieu, saying that perhaps a trip might do him good.

They had scarcely gone out and Kennedy closed the door carefully, when he turned and went directly to the instrument which I had seen him observing so interestedly.

Plainly, I could see that it was registering something.

"What's the matter?" I asked, non-plussed.

"Just a moment, Walter," he replied evasively, as if not quite sure of himself.

He walked fairly close to the window this time, keeping well out of the direct line of it, however, and there stood gazing out into the street.

A glint, as if of the sun shining on a pair of opera glasses could be seen from a window across the way.

"We are being watched," he said slowly, turning and looking at me fixedly, "but I don't dare investigate lest it cost the lives of more unfortunates."

He stood for a moment in deep thought. Then he pulled out a suitcase and began silently to pack it.

* * * * *

Arthur B. Reeve

Although we had not dared to investigate, we knew that from a building, across the street, emissaries of the Clutching Hand were watching for our signal of surrender.

The fact was, as we found out later, that in a poorly furnished room, much after the fashion of that which, with the help of the authorities, we had once raided in the suburbs, there were at that moment two crooks.

One of them was the famous, or rather the infamous, Professor LeCroix, with whom in a disguise as a doctor we had already had some experience when he stole from the Hillside Sanitarium the twilight sleep drugs. The other was the young secretary of the Clutching Hand who had given the warning at the suburban headquarters at the time when they were endeavoring to tranfuse Elaine Dodge's blood to save the life of the crook whom she had shot.

This was the new headquarters of the master criminal, very carefully guarded.

"Look!" cried LeCroix, very much elated at the effect that had been produced by his infra-red rays, "There is the sign—the vase of flowers. We have got him this time!"

LeCroix gleefully patted a peculiar instrument beside him. Apparently it was a combination of powerful electric arcs, the rays of which were shot through a funnel-like arrangement into a converter or, rather, a sort of concentration apparatus from which the dread power could be released through a tube-like affair at one end. It was his infra-red heat wave, F-ray, engine.

"I told you—it would work!" cried LeCroix.

* * * * *

I did not argue any further with Craig about his sudden resolution to go away. But it is a very solemn proceeding to pack up and admit defeat after such a brilliant succession of cases as had been his until we met this master criminal.

He was unshakeable, however, and the next morning we closed the laboratory and loaded our baggage, which was considerable, on a taxicab.

Neither of us said much, but I saw a quick look of appreciation on Craig's face as we pulled up at the wharf and saw that the Dodge car was already there. He seemed deeply moved that Elaine should come at such an early hour to have a last word.

Our cab stopped and Kennedy moved over toward her car, directing two porters, whom I noticed that he chose with care, to wait at one side. One of them was an old Irishman with a slight limp; the other a wiry Frenchman with a pointed beard.

In spite of her pleadings, however, Kennedy held to his purpose and, as we shook hands for the last time, I thought that Elaine would almost break down.

"Here, you fellows, now," directed Craig, turning brusquely to the porters, "hustle that baggage right aboard."

"Can't we go on the ship, too?" asked Elaine, appealingly.

"I'm sorry—I'm afraid there isn't time," apologized Craig.

We finally tore ourselves away, followed by the porters carrying as much as they could.

"Bon voyage!" cried Elaine, bravely keeping back a choke in

Arthur B. Reeve

her voice.

Near the gangplank, in the crowd, I noticed a couple of sinister faces watching the ship's officers and the passengers going aboard. Kennedy's quick eye spotted them, too, but he did not show in any way that he noticed anything as, followed by our two porters, we quickly climbed the gangplank.

A moment Craig paused by the rail and waved to Elaine and Bennett who returned the salute feelingly. I paused at the rail, too, speculating how we were to get the rest of our baggage aboard in time, for we had taken several minutes saying good-bye.

"In there," pointed Kennedy quickly to the porters, indicating our stateroom which was an outside room. "Come, Walter."

I followed him in with a heavy heart.

* * * * *

Outside could be seen the two sinister faces in the crowd watching intently, with eyes fixed on the stateroom. Finally one of the crooks boarded the ship hastily, while the other watched the two porters come out of the stateroom and pause at the window, speaking back into the room as though answering commands.

Then the porters quickly ran along the deck and down the plank, to get the rest of the luggage. As they approached the Dodge car, Elaine, Aunt Josephine and Perry Bennett were straining their eyes to catch a last glimpse of us.

The porters took a small but very heavy box and, lugging and tugging, hastened toward the boat with it. But they were too late. The gang plank was being hauled in.

They shouted, but the ship's officers waved them back.

"Too late!" one of the deckhands shouted, a little pleased to see that someone would be inconvenienced for tardiness.

The porters argued. But it was no use. All they could do was to carry the box back to the Dodge car.

Miss Dodge was just getting in as they returned.

"What shall we do with this and the other stuff?" asked the Irish porter.

She looked at the rest of the tagged luggage and the box which was marked:

Scientific Instruments Valuable Handle with care.

"Here—pile them in here," she said indicating the taxicab. "I'll take charge of them."

Meanwhile one of our sinister faced friends had just had time to regain the shore after following us aboard ship and strolling past the window of our stateroom. He paused long enough to observe one of the occupants studying a map, while the other was opening a bag.

"They're gone!" he said to the other as he rejoined him on the dock, giving a nod of his head and a jerk of his thumb at the ship.

"Yes," added the other crook, "and lost most of their baggage, too."

Slowly the Dodge car proceeded through the streets up from the river front, followed by the taxicab, until at last the Dodge mansion, was reached.

There Elaine and Aunt Josephine got out and Bennett stood talking with them a moment. Finally he excused himself reluctantly for it was now late, even for a lawyer, to get to his office.

As he hurried over to the subway, Elaine nodded to the porters in the taxicab, "Take that stuff in the house. We'll have to send it by the next boat."

Then she followed Aunt Josephine while the porters unloaded the boxes and bags.

Elaine sighed moodily as she walked slowly in.

"Here, Marie," she cried petulantly to her maid, "take these wraps of mine."

Marie ventured no remark, but, like a good servant, took them.

A moment later Aunt Josephine left her and Elaine went into the library and over to a table. She stood there an instant, then sank down into a chair, taking up Kennedy's picture and gazing at it with eyes filled by tears.

Just then Jennings came into the room, ushering the two porters laden with the boxes and bags.

"Where shall I have them put these things, Miss Elaine?" he inquired.

"Oh—anywhere," she answered hurriedly, replacing the picture.

Jennings paused. As he did so, one of the porters limped forward. "I've a message for you, Miss," he said in a rich Irish brogue, with a look at Jennings, "to be delivered in private."

Elaine glanced at him surprised. Then she nodded to Jennings who disappeared. As he did so, the Irishman limped to the door and drew together the portieres.

Then he came back closer to Elaine.

A moment she looked at him, not quite knowing from his strange actions whether to call for help or not.

* * * * *

At a motion from Kennedy, as he pulled off his wig, I pulled off the little false beard.

Elaine looked at us, transformed, startled.

"Wh—what—" she stammered. "Oh—I'm—so—glad. How—"

Kennedy said nothing. He was thoroughly enjoying her face.

"Don't you understand?" I explained, laughing merrily. "I admit that I didn't until that last minute in the stateroom on the boat when we didn't come back to wave a last good-bye. But all the care that Craig took in selecting the porters was the result of work he did yesterday, and the insistence with which he chose our travelling clothes had a deep-laid purpose."

She said nothing, and I continued.

"The change was made quickly in the stateroom. Kennedy's

Arthur B. Reeve

man threw on the coat and hat he wore, while Craig donned the rough clothes of the porter and added a limp and a wig. The same sort of exchange of clothes was made by me and Craig clapped a Van Dyck beard on my chin."

"I—I'm so glad," she repeated. "I didn't think you'd—"

She cut the sentence short, remembering her eyes and the photograph as we entered, and a deep blush crimsoned her face.

"Mum's the word," cautioned Kennedy, "You must smuggle us out of the house, some way."

* * * * *

Kennedy lost no time in confirming the suspicions of his bolometer as to the cause of the death of the two innocent victims of the machinations of the Clutching Hand.

Both of them, he had learned, had been removed to a nearby undertaking shop, awaiting the verdict of the coroner. We sought out the shop and prevailed on the undertaker to let us see the bodies.

As Kennedy pulled down the shroud from the face of the first victim, he disclosed on his forehead a round dark spot about the size of a small coin. Quickly, he moved to the next coffin and, uncovering the face, disclosed a similar mark.

"What is it?" I asked, awestruck.

"Why," he said, "I've heard of a certain Viennese, one LeCroix I believe, who has discovered or perfected an infra-red ray instrument which shoots its power a great distance with extreme accuracy and leaves a mark like these."

"Is he in New York?" I inquired anxiously.

"Yes, I believe he is."

Kennedy seemed indisposed to answer more until he knew more, and I saw that he would prefer not being questioned for the present.

We thanked the undertaker for his courtesy and went out.

* * * * *

Meanwhile Elaine had called up Perry Bennett.

"Mr. Bennett," she exclaimed over the wire, "just guess who called on me?"

"Who?" he answered, "I give it up."

"Mr. Kennedy and Mr. Jameson," she called back.

"Is that so?" he returned. "Isn't that fine? I didn't think he was the kind to run away like that. How did it happen?"

Elaine quickly told the story as I had told her.

Had she known it, however, Bennett's valet, Thomas, was at that very moment listening at the door, intensely interested.

As Bennett hung up the receiver, Thomas entered the room.

"If anyone calls me," ordered Bennett, "take the message, particularly if it is from Miss Dodge. I must get downtown— and tell her after I finish my court work for the day I shall be right up."

"Yes sir," nodded the valet with a covert glance at his master.

Then, as Bennett left, he followed him to the door, paused, thought a moment, then, as though coming to a sudden decision, went out by an opposite door.

It was not long afterward that a knock sounded at the door of the new headquarters of the Clutching Hand. LeCroix and the secretary were there, as well as a couple of others.

"The Chief!" exclaimed one.

The secretary opened the door, and, sure enough, the Clutching Hand entered.

"Well, how did your infra-red rays work?" he asked LeCroix.

"Fine."

"And they're gone?"

"Yes. The flowers were in the window yesterday. Two of our men saw them on the boat."

There came another knock. This time, as the door opened, it was Thomas, Bennett's faithless valet, who entered.

"Say," blurted out the informer, "do you know Kennedy and Jameson are back?"

"Back?" cried the crooks.

"Yes,—they didn't go. Changed clothes with the porters. I just heard Miss Dodge telling Mr. Bennett."

Clutching Hand eyed him keenly, then seemed to burst into an ungovernable fury.

Quickly he began volleying orders at the valet and the others. Then, with the secretary and two of the other crooks he left by another door from that by which he had sent the valet forth.

* * * * *

Leaving the undertaker's, Kennedy and I made our way, keeping off thoroughfares, to police headquarters, where, after making ourselves known, Craig made arrangements for a raid on the house across the street from the laboratory where we had seen the opera glass reflection.

Then, as secretly as we had come, we went out again, letting ourselves into the laboratory, stealthily looking up and down the street. We entered by a basement door, which Kennedy carefully locked again.

No sooner had we disappeared than one of the Clutching Hand's spies who had been watching behind a barrel of rubbish gave the signal of the hand down the street to a confederate and, going to the door, entered by means of a skeleton key.

We entered our laboratory which Kennedy had closed the day before. With shades drawn, it now looked deserted enough.

I dropped into a chair and lighted a cigarette with a sigh of relief, for really I had thought, until the boat sailed, that Kennedy actually contemplated going away.

Kennedy went over to a cabinet and, from it, took out a

Arthur B. Reeve

notebook and a small box. Opening the notebook on the laboratory table, he rapidly turned the pages.

"Here, Walter," he remarked. "This will answer your questions about the mysterious deadly ray."

I moved over to the table, eager to satisfy my curiosity and read the notes which he indicated with his finger.

INFRA-RED RAY NOTES

The infra-red ray which has been developed by LeCroix from the experiments of the Italian scientist Ulivi causes, when concentrated by an apparatus perfected by LeCroix, an instantaneous combustion of nonreflecting surfaces. It is particularly deadly in its effect on the brain centers.

It can be diverted, it is said however, by a shield composed of platinum backed by asbestos.

Next Kennedy opened the case which he had taken out of the cabinet and from it he took out the platinum-asbestos mirror, which was something of his own invention. He held it up and in pantomime showed me just how it would cut off the deadly rays.

He had not finished even that, when a peculiar noise in the laboratory itself disturbed him and he hastily thrust the asbestos platinum shield into his pocket.

Though we had not realized it, our return had been anticipated.

Suddenly, from a closet projected a magazine gun and before we could move, the Clutching Hand himself slowly appeared, behind us.

"Ah!" he exclaimed with mock politeness, "so, you thought you'd fool me, did you? Well!"

Just then, two other crooks, who had let themselves in by the skeleton key through the basement jumped into the room through that door covering us.

We started to our feet, but in an instant found ourselves both sprawling on the floor.

In the cabinet, beneath the laboratory table, another crook had been hidden and he tackled us with all the skill of an old football player against whom we had no defence.

Four of them were upon us instantly.

* * * * *

At the same time, Thomas, the faithless valet of Bennett, had been dispatched by the Clutching Hand to commandeer his master's roadster in his absence, and, carrying out the instructions, he had driven up before Elaine's house at the very moment when she was going out for a walk.

Thomas jumped out of the car and touched his hat deferentially.

"A message from Mr. Bennett, ma'am," he explained. "Mr. Kennedy and Mr. Bennett have sent me to ask you to come over to the laboratory."

Unsuspecting, Elaine stepped into the car and drove off.

Instead, however, of turning and pulling up on the laboratory side of the street, Thomas stopped opposite it. He got out and Elaine, thinking that perhaps it was to save time that he had not turned the car around, followed.

But when the valet, instead of crossing the street, went up to a door of a house and rang the bell, she began to suspect that all was not as it should be.

"What are you going here for, Thomas?" she asked. "There's the laboratory—over there."

"But, Miss Dodge," he apologized, "Mr. Kennedy and Mr. Bennett are here. They told me they'd be here."

The door was opened quickly by a lookout of the Clutching Hand and the valet asked if Craig and Elaine's lawyer were in. Of course the lookout replied that they were and, before Elaine knew it, she was jostled into the dark hallway and the door was banged shut.

Resistance was useless now and she was hurried along until another door was opened.

There she saw LeCroix and the other crooks.

And, as the door slammed, she caught sight of the fearsome Clutching Hand himself.

She drew back, but was too frightened even to scream.

With a harsh, cruel laugh, the super-criminal beckoned to her to follow him and look down through a small trap door.

Unable now to resist, she looked.

There she saw us. To that extent the valet had told the truth. Kennedy was standing in deep thought, while I sat on an old box, smoking a cigarette—very miserable.

Was this to be the sole outcome of Kennedy's clever ruse, I was wondering. Were we only to be shipwrecked in sight of port?

Watching his chance, when the street was deserted, the Clutching Hand and his followers had hustled us over to the new hangout across from the laboratory. There they had met more crooks and had thrust us into this vile hole. As the various ineffectual schemes for escape surged through my head, I happened to look up and caught a glance of horror on Craig's face. I followed his eyes. There, above us, was Elaine!

I saw her look from us to the Clutching Hand in terror. But none of us uttered a word.

"I will now show you, my dear young lady," almost hissed the Clutching Hand at length, "as pretty a game of hide and seek as you have ever seen."

As he said it, another trap door near the infra-red ray machine was opened and a beam of light burst through. I knew it was not that which we had to fear, but the invisible rays that accompanied it, the rays that had affected the bolometer.

Just then a spot of light showed near my foot, moving about the cement floor until it fell on my shoe. Instantly, the leather charred, even before I could move.

Kennedy and I leaped to our feet and drew back. The beam followed us. We retreated further. Still it followed, inexorably.

Clutching Hand was now holding Elaine near the door where she could not help seeing, laughing diabolically while he

Arthur B. Reeve

directed LeCroix and the rest to work the infra-red ray apparatus through the trap.

As we dodged from corner to corner, endeavoring to keep the red ray from touching us, the crooks seemed in no hurry, but rather to enjoy prolonging the torture as does a cat with a mouse.

"Please—oh, please—stop!" begged Elaine.

Clutching Hand only laughed with fiendish delight and urged his men on.

The thing was getting closer and closer.

Suddenly we heard a strange voice ring out above us.

"Police!"

"Where?" growled the Clutching Hand in fury.

"Outside—a raid! Run! He's told them!"

Already we could hear the hammers and axes of the police whom Kennedy had called upon before, as they battered at the outside door.

At that door a moment before, the lookout suddenly had given a startled stare and a suppressed cry. Glancing down the street he had seen a police patrol in which were a score or more of the strongarm squad. They had jumped out, some carrying sledgehammers, others axes.

Almost before he could cry out and retreat to give a warning, they had reached the door and the first resounding blows had been struck.

The lookout quickly had fled and drawn the bolts of a strong inner door, and the police began battering that impediment.

Instantly, Clutching Hand turned to LeCroix at the F-ray machine.

"Finish them!" he shouted.

We were now backed up against a small ell in the wall of the cellar. It was barely large enough to hold us, but by crowding we were able to keep out of the reach of the ray. The ray shot past the ell and struck a wall a couple of inches from us.

I looked. The cement began to crumble under the intense heat.

Meanwhile, the police were having great difficulty with the steelbolt-studded door into the room. Still, it was yielding a bit.

"Hurry!" shouted Clutching Hand to LeCroix.

Kennedy had voluntarily placed himself in front of me in the ell. Carefully, to avoid the ray, he took the asbestos-platinum shield from his pocket and slid it forward as best he could over the wall to the spot where the ray struck.

It deflected the ray.

But so powerful was it that even that part of the ray which was deflected could be seen to strike the ceiling in the corner which was of wood. Instantly, before Kennedy could even move the shield, the wood burst into flames.

Above us now smoke was pouring into the room where the deflected ray struck the floor and flames broke out.

Arthur B. Reeve

"Confound him!" ground out Clutching Hand, as they saw it.

The other crooks backed away and stood, hesitating, not knowing quite what to do.

The police had by this time finished battering in the door and had rushed into the outer passage.

While the flames leaped up, the crooks closed the last door into the room.

"Run!" shouted Clutching Hand, as they opened a secret gate disclosing a spiral flight of iron steps.

A moment later all had disappeared except Clutching Hand himself. The last door would hold only a few seconds, but Clutching Hand was waiting to take advantage of even that. With a last frantic effort he sought to direct the terrific ray at us. Elaine acted instantly. With all her strength she rushed forward, overturning the machine.

Clutching Hand uttered a growl and slowly raised his gun, taking aim with the butt for a well-directed blow at her head.

Just then the door yielded and a policeman stuck his head and shoulders through. His revolver rang out and Clutching Hand's automatic flew out of his grasp, giving him just enough time to dodge through and slam the secret door in the faces of the squad as they rushed in.

Back of the house, Clutching Hand and the other crooks were now passing through a bricked passage. The fire had got so far beyond control by this time that it drove the police back from their efforts to open the secret door. Thus the Clutching Hand had made good his escape through the passage which led out, as we later discovered, to the railroad tracks along the river.

"Down there—Mr. Kennedy—and Mr. Jameson," cried Elaine, pointing at the trap which was hidden in the stifle.

The fire had gained terrific headway, but the police seized a ladder and stuck it down into the basement.

Choking and sputtering, half suffocated, we staggered up.

"Are you hurt?" asked Elaine anxiously, taking Craig's arm.

"Not a bit—thanks to you!" he replied, forgetting all in meeting the eager questioning of her wonderful eyes.

Arthur B. Reeve

CHAPTER X

THE LIFE CURRENT

Assignments were being given out on the Star one afternoon, and I was standing talking with several other reporter in the busy hum of typewriters and clicking telegraphs.

"What do you think of that?" asked one of the fellows. "You're something of a scientific detective, aren't you?"

Without laying claim to such a distinction, I took the paper and read:

THE POISONED KISS AGAIN

Three More New York Women Report Being Kissed by Mysterious Stranger—Later Fell into Deep Unconsciousness. What Is It?

I had scarcely finished, when one of the copy boys, dashing past me, called, "You're wanted on the wire, Mr. Jameson."

I hurried over to the telephone and answered.

A musical voice responded to my hurried hello, and I hastened to adopt my most polite tone.

"Is this Mr. Jameson?" asked the voice.

"Yes," I replied, not recognizing it.

"Well, Mr. Jameson, I've heard of you on the Star and I've just had a very strange experience. I've had the poisoned kiss."

The woman did not pause to catch my exclamation of astonishment, but went on, "It was like this. A man ran up to me on the street and kissed me—and—I don't know how it was—but I became unconscious—and I didn't come to for an hour—in a hospital— fortunately. I don't know what would have happened if it hadn't been that someone came to my assistance and the man fled. I thought the Star would be interested."

"We are," I hastened to reply. "Will you give me your name?"

"Why, I am Mrs. Florence Leigh of number 20 Prospect Avenue," returned the voice. "Really, Mr. Jameson, some-thing ought to be done about these cases."

"It surely had," I assented, with much interest, writing her name eagerly down on a card. "I'll be out to interview you, directly."

The woman thanked me and I hung up the receiver.

"Say," I exclaimed, hurrying over to the editor's desk, "here's another woman on the wire who says she has received the poisoned kiss.

"Suppose you take that assignment," the editor answered, sensing a possible story.

I took it with alacrity, figuring out the quickest way by elevated and surface car to reach the address.

The conductor of the trolley indicated Prospect Avenue and I hurried up the street until I came to the house, a neat, unpretentious place. Looking at the address on the card first to make sure, I rang the bell.

I must say that I could scarcely criticize the poisoned kisser's taste, for the woman who had opened the door certainly was extraordinarily attractive.

"And you really were—put out by a kiss?" I queried, as she led me into a neat sitting room.

"Absolutely—as much as if it had been by one of these poisoned needles you read about," she replied confidently, hastening on to describe the affair volubly.

It was beyond me.

"May I use your telephone?" I asked.

"Surely," she answered.

I called the laboratory. "Is that you, Craig?" I inquired.

"Yes, Walter," he answered, recognizing my voice.

"Say, Craig," I asked breathlessly, "what sort of kiss would suffocate a person."

My only answer was an uproarious laugh from him at the idea.

"I know," I persisted, "but I've got the assignment from the

Star—and I'm out here interviewing a woman about it. It's all right to laugh—but here I am. I've found a case—names, dates and places. I wish you'd explain the thing, then."

"Oh, all right, Walter," he replied indulgently. "I'll meet you as soon as I can and help you out."

I hung up the receiver with an air of satisfaction. At least now I would get an explanation of the woman's queer story.

"I'll clear this thing up," I said confidently. "My friend, Craig Kennedy, the scientific detective is coming out here."

"Good! That fellow who attacked me ought to be shown up. All women may not be as fortunate as I."

We waited patiently. Her story certainly was remarkable. She remembered every detail up to a certain point—and then, as she said, all was blankness.

The bell rang and the woman hastened to the door admitting Kennedy.

"Hello, Walter," he greeted.

"This is certainly a most remarkable case, Craig," I said, introducing him, and telling briefly what I had learned.

"And you actually mean to say that a kiss had the effect—" Just then the telephone interrupted.

"Yes," she reasserted quickly. "Excuse me a second."

She answered the call. "Oh—why—yes, he's here. Do you want to speak to him? Mr. Jameson, it's the Star."

"Confound it!" I exclaimed, "isn't that like the old man—dragging me off this story before it's half finished in order to get another. I'll have to go. I'll get this story from you, Craig."

* * * * *

The day before, in the suburban house, the Clutching Hand had been talking to two of his emissaries, an attractive young woman and a man.

They were Flirty Florrie and Dan the Dude.

"Now, I want you to get Kennedy," he said. "The way to do it is to separate Kennedy and Elaine—see?"

"All right, Chief, we'll do it," they replied.

"I've rigged it so that you'll reach him through Jameson, understand?"

They nodded eagerly as he told them the subtle plan.

Clutching Hand had scarcely left when Flirty Florrie began by getting published in the papers the story which I had seen.

The next day she called me up from the suburban house. Having got me to promise to see her, she had scarcely turned from the telephone when Dan the Dude walked in from the next room.

"He's coming," she said.

Dan was carrying a huge stag head with a beautifully branched pair of antlers. Under his arm was a coil of wire which he had connected to the inside of the head.

"Fine!" he exclaimed. Then, pointing to the head, he added, "It's all ready. See how I fixed it? That ought to please the Chief."

Dan moved quickly to the mantle and mounted a stepladder there by which he had taken down the head, and started to replace the head above the mantle.

He hooked the head on a nail.

"There," he said, unscrewing one of the beautiful brown glass eyes of the stag.

Back of it could be seen a camera shutter. Dan worked the shutter several times to see whether it was all right.

"One of those new quick shutter cameras," he explained.

Then he ran a couple of wires along the moulding, around the room and into a closet, where he made the connection with a sort of switchboard on which a button was marked, "SHUTTER" and the switch, "WIND FILM."

"Now, Flirty," he said, coming out of the closet and pulling up the shade which let a flood of sunlight into the room, "you see, I want you to stand here—then, do your little trick. Get me?"

"I get you Steve," she laughed.

Just then the bell rang.

"That must be Jameson," she cried. "Now—get to your corner."

With a last look Dan went into the closet and shut the door.

Perhaps half an hour later, Clutching Hand himself called me up on the telephone. It was he—not the Star—as I learned only too late.

* * * * *

I had scarcely got out of the house, as Craig told me afterwards, when Flirty Florrie told all over again the embroidered tale that had caught my ear.

Kennedy said nothing, but listened intently, perhaps betraying in his face the scepticism he felt.

"You see," she said, still voluble and eager to convince him, "I was only walking on the street. Here,—let me show you. It was just like this."

She took his arm and before he knew it, led him to the spot on the floor near the window which Dan had indicated. Meanwhile Dan was listening attentively in his closet.

"Now—stand there. You are just as I was—only I didn't expect anything."

She was pantomiming someone approaching stealthily while Kennedy watched her with interest, tinged with doubt. Behind Craig, in his closet, Dan was reaching for the switchboard button.

"You see," she said advancing quickly and acting her words, "he placed his hands on my shoulders—so—then threw his arms about my neck—so."

She said no more, but imprinted a deep, passionate kiss on Kennedy's mouth, clinging closely to him. Before Kennedy could draw away, Dan, in the closet, had pressed the button and the switch several times in rapid succession.

"Th-that's very realistic," gasped Craig, a good deal taken aback by the sudden osculatory assault.

He frowned.

"I—I'll look into the case," he said, backing away. "There may be some scientific explanation—but—er—"

He was plainly embarrassed and hastened to make his adieux.

Kennedy had no more than shut the door before Dan, with a gleeful laugh, burst out of the closet and flung his own arms about Florrie in an embrace that might have been poisoned, it is true, but was none the less real for that.

* * * * *

How little impression the thing made on Kennedy can be easily seen from the fact that on the way downtown that afternoon he stopped at Martin's, on Fifth Avenue, and bought a ring—a very handsome solitaire, the finest Martin had in the shop.

It must have been about the time that he decided to stop at Martin's that the Dodge butler, Jennings, admitted a young lady who presented a card on which was engraved the name

Miss FLORENCE LEIGH 20 Prospect Avenue.

As he handed Elaine the card, she looked up from the book she was reading and took it.

"I don't know her," she said puckering her pretty brow. "Do

you? What does she look like?"

"I never saw her before, Miss Elaine," Jennings shrugged. "But she is very well dressed."

"All right, show her in, Jennings. I'll see her."

Elaine moved into the drawing room, Jennings springing forward to part the portieres for her and passing through the room quickly where Flirty Florrie sat waiting. Flirty Florrie rose and stood gazing at Elaine, apparently very much embarrassed, even after Jennings had gone.

There was a short pause. The woman was the first to speak.

"It IS embarrassing," she said finally, "but, Miss Dodge, I have come to you to beg for my love."

Elaine looked at her non-plussed.

"Yes," she continued, "you do not know it, but Craig Kennedy is infatuated with you." She paused again, then added, "But he is engaged to me."

Elaine stared at the woman. She was dazed. She could not believe it.

"There is the ring," Flirty Florrie added indicating a very impressive paste diamond.

Elaine frowned but said nothing. Her head was in a whirl. She could not believe. Although Florrie was very much embarrassed, she was quite as evidently very much wrought up. Quickly she reached into her bag and drew out two photographs, without a word, handing them to Elaine. Elaine took them reluctantly.

"There's the proof," Florrie said simply, choking a sob.

Elaine looked with a start. Sure enough, there was the neat living room in the house on Prospect Avenue. In one picture Florrie had her arms over Kennedy's shoulders. In the other, apparently, they were passionately kissing.

Elaine slowly laid the photographs on the table.

"Please—please, Miss Dodge—give me back my lost love. You are rich and beautiful—I am poor. I have only my good looks. But—I—I love him—and he—loves me—and has promised to marry me."

Filled with wonder, and misgivings now, and quite as much embarrassed at the woman's pleadings as the woman herself had acted a moment before, Elaine tried to wave her off.

"Really—I—I don't know anything about all this. It—it doesn't concern me. Please—go."

Florrie had broken down completely and was weeping softly into a lace handkerchief.

She moved toward the door. Elaine followed her.

"Jennings—please see the lady to the door."

Back in the drawing room, Elaine almost seized the photographs and hurried into the library where she could be alone. There she stood gazing at them—doubt, wonder, and fear battling on her plastic features.

Just then she heard the bell and Jennings in the hall.

She shoved the photographs away from her on the table.

It was Kennedy himself, close upon the announcement of the butler. He was in a particularly joyous and happy mood, for he had stopped at Martin's.

"How are you this afternoon?" he greeted Elaine gaily.

Elaine had been too overcome by what had just happened to throw it off so easily, and received him with a quickly studied coolness.

Still, Craig, man-like, did not notice it at once. In fact he was too busy gazing about to see that neither Jennings, Marie, nor the duenna Aunt Josephine were visible. They were not and he quickly took the ring from his pocket. Without waiting, he showed it to Elaine. In fact, so sure had he been that everything was plain sailing, that he seemed to take it almost for granted. Under other circumstances, he would have been right. But not tonight.

Elaine very coolly admired the ring, as Craig might have eyed a specimen on a microscope slide. Still, he did not notice.

He took the ring, about to put it on her finger. Elaine drew away. Concealment was not in her frank nature.

She picked up the two photographs.

"What have you to say about those?" she asked cuttingly.

Kennedy, quite surprised, took them and looked at them. Then he let them fall carelessly on the table and dropped into a chair, his head back in a burst of laughter.

"Why—that was what they put over on Walter," he said. "He called me up early this afternoon—told me he had discovered one of these poisoned kiss cases you have read about in the papers. Think of it—all that to pull a concealed camera! Such an elaborate business—just to get me where they could fake this thing. I suppose they've put some one up to saying she's engaged?"

Elaine was not so lightly affected. "But," she said severely, repressing her emotion, "I don't understand, MR. Kennedy, how scientific inquiry into 'the poisoned kiss' could necessitate this sort of thing."

She pointed at the photographs accusingly.

"But," he began, trying to explain.

"No buts," she interrupted.

"Then you believe that I—"

"How can you, as a scientist, ask me to doubt the camera," she insinuated, very coldly turning away.

Kennedy rapidly began to see that it was far more serious than he had at first thought.

"Very well," he said with a touch of impatience, "if my word is not to be taken—I—I'll—"

He had seized his hat and stick.

Elaine did not deign to answer.

Then, without a word he stalked out of the door.

As he did so, Elaine hastily turned and took a few steps after him, as if to recall her words, then stopped, and her pride got the better of her.

She walked slowly back to the chair by the table—the chair he had been sitting in—sank down into it and cried.

* * * * *

Kennedy was moping in the laboratory the next day when I came in.

Just what the trouble was, I did not know, but I had decided that it was up to me to try to cheer him up.

"Say, Craig," I began, trying to overcome his fit of blues.

Kennedy, filled with his own thoughts, paid no attention to me. Still, I kept on.

Finally he got up and, before I knew it, he took me by the ear and marched me into the next room.

I saw that what he needed chiefly was to be let alone, and he went back to his chair, dropping down into it and banging his fists on the table. Under his breath he loosed a small volley of bitter expletives. Then he jumped up.

"By George—I WILL," he muttered.

I poked my head out of the door in time to see him grab up his hat and coat and dash from the room, putting his coat on as he went.

"He's a nut today," I exclaimed to myself.

Though I did not know, yet, of the quarrel, Kennedy had really struggled with himself until he was willing to put his pride in his pocket and had made up his mind to call on Elaine again.

As he entered, he saw that it was really of no use, for only Aunt Josephine was in the library.

"Oh, Mr. Kennedy," she said innocently enough, "I'm so sorry she isn't here. There's been something troubling her and she won't tell me what it is. But she's gone to call on a young woman, a Florence Leigh, I think."

"Florence Leigh!" exclaimed Craig with a start and a frown. "Let me use your telephone."

I had turned my attention in the laboratory to a story I was writing, when I heard the telephone ring. It was Craig. Without a word of apology for his rudeness, which I knew had been purely absent-minded, I heard him saying, "Walter—meet me in half an hour outside that Florence Leigh's house."

He was gone in a minute, giving me scarcely time to call back that I would.

Then, with a hasty apology for his abruptness, he excused himself, leaving Aunt Josephine wondering at his strange actions.

At about the same time that Craig had left the laboratory, at the Dodge house Elaine and Aunt Josephine had been in the hall near the library. Elaine was in her street dress.

"I'm going out, Auntie," she said with an attempted gaiety. "And," she added, "if anyone should ask for me, I'll be there."

Arthur B. Reeve

She had showed her a card on which was engraved, the name and address of Florence Leigh.

"All right, dear," answered Aunt Josephine, not quite clear in her mind what subtle change there was in Elaine.

* * * * *

Half an hour later I was waiting near the house in the suburbs to which I had been directed by the strange telephone call the day before. I noticed that it was apparently deserted. The blinds were closed and a "To Let" sign was on the side of the house.

"Hello, Walter," cried Craig at last, bustling along. He stopped a moment to look at the house. Then, together, we went up the steps and we rang the bell, gazing about.

"Strange," muttered Craig. "The house looks deserted."

He pointed out the sign and the generally unoccupied look of the place. Nor was there any answer to our ring. Kennedy paused only a second, in thought.

"Come on, Walter," he said with a sudden decision. "We've got to get in here somehow."

He led the way around the side of the house to a window, and with a powerful grasp, wrenched open the closed shutters. He had just smashed the window viciously with his foot when a policeman appeared.

"Hey, you fellows—what are you doing there?" he shouted.

Craig paused a second, then pulled his card from his pocket.

"Just the man I want," he parried, much to the policeman's surprise, "There's something crooked going on here. Follow us in."

We climbed into the window. There was the same living room we had seen the day before. But it was now bare and deserted. Everything was gone except an old broken chair. Craig and I were frankly amazed at the complete and sudden change and I think the policeman was a little surprised, for he had thought the place occupied.

"Come on," cried Kennedy, beckoning us on.

Quickly he rushed through the house. There was not a thing in it to change the deserted appearance of the first floor. At last it occurred to Craig to grope his way down cellar. There was nothing there, either, except a bin, as innocent of coal as Mother Hubbard's cupboard was of food. For several minutes we hunted about without discovering a thing.

Kennedy had been carefully going over the place and was at the other side of the cellar from ourselves when I saw him stop and gaze at the floor. He was not looking, apparently, so much as listening. I strained my ears, but could make out nothing. Before I could say anything, he raised his hand for silence. Apparently he had heard something.

"Hide," he whispered suddenly to us.

Without another word, though for the life of me I could make nothing out of it, I pulled the policeman into a little angle of the wall nearby, while Craig slipped into a similar angle.

We waited a moment. Nothing happened. Had he been seeing things or hearing things, I wondered?

From our hidden vantage we could now see a square piece in the floor, perhaps five feet in diameter, slowly open up as though on a pivot. Beneath it we could make out a tube-like hole, perhaps three feet across, with a covered top. It slowly opened.

A weird and sinister figure of a man appeared. Over his head he wore a peculiar helmet with hideous glass pieces over the eyes, and tubes that connected with a tank which he carried buckled to his back. As he slowly dragged himself out, I could wonder only at the outlandish headgear.

Quickly he closed down the cover of the tube, but not before a vile effluvium seemed to escape, and penetrate even to us in our hiding places. As he moved forward, Kennedy gave a flying leap at him, and we followed with a regular football interference.

It was the work of only a moment for us to subdue and hold him, while Craig ripped off the helmet.

It was Dan the Dude.

"What's that thing?" I puffed, as I helped Craig with the headgear.

"An oxygen helmet," he replied. "There must be air down the tube that cannot be breathed."

He went over to the tube. Carefully he opened the top and gazed down, starting back a second later, with his face puckered up at the noxious odor.

"Sewer gas," he ejaculated, as he slammed the cover down. Then he added to the policeman, "Where do you suppose it comes from?"

"Why," replied the officer, "the St. James Drain—an old sewer—is somewhere about these parts."

Kennedy puckered his face as he gazed at our prisoner. He reached down quickly and lifted something off the man's coat.

"Golden hair," he muttered. "Elaine's!"

A moment later he seized the man and shook him roughly.

"Where is she—tell me?" he demanded.

The man snarled some kind of reply, refusing to say a word about her.

"Tell me," repeated Kennedy.

"Humph!" snorted the prisoner, more close-mouthed than ever.

Kennedy was furious. As he sent the man reeling away from him, he seized the oxygen helmet and began putting it on. There was only one thing to do—to follow the clue of the golden strands of hair.

Down into the pest hole he went, his head protected by the oxygen helmet. As he cautiously took one step after another down a series of iron rungs inside the hole, he found that the water was up to his chest. At the bottom of the perpendicular pit was a narrow low passage way, leading off. It was just about big enough to get through, but he managed to grope along it. He came at last to the main drain, an old stone-walled sewer, as murky a place as could well be imagined, filled with the foulest sewer gas. He was hardly able to keep his feet in the swirling, bubbling water that swept past,

Arthur B. Reeve

almost up to his neck.

The minutes passed as the policeman and I watched our prisoner in the cellar, by the tube. I looked anxiously at my watch.

"Craig!" I shouted at last, unable to control my fears for him.

No answer. To go down after him seemed out of the question.

By this time, Craig had come to a small open chamber into which the sewer widened. On the wall he found another series of iron rungs up which he climbed. The gas was terrible.

As he neared the top of the ladder, he came to a shelf-like aperture in the sewer chamber, and gazed about. It was horribly dark. He reached out and felt a piece of cloth. Anxiously he pulled on it. Then he reached further into the darkness.

There was Elaine, unconscious, apparently dead.

He shook her, endeavoring to wake her up. But it was no use.

In desperation Craig carried her down the ladder.

With our prisoner, we could only look helplessly around. Again and again I looked at my watch as the minutes lengthened. Suppose the oxygen gave out?

"By George, I'm going down after him," I cried in desperation.

"Don't do it," advised the policeman. "You'll never get out."

One whiff of the horrible gas told me that he was right. I should not have been able to go fifty feet in it. I looked at him in despair. It was impossible.

"Listen," said the policeman, straining his ears.

There was indeed a faint noise from the black depths below us. A rope alongside the rough ladder began to move, as though someone was pulling it taut. We gazed down.

"Craig! Craig!" I called. "Is that you?"

No answer. But the rope still moved. Perhaps the helmet made it impossible for him to hear.

He had struggled back in the swirling current almost exhausted by his helpless burden. Holding Elaine's head above the surface of the water and pulling on the rope to attract my attention, for he could neither hear nor shout, he had taken a turn of the rope about Elaine. I tried pulling on it. There was something heavy on the other end and I kept on pulling.

At last I could make out Kennedy dimly mounting the ladder. The weight was the unconscious body of Elaine which he steadied as he mounted. I tugged harder and he slowly came up.

Together, at last, the policeman and I reached down and pulled them out.

We placed Elaine on the cellar floor, as comfortably as was possible, and the policeman began his first-aid motions for resuscitation.

"No—no," cried Kennedy, "Not here—take her up where the air is fresher."

With his revolver still drawn to overawe the prisoner, the policeman forced him to aid us in carrying her up the rickety flight of cellar steps. Kennedy followed quickly, unscrewing the oxygen helmet as he went.

In the deserted living room we deposited our senseless burden, while Kennedy, the helmet off now, bent over her.

"Quick—quick!" he cried to the officer, "An ambulance!"

"But the prisoner," the policeman indicated.

"Hurry—hurry—I'll take care of him," urged Craig, seizing the policeman's pistol and thrusting it into his pocket. "Walter—help me."

He was trying the ordinary methods of resuscitation. Meanwhile the officer had hurried out, seeking the nearest telephone, while we worked madly to bring Elaine back.

Again and again Kennedy bent and outstretched her arms, trying to induce respiration. So busy was I that for the moment I forgot our prisoner.

But Dan had seen his chance. Noiselessly he picked up the old chair in the room and with it raised was approaching Kennedy to knock him out.

Before I knew it myself, Kennedy had heard him. With a half instinctive motion, he drew the revolver from his pocket and, almost before I could see it, had shot the man. Without a word he returned the gun to his pocket and again bent over Elaine, without so much as a look at the crook who sank to the floor, dropping the chair from his nerveless hands.

Already the policeman had got an ambulance which was now

tearing along to us.

Frantically Kennedy was working.

A moment he paused and looked at me—hopeless.

Just then, outside, we could hear the ambulance, and a doctor and two attendants hurried up to the door. Without a word the doctor seemed to appreciate the gravity of the case.

He finished his examination and shook his head.

"There is no hope—no hope," he said slowly.

Kennedy merely stared at him. But the rest of us instinctively removed our hats.

Kennedy gazed at Elaine, overcome. Was this the end?

It was not many minutes later that Kennedy had Elaine in the little sitting room off the laboratory, having taken her there in the ambulance, with the doctor and two attendants.

Elaine's body had been placed on a couch, covered by a blanket, and the shades were drawn. The light fell on her pale face.

There was something incongruous about death and the vast collection of scientific apparatus, a ghastly mocking of humanity. How futile was it all in the presence of the great destroyer?

Aunt Josephine had arrived, stunned, and a moment later, Perry Bennett. As I looked at the sorrowful party, Aunt Josephine rose slowly from her position on her knees where she had been weeping silently beside Elaine, and pressed her hands over her eyes, with every indication of faintness.

Before any of us could do anything, she had staggered into the laboratory itself, Bennett and I following quickly. There I was busy for some time getting restoratives.

Meanwhile Kennedy, beside the couch, with an air of desperate determination, turned away and opened a cabinet. From it he took a large coil and attached it to a storage battery, dragging the peculiar apparatus near Elaine's couch.

To an electric light socket, Craig attached wires. The doctor watched him in silent wonder.

"Doctor," he asked slowly as he worked, "do you know of Professor Leduc of the Nantes Ecole de Medicin?"

"Why—yes," answered the doctor, "but what of him?"

"Then you know of his method of electrical resuscitation."

"Yes—but—" He paused, looking apprehensively at Kennedy.

Craig paid no attention to his fears, but approaching the couch on which Elaine lay, applied the electrodes. "You see," he explained, with forced calmness, "I apply the anode here—the cathode there."

The ambulance surgeon looked on excitedly, as Craig turned on the current, applying it to the back of the neck and to the spine.

For some minutes the machine worked.

Then the young doctor's eyes began to bulge.

"My heavens!" he cried under his breath. "Look!"

Elaine's chest had slowly risen and fallen. Kennedy, his attention riveted on his work, applied himself with redoubled efforts. The young doctor looked on with increased wonder.

"Look! The color in her face! See her lips!" he cried.

At last her eyes slowly fluttered open—then closed.

Would the machine succeed? Or was it just the galvanic effect of the current? The doctor noticed it and quickly placed his ear to her heart. His face was a study in astonishment. The minutes sped fast.

To us outside, who had no idea what was transpiring in the other room, the minutes were leaden-feeted. Aunt Josephine, weak but now herself again, was sitting nervously.

Just then the door opened.

I shall never forget the look on the young ambulance surgeon's face, as he murmured under his breath, "Come here—the age of miracles is not passed—look!"

Raising his finger to indicate that we were to make no noise, he led us into the other room.

Kennedy was bending over the couch.

Elaine, her eyes open, now, was gazing up at him, and a wan smile flitted over her beautiful face.

Kennedy had taken her hand, and as he heard us enter, turned half way to us, while we stared in blank wonder from Elaine to the weird and complicated electrical apparatus.

"It is the life-current," he said simply, patting the Leduc apparatus with his other hand.

CHAPTER XI

THE HOUR OF THREE

With the ominous forefinger of his Clutching Hand extended, the master criminal emphasized his instructions to his
minions.

"Perry Bennett, her lawyer, is in favor again with Elaine
Dodge," he was saying. "She and Kennedy are on the outs
even yet. But they may become reconciled. Then she'll have
that fellow on our trail again. Before that happens, we must
'get' her—see?"

It was in the latest headquarters to which Craig had chased
the criminal, in one of the toughest parts of the old
Greenwich village, on the west side of New York, not far
from the river front.

They were all seated in a fairly large but dingy old room, in
which were several chairs, a rickety table and, against the
wall, a roll-top desk on the top of which was a telephone.

Several crooks of the gang were sitting about, smoking.

"Now," went on Clutching Hand, "I want you, Spike, to
follow them. See what they do—where they go. It's her

birthday. Something's bound to occur that will give you a lead. All you've got to do is to use your head. Get me?"

Spike rose, nodded, picked up his hat and coat and squirmed out on his mission, like the snake that he was.

* * * * *

It was, as Clutching Hand had said, Elaine's birthday. She had received many callers and congratulations, innumerable costly and beautiful tokens of remembrance from her count-less friends and admirers. In the conservatory of the Dodge house Elaine, Aunt Josephine, and Susie Martin were sitting discussing not only the happy occasion, but, more, the many strange events of the past few weeks.

"Well," cried a familiar voice behind them. "What would a certain blonde young lady accept as a birthday present from her family lawyer?"

All three turned in surprise.

"Oh, Mr. Bennett," cried Elaine. "How you startled us!"

He laughed and repeated his question, adopting the tone that he had once used in the days when he had been more in favor with the pretty heiress, before the advent of Kennedy.

Elaine hesitated. She was thinking not so much of his words as of Kennedy. To them all, however, it seemed that she was unable to make up her mind what, in the wealth of her luxury, she would like.

Susie Martin had been wondering whether, now that Bennett was here, she were not de trop, and she looked at her wrist watch mechanically. As she did so, an idea occurred to her.

"Why not one of these?" she cried impulsively, indicating the watch. "Father has some beauties at the shop."

"Oh, good," exclaimed Elaine, "how sweet!"

She welcomed the suggestion, for she had been thinking that perhaps Bennett might be hinting too seriously at a solitaire.

"So that strikes your fancy?" he asked. "Then let's all go to the shop. Miss Martin will personally conduct the tour, and we shall have our pick of the finest stock."

A moment later the three young people went out and were quickly whirled off down the Avenue in the Dodge town car.

It was too gay a party to notice a sinister figure following them in a cab. But as they entered the fashionable jewelry shop, Spike, who had alighted, walked slowly down the street.

Chatting with animation, the three moved over to the watch counter, while the crook, with a determination not to risk missing anything, entered the shop door, too.

"Mr. Thomas," asked Susie as her father's clerk bowed to them, "please show Miss Dodge the wrist watches father was telling about."

With another deferential bow, the clerk hastened to display a case of watches and they bent over them. As each new watch was pointed out, Elaine was delighted.

Unobserved, the crook walked over near enough to hear what was going on.

At last, with much banter and yet care, Elaine selected one

that was indeed a beauty and was about to snap it on her dainty wrist, when the clerk interrupted.

"I beg pardon," he suggested, "but I'd advise you to leave it to be regulated, if you please."

"Yes, indeed," chimed in Susie. "Father always advises that."

Reluctantly, Elaine handed it over to the clerk.

"Oh, thank you, ever so much, Mr. Bennett," she said as he unobtrusively paid for the watch and gave the address to which it was to be sent when ready.

A moment later they went out and entered the car again.

As they did so, Spike, who had been looking various things in the next case over as if undecided, came up to the watch counter.

"I'm making a present," he remarked confidentially to the clerk. "How about those bracelet watches?"

The clerk pulled out some of the cheaper ones.

"No," he said thoughtfully, pointing out a tray in the show case, "something like those."

He ended by picking out one identically like that which Elaine had selected, and started to pay for it.

"Better have it regulated," repeated the clerk.

"No," he objected hastily, shaking his head and paying the money quickly. "It's a present—and I want it tonight."

He took the watch and left the store hurriedly.

* * * * *

In the laboratory, Kennedy was working over an oblong oak box, perhaps eighteen inches in length and half as high. In the box I could see, besides other apparatus, two good sized spools of fine wire.

"What's all that?" I asked inquisitively.

"Another of the new instruments that scientific detectives use," he responded, scarcely looking up, "a little magnetic wizard, the telegraphone."

"Which is?" I prompted.

"Something we detectives might use to take down and 'can' telephone and other conversations. When it is attached properly to a telephone, it records everything that is said over the wire."

"How does it work?" I asked, much mystified.

"Well, it is based on an entirely new principle, in every way different from the phonograph," he explained. "As you can see there are no discs or cylinders, but these spools of extremely fine steel wire. The record is not made mechanically on a cylinder, but electromagnetically on this wire."

"How?" I asked, almost incredulously.

"To put it briefly," he went on, "small portions of magnetism, as it were, are imparted to fractions of the steel wire as it passes between two carbon electric magnets. Each

248   Arthur B. Reeve

impression represents a sound wave. There is no apparent difference in the wire, yet each particle of steel undergoes an electromagnetic transformation by which the sound is indelibly imprinted on it."

"Then you scrape the wire, just as you shave records to use it over again?" I suggested.

"No," he replied. "You pass a magnet over it and the magnet automatically erases the record. Rust has no effect. The record lasts as long as steel lasts."

Craig continued to tinker tantalizingly with the machine which had been invented by a Dane, Valdemar Poulsen.

He had scarcely finished testing out the telegraphone, when the laboratory door opened and a clean-cut young man entered.

Kennedy, I knew, had found that the routine work of the Clutching Hand case was beyond his limited time and had retained this young man, Raymond Chase, to attend to that.

Chase was a young detective whom Craig had employed on shadowing jobs and as a stool pigeon on other cases, and we had all the confidence in the world in him.

Just now what worried Craig was the situation with Elaine, and I fancied that he had given Chase some commission in connection with that.

"I've got it, Mr. Kennedy," greeted Chase with quiet modesty.

"Good," responded Craig heartily. "I knew you would."

"Got what?" I asked a moment later.

Kennedy nodded for Chase to answer.

"I've located the new residence of Flirty Florrie," he replied.

I saw what Kennedy was after at once. Flirty Florrie and Dan the Dude had caused the quarrel between himself and Elaine. Dan the Dude was dead. But Flirty Florrie might be forced to explain it.

"That's fine," he added, exultingly. "Now, I'll clear that thing up."

He took a hasty step to the telephone, put his hand on the receiver and was about to take it off the hook. Then he paused, and I saw his face working. The wound Elaine had given his feelings was deep. It had not yet quite healed.

Finally, his pride, for Kennedy's was a highly sensitive nature, got the better of him.

"No," he said, half to himself, "not—yet."

Elaine had returned home.

Alone, her thoughts naturally went back to what had happened recently to interrupt a friendship which had been the sweetest in her life.

"There MUST be some mistake," she murmured pensively to herself, thinking of the photograph Flirty had given her. "Oh, why did I send him away? Why didn't I believe him?"

Then she thought of what had happened, of how she had been seized by Dan the Dude in the deserted house, of how

Arthur B. Reeve

the noxious gas had overcome her.

They had told her of how Craig had risked his life to save her, how she had been brought home, still only half alive, after his almost miraculous work with the new electric machine.

There was his picture. She had not taken that away. As she looked at it, a wave of feeling came over her. Mechanically, she put out her hand to the telephone.

She was about to take off the receiver, when something seemed to stay her hand. She wanted him to come to her.

And, if either of them had called the other just then, they would have probably crossed wires.

Of such stuff are the quarrels of lovers.

Craig's eye fell on the telegraphone, and an idea seemed to occur to him.

"Walter, you and Chase bring that thing along," he said a moment later.

He paused long enough to take a badge from the drawer of a cabinet, and went out. We followed him, lugging the telegraphone.

At last we came to the apartment house at which Chase had located the woman.

"There it is," he pointed out, as I gave a groan of relief, for the telegraphone was getting like lead.

Kennedy nodded and drew from his pocket the badge I had

seen him take from the cabinet.

"Now, Chase," he directed, "you needn't go in with us. Walter and I can manage this, now. But don't get out of touch with me. I shall need you any moment—certainly tomorrow."

I saw that the badge read, Telephone Inspector.

"Walter," he smiled, "you're elected my helper."

We entered the apartment house hall and found a Negro boy in charge of the switchboard. It took Craig only a moment to convince the boy that he was from the company and that complaints had been made by some anonymous tenant.

"You look over that switchboard, Kelly," he winked at me, "while I test out the connections back here. There must be something wrong with the wires or there wouldn't be so many complaints."

He had gone back of the switchboard and the Negro, still unsuspicious, watched without understanding what it was all about.

"I don't know," Craig muttered finally for the benefit of the boy, "but I think I'll have to leave that tester after all. Say, if I put it here, you'll have to be careful not to let anyone meddle with it. If you do, there'll be the deuce to pay. See?"

Kennedy had already started to fasten the telegraphone to the wires he had selected from the tangle.

At last he finished and stood up.

"Don't disturb it and don't let anyone else touch it," he

ordered. "Better not tell anyone—that's the best way. I'll be back for it tomorrow probably."

"Yas sah," nodded the boy, with a bow, as we went out.

We returned to the laboratory, where there seemed to be nothing we could do now except wait for something to happen.

Kennedy, however, employed the time by plunging into work, most of the time experimenting with a peculiar little coil to which ran the wires of an ordinary electric bell.

Back in the new hang-out, the Clutching Hand was laying down the law to his lieutenants and heelers, when Spike at last entered.

"Huh!" growled the master criminal, covering the fact that he was considerably relieved to see him at last, "where have YOU been? I've been off on a little job myself and got back."

Spike apologized profusely. He had succeeded so easily that he had thought to take a little time to meet up with an old pal whom he ran across, just out of prison.

"Yes sir," he replied hastily, "well, I went over to the Dodge house, and I saw them finally. Followed them into a jewelry shop. That lawyer bought her a wrist watch. So I bought one just like it. I thought perhaps we could—" "Give it to me," growled Clutching Hand, seizing it the moment Slim displayed it. "And don't butt in—see?"

From the capacious desk, the master criminal pulled a set of small drills, vices, and other jeweler's tools and placed them on the table.

"All right," he relented. "Now, do you see what I have just thought of—no? This is just the chance. Look at me."

The heelers gathered around him, peering curiously at their master as he worked at the bracelet watch.

Carefully he plied his hands to the job, regardless of time.

"There," he exclaimed at last, holding the watch up where they could all see it. "See!"

He pulled out the stem to set the hands and slowly twisted it between his thumb and finger. He turned the hands until they were almost at the point of three o'clock.

Then he held the watch out where all could see it.

They bent closer and strained their eyes at the little second hand ticking away merrily.

As the minute hand touched three, from the back of the case, as if from the casing itself, a little needle, perhaps a quarter of an inch, jumped out. It seemed to come from what looked like merely a small inset in the decorations.

"You see what will happen at the hour of three?" he asked.

No one said a word, as he held up a vial which he had drawn from his pocket. On it they could read the label, "Ricinus."

"One of the most powerful poisons in the world!" he exclaimed. "Enough here to kill a regiment!"

They fairly gasped and looked at it with horror, exchanging glances. Then they looked at him in awe. There was no wonder that Clutching Hand kept them in line, once he had a

Arthur B. Reeve

crook in his power.

Opening the vial carefully, he dipped in a thin piece of glass and placed a tiny drop in a receptacle back of the needle and on the needle itself.

Altogether it savored of the ancient days of the Borgias with their weird poisoned rings.

Then he dropped the vial back into his pocket, pressed a spring, and the needle went back into its unsuspected hiding place.

"I've set my invention to go off at three o'clock," he concluded. "Tomorrow forenoon, it will have to be delivered early—and I don't believe we shall be troubled any longer by Miss Elaine Dodge," he added venomously.

Even the crooks, hardened as they were, could only gasp.

Calmly he wrapped up the apparently innocent engine of destruction and handed it to Spike.

"See that she gets it in time," he said merely.

"I will, sir," answered Spike, taking it gingerly.

Flirty Florrie had returned that afternoon, late, from some expedition on which she had been sent.

Rankling in her heart yet was the death of her lover, Dan the Dude. For, although in her sphere of crookdom they are neither married nor given in marriage, still there is a brand of loyalty that higher circles might well copy. Sacred to the memory of the dead, however, she had one desire—revenge.

Thus when she arrived home, she went to the telephone to report and called a number, 4494 Greenwich.

"Hello, Chief," she repeated. "This is Flirty. Have you done anything yet in the little matter we talked about?"

"Say—be careful of names—over the wire," came a growl.

"You know—what I mean."

"Yes. The trick will be pulled off at three o'clock." "Good!" she exclaimed. "Good-bye and thank you."

With his well-known caution Clutching Hand did not even betray names over the telephone if he could help it.

Flirty hung up the receiver with satisfaction. The manes of the departed Dan might soon rest in peace!

The next day, early in the forenoon, a young man with a small package carefully done up came to the Dodge house.

"From Martin's, the jeweler's, for Miss Dodge," he said to Jennings at the door.

Elaine and Aunt Josephine were sitting in the library when Jennings announced him.

"Oh, it's my watch," cried Elaine. "Show him in."

Jennings bowed and did so. Spike entered, and handed the package to Elaine, who signed her name excitedly and opened it.

"Just look, Auntie," she exclaimed. "Isn't it stunning?"

"Very pretty," commented Aunt Josephine.

Elaine put the watch on her wrist and admired it.

"Is it all right?" asked Spike.

"Yes, yes," answered Elaine. "You may go."

He went out, while Elaine gazed rapturously at the new trinket while it ticked off the minutes—this devilish instrument.

Early the same morning Kennedy went around again to the apartment house and, cautious not to be seen by Flirty, recovered the telegraphone. Together we carried it to the laboratory.

There he set up a little instrument that looked like a wedge sitting up on end, in the face of which was a dial. Through it he began to run the wire from the spools, and, taking an earpiece, put another on my head over my ears.

"You see," he explained, "the principle on which this is based is that a mass of tempered steel may be impressed with and will retain magnetic fluxes varying in density and in sign in adjacent portions of itself—little deposits of magnetic impulse.

"When the telegraphone is attached to the telephone wire, the currents that affect the receiver also affect the coils of the telegraphone and the disturbance set up causes a deposit of magnetic impulse on the steel wire.

"When the wire is again run past these coils with a receiver such as I have here in circuit with the coils, a light vibration is set up in the receiver diaphragm which reproduces the sound of speech." He turned a switch and we listened eagerly. There was no grating and thumping, as he controlled the running off of the wire. We were listening to everything that had been said over the telephone during the time since we left the machine.

First came several calls from people with bills and she put them off most adroitly.

Then we heard a call that caused Kennedy to look at me quickly, stop the machine and start at that point over again.

"That's what I wanted," he said as we listened in:

"Give me 4494 Greenwich."

"Hello."

"Hello, Chief. This is Flirty. Have you done anything yet in the little matter we talked about?

"Say—be careful of names—over the wire."

"You know—what I mean."

"Yes, the trick will be pulled off at three o'clock.

"Good! Good-bye and thank you!"

"Good-bye."

Kennedy stopped the machine and I looked at him blankly.

"She called Greenwich 4494 and was told that the trick would be pulled off at three o'clock today," he ruminated.

"What trick?" I asked.

He shook his head. "I don't know. That is what we must find out. I hadn't expected a tip like that. What I wanted was to find out how to get at the Clutching Hand."

He paused and considered a minute, then moved to the telephone.

"There's only one thing to do and that's to follow out my original scheme," he said energetically. "Information, please."

"Where is Greenwich 4494?" he asked a moment later.

The minutes passed. "Thank you," he cried, writing down on a pad an address over on the west side near the river front. Then turning to me he explained, "Walter, we've got him at last!"

Craig rose and put on his hat and coat, thrusting a pair of opera glasses into his pocket, in case we should want to observe the place at a distance. I followed him excitedly. The trail was hot.

Kennedy and I came at last to the place on the West Side where the crooked streets curved off.

Instead of keeping on until he came to the place we sought, he turned and quickly slipped behind the shelter of a fence. There was a broken board in the fence and he bent down, gazing through with the opera glasses.

Across the lot was the new headquarters, a somewhat dilapidated old-fashioned brick house of several generations back. Through the glass we could see an evil-countenanced crook slinking along. He mounted the steps and rang the bell, turning as he waited.

From a small aperture in the doorway looked out another face, equally evil. Under cover, the crook made the sign of the clutching hand twice and was admitted.

"That's the place, all right," whispered Kennedy with satisfaction.

He hurried to a telephone booth where he called several numbers. Then we returned to the laboratory, while Kennedy quickly figured out a plan of action. I knew Chase was expected there soon.

From the table he picked up the small coil over which I had seen him working, and attached it to the bell and some batteries. He replaced it on the table, while I watched curiously.

"A selenium cell," he explained. "Only when light falls on it does it become a good conductor of electricity. Then the bell will ring."

Just before making the connection he placed his hat over the cell. Then he lifted the hat. The light fell on it and the bell rang. He replaced the hat and the bell stopped. It was evidently a very peculiar property of the substance, selenium.

Just then there came a knock at the door. I opened it.

"Hello, Chase," greeted Kennedy. "Well, I've found the new headquarters all right,—over on the west side."

Kennedy picked up the selenium cell and a long coil of fine wire which he placed in a bag. Then he took another bag already packed and, shifting them between us, we hurried down town.

Near the vacant lot, back of the new headquarters, was an old broken down house. Through the rear of it we entered.

I started back in astonishment as we found eight or ten policemen already there. Kennedy had ordered them to be ready for a raid and they had dropped in one at a time without attracting attention.

"Well, men," he greeted them, "I see you found the place all right. Now, in a little while Jameson will return with two wires. Attach them to the bell which I will leave here. When it rings, raid the house. Jameson will lead you to it. Come, Walter," he added, picking up the bags.

Ten minutes later, outside the new headquarters, a crouched up figure, carrying a small package, his face hidden under his soft hat and up-turned collar, could have been seen slinking along until he came to the steps.

He went up and peered through the aperture of the doorway. Then he rang the bell. Twice he raised his hand and clenched it in the now familiar clutch.

A crook inside saw it through the aperture and opened the door. The figure entered and almost before the door was shut tied the masking handkerchief over his face, which hid his identity from even the most trusted lieutenants. The crook bowed to the chief, who, with a growl as though of recognition, moved down the hall.

As he came to the room from which Spike had been sent on his mission, the same group was seated in the thick tobacco smoke.

"You fellows clear out," he growled. "I want to be alone."

"The old man is peeved," muttered one, outside, as they left.

The weird figure gazed about the room to be sure that he was alone.

When Craig and I left the police he had given me most minute instructions which I was now following out to the letter.

"I want you to hide there," he said, indicating a barrel back of the house next to the hang-out. "When you see a wire come down from the headquarters, take it and carry it across the lot to the old house. Attach it to the bell; then wait. When it rings, raid the Clutching Hand joint."

I waited what seemed to be an interminable time back of the barrel and it is no joke hiding back of a barrel.

Finally, however, I saw a coil of fine wire drop rapidly to the ground from a window somewhere above. I made a dash for it, as though I were trying to rush the trenches, seized my prize and without looking back to see where it came from, beat a hasty retreat.

Around the lot I skirted, until at last I reached the place where the police were waiting. Quickly we fastened the wire to the bell.

We waited.

Not a sound from the bell.

Up in the room in the joint, the hunched up figure stood by the table. He had taken his hat off and placed it carefully on the table, and was now waiting.

Suddenly a noise at the door startled him. He listened. Then he backed away from the door and drew a revolver.

As the door slowly opened there entered another figure, hat over his eyes, collar up, a handkerchief over his face, the exact counterpart of the first!

For a moment each glared at the other.

"Hands up!" shouted the first figure, hoarsely, moving the gun and closing the door, with his foot.

The newcomer slowly raised his crooked hand over his head, as the blue steel revolver gaped menacingly.

With a quick movement of the other hand, the first sinister figure removed the handkerchief from his face and straight-tened up.

It was Kennedy!

"Come over to the center of the room," ordered Kennedy.

Clutching Hand obeyed, eyeing his captor closely.

"Now lay your weapons on the table."

He tossed down a revolver.

The two still faced each other.

"Take off that handkerchief!"

It was a tense moment. Slowly Clutching Hand started to obey. Then he stopped. Kennedy was just about to thunder, "Go on," when the criminal calmly remarked, "You've got

ME all right, Kennedy, but in twenty minutes Elaine Dodge will be dead!"

He said it with a nonchalance that might have deceived anyone less astute than Kennedy. Suddenly there flashed over Craig the words: "THE TRICK WILL BE PULLED OFF AT THREE O'CLOCK!"

There was no fake about that. Kennedy frowned. If he killed Clutching Hand, Elaine would die. If he fought, he must either kill or be killed. If he handed Clutching Hand over, all he had to do was to keep quiet. He looked at his watch. It was twenty-five minutes of three.

What a situation!

He had caught a prisoner he dared not molest—yet.

"What do you mean—tell me?" demanded Kennedy with forced calm.

"Yesterday Mr. Bennett bought a wrist watch for Elaine," the Clutching Hand said quietly. "They left it to be regulated. One of my men bought one just like it. Mine was delivered to her today."

"A likely story!" doubted Kennedy.

For answer, the Clutching Hand pointed to the telephone.

Kennedy reached for it.

"One thing," interrupted the Clutching Hand. "You are a man of honor."

"Yes—yes. Go on."

Arthur B. Reeve

"If I tell you what to do, you must promise to give me a fighting chance."

"Yes, yes."

"Call up Aunt Josephine, then. Do just as I say."

Covering Clutching Hand, Kennedy called a number. "This is Mr. Kennedy, Mrs. Dodge. Did Elaine receive a present of a wrist watch from Mr. Bennett?"

"Yes," she replied, "for her birthday. It came this forenoon."

Kennedy hung up the receiver and faced Clutching Hand puzzled as the latter said, "Call up Martin, the jeweler."

Again Kennedy obeyed.

"Has the watch purchased for Miss Elaine Dodge been delivered?" he asked the clerk.

"No," came back the reply, "the watch Mr. Bennett bought is still here being regulated."

Kennedy hung up the receiver. He was stunned.

"The watch will cause her death at three o'clock," said the Clutching Hand. "Swear to leave here without discovering my identity and I will tell you how. You can save her!"

A moment Kennedy thought. Here was a quandary.

"No," he shouted, seizing the telephone.

Before Kennedy could move, Clutching Hand had pulled the telephone wires with almost superhuman strength from the junction box.

"In that watch," he hissed, "I have set a poisoned needle in a spring that will be released and will plunge it into her arm at exactly three o'clock. On the needle is ricinus!"

Craig advanced, furious. As he did so, Clutching Hand pointed calmly to the clock. It was twenty minutes of three!

With a mental struggle, Kennedy controlled his loathing of the creature before him.

"All right—but you'll hear from me—sooner than you suspect," he shouted, starting for the door.

Then he came back and lifted his hat, hiding as much as possible the selenium cell, letting the light fall on it.

"Only Elaine's life has saved you."

With a last threat he dashed out. He hailed a cab, returning from some steamship wharves not far away.

"Quick!" he ordered, giving the Dodge address on Fifth Avenue.

Minute after minute the police and I waited. Was anything wrong? Where was Craig?

Just then a tremor grew into a tinkle, then came the strong burr of the bell. Kennedy needed us.

With a shout of encouragement to the men I dashed out and over to the old house.

Meanwhile Clutching Hand himself had approached the table

to recover his weapon and had noticed the queer little selenium cell. He picked it up and for the first time saw the wire leading out.

"The deuce!" he cried. "He's planned to get me anyhow!"

Clutching Hand rushed to the door—then stopped short. Outside he could hear the police and myself. We had shot the lock on the outside and were already inside.

Clutching Hand slammed shut his door and pulled down over it a heavy wooden bar. A few steps took him to the window. There were police in the back yard, too. He was surrounded.

But he did not hurry. He knew what to do with every second.

At the desk he paused and took out a piece of cardboard. Then with a heavy black marking pencil, he calmly printed on it, while we battered at the barricaded door, a few short feet away.

He laid the sign on the desk, then on another piece of cardboard, drew crudely a hand with the index finger, pointing. This he placed on a chair, indicating the desk.

Just as the swaying and bulging door gave way, Clutching Hand gave the desk a pull. It opened up—his getaway.

He closed it with a sardonic smile in our direction, just before the door crashed in.

We looked about. There was not a soul in the room, nothing but the selenium cell, the chairs, the desk.

"Look!" I cried catching sight of the index finger, and going over to the desk.

We rolled back the top. There on the flat top was a sign:

Dear Blockheads:

Kennedy and I couldn't wait.

Yours as ever,

Then came that mysterious sign of the Clutching Hand.

We hunted over the rooms, but could find nothing that showed a clue. Where was Clutching Hand? Where was Kennedy?

In the next house Clutching Hand had literally come out of an upright piano into the room corresponding to that he had left. Hastily he threw off his handkerchief, slouch hat, old coat and trousers. A neat striped pair of trousers replaced the old, frayed and baggy pair. A new shirt, then a sporty vest and a frock coat followed. As he put the finishing touches on, he looked for all the world like a bewhiskered foreigner.

With a silk hat and stick, he surveyed himself, straightening his tie. At the door of the new headquarters, a few seconds later, I stood with the police.

"Not a sign of him anywhere," growled one of the officers.

Nor was there. Down the street we could see only a straight well- dressed, distinguished looking man who had evidently walked down to the docks to see a friend off, perhaps.

Elaine was sitting in the library reading when Aunt Josephine turned to her.

"What time is it, dear?" she asked.

Elaine glanced at her pretty new trinket.

"Nearly three, Auntie—a couple of minutes," she said.

Just then there came the sound of feet running madly down the hall way. They jumped up, startled.

Kennedy, his coat flying, and hat jammed over his eyes, had almost bowled over poor Jennings in his mad race down the hall.

"Well," demanded Elaine haughtily, "what's—"

Before she knew what was going on, Craig hurried up to her and literally ripped the watch off her wrist, breaking the beautiful bracelet.

He held it up, gingerly. Elaine was speechless. Was this Kennedy? Was he possessed by such an inordinate jealousy of Bennett?

As he held the watch up, the second hand ticked around and the minute hand passed the meridian of the hour.

A viciously sharp little needle gleamed out—then sprang back into the filigree work again.

"Well," she gasped again, "what's the occasion of THIS?"

Craig gazed at Elaine in silence.

Should he defend his rudeness, if she did not understand? She stamped her foot, and repeated the question a third time.

"What do you mean, sir, by such conduct?"

Slowly he bowed.

"I just don't like the kind of birthday presents you receive," he said, turning on his heel. "Good afternoon."

Arthur B. Reeve

CHAPTER XII

THE BLOOD CRYSTALS

"On your right is the residence of Miss Elaine Dodge, the heiress, who is pursuing the famous master criminal known as the Clutching Hand."

The barker had been grandiloquently pointing out the residences of noted New Yorkers as the big sightseeing car lumbered along through the streets. The car was filled with people and he plied his megaphone as though he were on intimate terms with all the city's notables.

No one paid any attention to the unobtrusive Chinaman who sat inconspicuously in the middle of the car. He was Mr. Long Sin, but no one saw anything particularly mysterious about an oriental visitor more or less viewing New York City.

Long was of the mandarin type, with drooping mustache, well dressed in American clothes, and conforming to the new customs of an occidentalized China.

Anyone, however, who had been watching Long Sin would have seen that he showed much interest whenever any of the wealthy residents of the city were mentioned. The name of

Elaine Dodge seemed particularly to strike him. He listened with subtle interest to what the barker said and looked keenly at the Dodge house.

The sight-seeing car had passed the house, when he rose slowly and motioned that he wanted to be let off. The car stopped, he alighted and slowly rambled away, evidently marvelling greatly at the strange customs of these uncouth westerners.

Elaine was going out, when she met Perry Bennett almost on the steps of the house.

"I've brought you the watch," remarked Bennett; "thought I'd like to give it to you myself."

He displayed the watch which he himself had bought a couple of days before for her birthday. He had called for it himself at the jeweller's where it had now been regulated.

"Oh, thank you," exclaimed Elaine. "Won't you come in?"

They had scarcely greeted each other, when Long Sin strolled along. Neither of them, however, had time to notice the quiet Chinaman who passed the house, looking at Elaine sharply out of the corner of his eye. They entered and Long disappeared down the street.

"Isn't it a beauty?" cried Elaine, holding it out from her, as they entered the library and examining it with great appreciation. "And, oh, do you know, the strangest thing happened yesterday? Sometimes Mr. Kennedy acts too queerly for anything."

She related how Craig had burst in on her and Aunt Josephine and had almost torn the other watch off her wrist.

"Another watch?" repeated Bennett, amazed. "It must have been a mistake. Kennedy is crazy."

"I don't understand it, myself," murmured Elaine.

Long Sin had continued his placid way, revolving some dark and devious plan beneath his impassive Oriental countenance. He was no ordinary personage. In fact he was astute enough to have no record. He left that to his tools.

This remarkable criminal had established himself in a hired apartment downtown. It was furnished in rather elegant American style, but he had added to it some most valuable Oriental curios which gave it a fascinating appearance.

Long Sin, now in rich Oriental costume, was reclining on a divan smoking a strange looking pipe and playing with two pet white rats. Each white rat had a gold band around his leg, to which was connected a gold chain about a foot in length, and the chains ended in rings which were slipped over Long's little fingers. Ordinarily, he carried the pets up the capacious sleeve of each arm.

A servant, also in native costume, entered and bowed deferentially.

"A Miss Mary Carson," she lisped in soft English.

"Let the lady enter," waved Long Sin, with a smile of subtle satisfaction.

The girl bowed again and silently left the room, returning with a handsome, very well dressed white woman.

It would be difficult to analyze just what the fascination was that Long Sin exercised over Mary Carson. But as the servant left the room, Mary bowed almost as deferentially as the little Chinese girl. Long merely nodded in reply.

After a moment, he slowly rose and took from a drawer a newspaper clipping. Without a word, he handed it to Mary. She looked at it with interest, as one woman always does at the picture of another pretty woman. It was a newspaper cut of Elaine, under which was:

ELAINE DODGE, THE HEIRESS, WHOSE BATTLE WITH THE CLUTCHING HAND IS CREATING WORLD WIDE INTEREST.

"Now," he began, at last, breaking the silence, "I'll show you just what I want you to do."

He went over to the wall and took down a curious long Chinese knife from a scabbard which hung there conspicuously.

"See that?" he added, holding it up.

Before she could say a word, he had plunged the knife, apparently, into his own breast.

"Oh!" cried Mary, startled.

She expected to see him fall. But nothing happened. Long Sin laughed. It was an Oriental trick knife in which the blade telescoped into the handle.

"Look at it," he added, handing it to her.

Long Sin took a bladder of water from a table nearby and concealed it under his coat. "Now, you stab me," he directed.

Mary hesitated. But he repeated the command and she

plunged the knife gingerly at him. It telescoped. He made her try it over and she stabbed more resolutely. The water from the bladder poured out.

"Good!" cried Long Sin, much pleased. "Now," he added, seating himself beside her, "I want you to lure Elaine here."

Mary looked at him inquiringly as he returned the knife to its scabbard on the wall. "Remember where it is," he continued. "Now, if you will come into the other room I will show you how to get her."

I had been amusing myself by rigging up a contrivance by which I could make it possible to see through or rather over, a door. The idea had been suggested to me by the cystoscope which physicians use in order to look down one's throat, and I had calculated that by using three mirrors placed at proper angles, I could easily reflect rays down to the level of my eye.

Kennedy, who had been busy in the other end of the laboratory, happened to look over in my direction. "What's the big idea, Walter?" he asked.

It was, I admit, a rather cumbersome and clumsy affair.

"Well, you see, Craig," I explained, "you put the top mirror through the transom of a door and—"

Kennedy interrupted with a hearty burst of laughter. "But suppose the door has no transom?" he asked, pointing to our own door.

I scratched my head, thoughtfully. I had assumed that the door would have a transom. A moment later, Craig went to the cabinet and drew out a tube about as big around as a putty blower and as long.

"Now, here's what I call my detectascope," he remarked. "None of your mirrors for me."

"I know," I said somewhat nettled, "but what can you see through that putty blower? A key hole is just as good."

"Do you realize how little you can really see through a key hole?" he replied confidently. "Try it over there."

I did and to tell the truth I could see merely a little part of the hall. Then Kennedy inserted the detectascope.

"Look through that," he directed.

I put my eye to the eye-piece and gazed through the bulging lens of the other end. I could see almost the whole hall.

"That," he explained, "is what is known as a fish-eye lens—a lens that looks through an angle of some 180 degrees, almost twice that of the widest angle lens I know of."

I said nothing, but tossed my own crude invention into the corner, while Craig went back to work.

Elaine was playing with "Rusty" when Jennings brought in a card on which was engraved the name, "Miss Mary Carson," and underneath, in pencil, was written "Belgian Relief Committee."

"How interesting," commented Elaine, rising and accompanying Jennings back into the drawing room. "I wonder what she wants. Very pleased to meet you, Miss Carson," she greeted her visitor.

Arthur B. Reeve

"You see, Miss Dodge," began Mary, "we're getting up this movement to help the Belgians and we have splendid backing. Just let me show you some of the names on our committee."

She handed Elaine a list which read:

BELGIAN RELIEF COMMITTEE

Mrs. Warburton Fish Mrs. Hamilton Beekman Mrs. C. August Iselm Mrs. Belmont Rivington Mrs. Rupert Solvay.

"I've just been sent to see if I cannot persuade you to join the committee and attend a meeting at Mrs. Rivington's," she went on.

"Why, er," considered Elaine thoughtfully, "er—yes. It must be all right with such people in it."

"Can you go with me now?"

"Just as well as later," agreed Elaine.

They went out together, and, as they were leaving the house a man who had been loitering outside looked at Elaine, then fixedly at her companion.

No sooner had they gone than he sped off to a car waiting around the corner. In the dark depths was a sinister figure, the master criminal himself. The watcher had been an emissary of the Clutching Hand.

"Chief," he whispered eagerly, "You know Adventuress Mary? Well, she's got Elaine Dodge in tow!"

"The deuce!" cried Clutching Hand. "Then we must teach

Mary Carson, or whoever she is working for, a lesson. No one shall interfere with our affairs. Follow them!"

Elaine and Mary had gone downtown, talking animatedly, and walked down the avenue toward Mrs. Rivington's apartment.

Meanwhile, Long Sin, still in his Chinese costume, was explaining to the servant just what he wished done, pointing out the dagger on the wall and replacing the bladder under his jacket. A box of opium was on the table, and he was giving most explicit directions. It was into such a web that Elaine was being unwittingly led by Mary.

Entering the hallway of the apartment, Mary rang the bell.

Long heard it. "Answer it," he directed the servant who hastened to do so, while Long glided like a serpent into a back room.

The servant opened the door and Elaine and Mary entered. He closed the door and almost before they knew locked it and was gone into the back room.

Elaine gazed about in trepidation. But before she could say anything, Mary, with a great show of surprise, exclaimed, "Why, I must have made a mistake. This isn't Mrs. Rivington's apartment. How stupid of me."

They looked at each other a moment. Then each laughed nervously, as together they started to go out of the door. It was locked!

Quickly they ran to another door. It was locked, also.

Then they went to the windows. Behind the curtains they

were barred and looked out on a blank brick wall in a little court.

"Oh," cried Mary wringing her hands, stricken in mock panic, "oh, I'm so frightened. This may be the den of Chinese white slavers!"

She had picked up some Chinese articles on a table, including the box that Long had left there. It had a peculiar odor.

"Opium!" she whispered, showing it to Elaine.

The two looked at each other, Elaine genuinely worried now.

Just then, the Chinaman entered and stood a moment gazing at them. They turned and Elaine recoiled from him. Long bowed.

"Oh sir," cried Mary, "We've made a mistake. Can't you tell us how to get out?"

Long's only answer was to spread out his hands in polite deprecation and shrug his suave shoulders.

"No speke Englis," he said, gliding out again from the room and closing the door.

Elaine and Mary looked about in despair.

"What shall we do?" asked Elaine.

Mary said nothing, but with a hasty glance discovered on the wall the knife which Long had already told her about. She took it from its scabbard. As she did so the Chinaman returned with a tray on which were queer drinks and glasses.

At the sight of Mary with the knife he scowled blackly, laid the tray down, and took a few steps in her direction. She brandished the knife threateningly, then, as if her nerve failed her, fainted letting the knife fall carefully on the floor so that it struck on the handle and not on the blade.

Long quickly caught her as she fainted and carried her out of the room, banging shut the door. Elaine followed in a moment, loyally, to protect her supposed friend, but found that the door had a snap lock on the other side.

She looked about wildly and in a moment Long reappeared. As he advanced slowly and insinuatingly, she drew back, pleading. But her words fell on seemingly deaf ears.

She had picked up the knife which Mary had dropped and when at last Long maneuvred to get her cornered and was about to seize her, she nerved herself up and stabbed him resolutely.

Long staggered back—and fell.

As he did so, he pressed the bladder which he had already placed under his coat. A dark red fluid, like blood, oozed out all over him and ran in a pool on the floor.

Elaine, too horror-stricken at what had happened even to scream, dropped the knife and bent over him. He did not move. She staggered back and ran through the now open door. As she did so, Long seemed suddenly to come to life. He raised himself and looked after her, then with a subtle smile sank back into his former assumed posture on the floor.

When Elaine reached the other room, she found Mary there with the Chinese servant who was giving her a glass of

Arthur B. Reeve

water. At the sight of her, the servant paused, then withdrew into another room further back. Mary, now apparently recovering from her faintness, smiled wanly at Elaine.

"It's all right," she murmured. "He is a Chinese prince who thought we were callers."

At the reassuring nod of Mary toward the front room, Elaine was overcome.

"I—I killed him!" she managed to gasp.

"What?" cried Mary, starting up and trembling violently. "You killed him?"

"Yes," sobbed Elaine, "he came at me—I had the knife—I struck at him—"

The two girls ran into the other room. There Mary looked at the motionless body on the floor and recoiled, horrified.

Elaine noticing some spots on her hands and seeing that they were stained by the blood of Long Sin, wiped the spots off on her hankerchief, dropping it on the floor.

"Ugh!" exclaimed a guttural voice behind them.

It was the servant who had come in. Even his ordinarily impassive Oriental face could not conceal the horror and fear at the sight of his master lying on the floor in a pool of gore. Elaine was now more frightened than ever, if that were possible.

"You—kill him—with knife?" insinuated the Chinese.

Elaine was dumb. The servant did not wait for an answer, but hastily opened the hall door.

To Elaine it seemed that something must be done quickly. A moment and all the house would be in uproar.

Instead, he placed his finger on his lips. "Quick—no word," he said, leading the way to the hall door, "and—you must not leave that—it will be a clue," he added, picking up the bloody handkerchief and pressing it into Elaine's hand.

They quickly ran out into the hall.

"Go—quick!" he urged again, "and hide the handkerchief in the bag. Let no one see it!"

He shut the door. As they hurried away, Elaine breathed a sigh of relief.

"Why did he let us go, though?" she whispered, her head in a whirl.

"I don't know," panted Mary, "but anyhow, thank heaven, we are out of it. Come," she added, taking Elaine's arm, "not a soul has seen us except the servant. Let us get away as quietly as we can."

They had reached the street. Afraid to run, they hurried as fast as they could until they turned the first corner.

Elaine looked back. No one was pursuing.

"We must separate," added Mary. "Let us go different ways. I will see you later. Perhaps they will think some enemy has murdered him."

They pressed each other's hands and parted.

Meanwhile in the front room, Long Sin was on his feet again brushing himself off and mopping up the blood.

"It worked very well, Sam," he said to the servant.

They were conversing eagerly and laughing and did not hear a noise in the back room.

A sinister figure had made its way by means of a fire-escape to a rear window that was not barred, and silently he had stolen in on them.

Cat-like, he advanced, but instead of striking at them, he quietly took a seat in a chair close behind them, a magazine revolver in his hand.

They turned at a slight noise and saw him. Genuine fright was now on their faces as they looked at him, open mouthed.

"What's all this?" he growled. "I am known as the Clutching Hand. I allow no interferences with my affairs. Tell me what you are doing here with Elaine Dodge."

Their beady almond eyes flashed fear. Clutching Hand moved menacingly. There was nothing for the astute Long Sin to do but to submit. Cowed by the well-known power of the master criminal, he took Clutching Hand into his confidence.

With a low bow, Long Sin spread out his hands in surrender and submission.

"I will tell you, honorable sir," he said at length.

"Go on!" growled the criminal.

Quickly Long rehearsed what had happened, from the moment the idea of blackmail had entered his head.

"How about Mary Carson?" asked Clutching Hand. "I saw her here."

Long gave a glance of almost superstitious dread at the man, as if he had an evil eye.

"She will be back—is here now," he added, opening the door at a knock and admitting her.

Adventuress Mary had hurried back to see that all was right. This time Mary was genuinely scared at the forbidding figure of which she had heard.

"It is all right," pacified Long. "Henceforth we work with the honorable Clutching Hand."

Clutching Hand continued to emphasize his demands on them, punctuating his sentences by flourishes of the gun as he gave them the signs and passwords which would enable them to work with his own emissaries.

It was a strange initiation.

At home at last, Elaine sank down into a deep library chair and stared straight ahead. She saw visions of arrest and trial, of the terrible electric chair with herself in it, bound, and of the giving of the fatal signal for turning on the current.

Were such things as these going to happen to her, without Kennedy's help? Why had they quarreled? She buried her face in her hands and wept.

Then she could stand it no longer. She had not taken off her

Arthur B. Reeve

street clothes. She rose and almost fled from the house.

Kennedy and I were still in the laboratory when a knock sounded at the door. I went to the door and opened it. There stood Elaine Dodge.

It was a complete surprise to Craig. There was silence between them for a moment and they merely looked at each other. Elaine was pale and woebegone.

At last Kennedy took a quick step toward her and led her to a chair. Still he felt a sort of constraint.

"What IS the matter?" he asked at length.

She hesitated, then suddenly burst out, "Craig—I—I am—a murderess!"

I have never seen such a look on Craig's face. I know he wanted to laugh and say, "YOU—a murderess?" yet he would not have offended even her self accusation for the world. He managed to do the right thing and say nothing.

Then she poured forth the story substantially as I have set it down, but without the explanation which at that time was not known to any of us.

"Oh," expostulated Craig, "there must be some mistake. It's impossible—impossible."

"No," she asserted. "Look—here's my handkerchief all spotted with blood."

She opened the bag and displayed the blood-spotted hand-kerchief. He took it and examined it carefully.

"Elaine," he said earnestly, not at all displeased, I could see that something had come up that might blot out the past unfortunate misunderstanding, "there simply must be something wrong here. Leave this handkerchief with me. I'll do my best."

There was still a little restraint between them. She was almost ready to beg his pardon, for all the coolness there had been between them, yet still hesitated.

"Thank you," she said simply as she left the laboratory.

Craig went to work abruptly without a word. On the laboratory table he placed his splendid microscope and several cases of slides as well as innumerable micro-photographs. He had been working for some time when he looked up.

"Ever hear of Dr. Edward Reichert of the University of Pennsylvania and his wonderful discoveries of how blood crystals vary in different species?" he asked.

I had not, but did not admit it.

"Well," he went on, "there is a blood test so delicate that one might almost say that he could identify a criminal by the finger prints, so to speak, of his blood crystals. The hemoglobin or red coloring matter forms crystals and the variations of these crystals both in form and molecular construction are such that they set apart every species of animal from every other, and even the races of men—perhaps may even set apart individuals. Here, Walter, we have sample of human blood crystals."

I looked through the microscope as he directed. There I could see the crystals sharply defined.

"And here," he added, "are the crystals of the blood on Elaine's handkerchief."

I looked again as he changed the slides. There was a marked difference and I looked up at him quickly.

"It is dog's blood—not human blood," he said simply.

I looked again at the two sets of slides. There could be no doubt that there was a plain difference.

"Wonderful!" I exclaimed.

"Yes—wonderful," he agreed, "but what's the game back of all this—that's the main question now."

Long after Clutching Hand had left, Long Sin was giving instructions to his servant and Adventuress Mary just how he had had to change his plans as a result of the unexpected visit.

"Very well," nodded Mary as she left him, "I will do as you say—trust me."

It was not much later, then, that Elaine received a second visit from Mary.

"Show her in, Jennings," she said to the butler nervously.

Indeed, she felt that every eye must be upon her. Even Jennings would know of her guilt soon.

Anxiously, therefore, Elaine looked at her visitor.

"Do you know why the servant allowed us to leave the apartment?" whispered Mary with a glance about fearfully, as if the walls had ears.

"No—why?" inquired Elaine anxiously.

"He's a tong man who has been chosen to do away with the Prince. He followed me, and says you have done his work for him. If you will give him ten thousand dollars for expenses, he will attend to hiding the body."

Here at least was a way out.

"But do you think that is all right? Can he do it?" asked Elaine eagerly.

"Do it? Why those tong men can do anything for money. Only one must be careful not to offend them."

Mary was very convincing.

"Yes, I suppose you are right," agreed Elaine, finally. "I had better do as you say. It is the safest way out of the trouble. Yes, I'll do it. I'll stop at the bank now and get the money."

They rose and Mary preceded her, eager to get away from the house. At the door, however, Elaine asked her to wait while she ran back on some pretext. In the library she took off the receiver of the telephone and quickly called a number.

Our telephone rang in the middle of our conversation on blood crystals and Kennedy himself answered it.

It was Elaine asking Craig's advice.

"They have offered to hush the thing up for ten thousand dollars," she said, in a muffled voice.

She seemed bent on doing it and no amount of argument from him could stop her. She simply refused to accept the evidence of the blood crystals as better than what her own eyes told her she had seen and done.

"Then wait for half an hour," he answered, without arguing further. "You can do that without exciting suspicion. Go with her to her hotel and hand her over the money."

"All right—I'll do it," she agreed.

"What is the hotel?"

Craig wrote on a slip of paper what she told him—"Room 509, Hotel La Coste."

"Good—I'm glad you called me. Count on me," he finished as he hung up the receiver.

Hastily he threw on his street coat. "Go into the back room and get me that brace and bit, Walter," he asked.

I did so. When I returned, I saw that he had placed the detectascope and some other stuff in a bag. He shoved in the brace and bit also.

"Come on—hurry!" he urged.

We must have made record time in getting to the Coste. It was an ornate place, where merely to breathe was expensive. We entered and by some excuse Kennedy contrived to get past the vigilant bellhops. We passed the telephone switchboard and entered the elevator, getting off at the fifth floor.

With a hasty glance up and down the corridor, to make sure no one was about, Kennedy came to room 509, then passed to the next, 511, opening the door with a skeleton key. We entered and Craig locked the door behind us. It was an ordinary hotel room, but well- furnished. Fortunately it was unoccupied.

Quietly Craig went to the door which led to the next room. It was, of course, locked also. He listened a moment carefully. Not a sound. Quickly, with an exclamation of satisfaction, he opened that door also and went into 509.

This room was much like that in which we had already been. He opened the hall door.

"Watch here, Walter," he directed, "Let me know at the slightest alarm."

Craig had already taken the brace and bit from the bag and started to bore through the wall into room 511, selecting a spot behind a picture of a Spanish dancer—a spot directly back of her snapping black eyes. He finished quickly and inserted the detectascope so that the lens fitted as an eye in the picture. The eye piece was in Room 511. Then he started to brush up the pieces of plaster on the floor.

"Craig," I whispered hastily as I heard an elevator door, "someone's coming!"

He hurried to the door and looked. "There they are," he said, as we saw Elaine and Mary rounding the corner of the hall.

Across the hall, although we did not know it at the time, in room 540, already, Long Sin had taken up his station, just to be handy. There he had been with his servant, playing with his two trained white rats.

Long placed them up his capacious sleeves and carefully

Arthur B. Reeve

opened the door to look out. Unfortunately he, was just in time to see the door of 509 open and disclose us.

His subtle glance detected our presence without our knowing it.

Hastily picking up the brace and bit and the rest of the debris, and with a last look at the detectascope, which was hardly noticeable, even if one already knew it was there, we hurried into 511 and shut the door.

Kennedy mounted a chair and applied his eye to the detectascope. Just then Mary and Elaine entered the next room, Mary opening the door with a regular key.

"Won't you step in?" she asked.

Elaine did so and Mary hesitated in the hall. Long Sin had slipped out on noiseless feet and taken refuge behind some curtains. As he saw her alone, he beckoned to Mary.

"There's a stranger in the next room," he whispered. "I don't like him. Take the money and as quickly as possible get out and go to my apartment."

At the news that there was a suspicious stranger about, Mary showed great alarm. Everything was so rapid, now, that the slightest hesitation meant disaster. Perhaps, by quickness, even a suspicious stranger could be fooled, she reasoned. At any rate, Long Sin was resourceful. She had better trust him.

Mary followed Elaine into the room, where she had seated herself already, and locked the door.

"Have you the money there?" she asked.

"Yes," nodded Elaine, taking out the package of bills which she had got from the bank during the half hour delay.

All this we could see by gazing alternately through the detectascope.

Elaine handed Mary the money. Mary counted it slowly. At last she looked up.

"It's all right," she said. "Now, I'll take this to that tong leader—he's in a room only just across the hall."

She went out.

Kennedy at the detectascope was very excited as this went on. He now jumped off the chair on which he had been standing and rushed to the door to head her off.

To our surprise, in spite of the fact that we could turn the key in the lock, it was impossible to open it!

It was only a moment that Craig paused at the door. The next moment he burst into 509, followed closely by me.

With a scream, Elaine was on her feet in an instant.

There was no time for explanations, however.

He rushed to the door to go out, but it was locked—somehow, on the outside. The skeleton key would not work, at any rate.

He shot the lock, and dashed out, calling back, "Walter, stay there—with Elaine."

Mary had just succeeded in getting on the elevator as

Arthur B. Reeve

Kennedy hurried down the hall. The door was closed and the car descended. He rang the push bell furiously, but there was no answer.

Had he got so far in the chase, only to be outwitted?

He dashed back to the room, with us, and jerked down the telephone receiver.

"Hello—hello—hello!" he called.

No answer.

There seemed to be no way to get a connection. What was the matter?

He hurried down the hall again.

No sooner had Elaine and Mary actually gone into the room, than Long and his servant stole out of 540, across the hall. Somewhere they had obtained a strong but thin rope.

Quickly and silently Long tied the handle of the door 511 in which we were to the handle of 540 which he was vacating. As both doors opened inward and were opposite, they were virtually locked.

Then Long and his servant hurried down the hallway to the elevator.

Down in the hotel lobby, with his followers, the Chinaman paused before the telephone switchboard where two girls were at work.

"You may go," ordered Long, and, as his man left, he moved over closer to the switchboard.

He was listening eagerly and also watching an indicator that told the numbers of the rooms which called, as they flashed into view.

Just as a call from "509" flashed up, Long slipped the rings off his little fingers and loosened the white rats on the telephone switchboard itself.

With a shriek, the telephone system of the Coste went temporarily out of business.

The operators fled to the nearest chairs, drawing their skirts about them.

There was the greatest excitement among all the women in the corridor. Such a display of hosiery was never contemplated by even the most daring costumers.

Shouts from the bellboys who sought to catch the rats who scampered hither and thither in frightened abandon mingled with the shrieks of the ladies.

Kennedy had succeeded in finding the alcove of the floor clerk in charge of the fifth floor. There on his desk was an instrument having a stylus on the end of two arms, connected to a system of magnets. It was a telautograph.

Unceremoniously, Craig pushed the clerk out of his seat and sat down himself. It was a last chance, now that the telephone was out of commission.

Downstairs, in the hotel office, where the excitement had not spread to everyone, was the other end of the electric long distance writer.

It started to write, as Kennedy wrote, upstairs:

"HOUSE DETECTIVE—QUICK—HOLD WOMAN WITH BLUE CHATELAINE BAG, GETTING OUT OF ELEVATOR."

The clerks downstairs saw it and shouted above the din of the rat- baiting.

"McCann—McCann!"

The clerk had torn off the message from the telautograph register, and handed it to the house man who pushed his way to the desk.

Quickly the detective called to the bell-hops. Together they hurried after the well-dressed woman who had just swept out of the elevator. Mary had already passed through the excited lobby and out, and was about to cross the street—safe.

McCann and the bell-hops were now in full cry after her. Flight was useless. She took refuge in indignation and threats.

But McCann was obdurate. She passed quickly to tears and pleadings. It had no effect. They insisted on leading her back. The game was up.

Even an offer of money failed to move their adamantine hearts. Nothing would do but that she must face her accusers.

In the meantime Long Sin had recovered his precious and useful pets. Life in the Coste had assumed something of its normal aspect, and Craig had succeeded in getting an elevator.

It was just as Mary was led in threatening and pleading by turns that he stepped off in the lobby.

There was, however, still just enough excitement to cover a little pantomime. Long Sin had been about to slip out of a side door, thinking all was well, when he caught sight of Mary being led back. She had also seen him, and began to struggle again.

Quickly he shook his head, indicating for her to stop. Then slowly he secretly made the sign of the Clutching Hand at her. It meant that she must not snitch.

She obeyed instantly, and he quietly disappeared.

"Here," cried Kennedy, "take her up in the elevator. I'll prove the case."

With the house detective and Kennedy, Mary was hustled into the elevator and whisked back as she had escaped.

In the meantime I had gathered up what stuff we had in the room we had entered and had returned with Kennedy's bag.

"Wh—what's it all about?" inquired Elaine excitedly.

I tried to explain.

Just then, out in the hall we could hear loud voices, and that of Mary above the rest. Kennedy, a man who looked like a detective, and some bell-boys were leading her toward us.

"Now—not a word of who she is in the papers, McCann," Kennedy was saying, evidently about Elaine. "You know it wouldn't sound well for La Coste. As for that woman—well, I've got the money back. You can take her off—make the charge."

As the house man left with Mary, I handed Craig his bag.

We moved toward the door, and as we stood there a moment with Elaine, he quietly handed over to her the big roll of bills.

She took it, with surprise still written in her big blue eyes. "Oh—thank you—I might have known it was only a black-mail scheme," she cried eagerly.

Craig held out his hand and she took it quickly, gazing into his eyes. Craig bowed politely, not quite knowing what to do under the circumstances.

If he had been less of a scientist, he might have understood the look on her face, but, with a nod to me, he turned, and went.

As she looked first at him, then at the paltry ten thousand in her hand, Elaine stamped her little foot in vexation.

"I'm glad I DIDN'T say anything more," she cried. "No—no—he shall beg my pardon first—there!"

CHAPTER XIII

THE DEVIL WORSHIPPERS

Elaine was seated in the drawing room with Aunt Josephine one afternoon, when her lawyer, Perry Bennett, dropped in unexpectedly.

He had hardly greeted them when the butler, Jennings, in his usual impassive manner announced that Aunt Josephine was wanted on the telephone.

No sooner were Elaine and Bennett alone, than Elaine, turning to him, exclaimed impulsively, "I'm so glad you have come. I have been longing to see you and to tell you about a strange dream I have had."

"What was it?" he asked, with instant interest.

Leaning back in her chair and gazing before her tremulously, Elaine continued, "Last night, I dreamed that father came to me and told me that if I would give up Kennedy and put my trust in you, I would find the Clutching Hand. I don't know what to think of it."

Bennett, who had been listening intently, remained silent for a few moments. Then, putting down his tea cup, he moved over nearer to Elaine and bent over her.

"Elaine," he said in a low tone, his remarkable eyes looking straight into her own, "you must know that I love you. Then give me the right to protect you. It was your father's dearest wish, I believe, that we should marry. Let me share your dangers and I swear that sooner or later there will be an end to the Clutching Hand. Give me your answer, Elaine," he urged, "and make me the happiest man in all the world."

Elaine listened, and not unsympathetically, as Bennett continued to plead for her answer.

"Wait a little while—until to-morrow," she replied finally, as if overcome by the recollections of her weird dream and the unexpected sequel of his proposal.

"Let it be as you wish, then," agreed Bennett quietly.

He took her hand and kissed it passionately.

An instant later Aunt Josephine returned. Elaine, unstrung by what had happened, excused herself and went into the library.

She sank into one of the capacious arm chairs, and passing her hand wearily over her throbbing forehead, closed her eyes in deep thought. Involuntarily, her mind travelled back over the rapid succession of events of the past few weeks and the part that she had thought, at least, Kennedy had come to play in her life.

Then she thought of their recent misunderstanding. Might there not be some simple explanation of it, after all, which she had missed? What should she do?

She solved the problem by taking up the telephone and asking for Kennedy's number.

I was chatting with Craig in his laboratory, and, at the same time, was watching him in his experimental work. Just as a call came on the telephone, he was pouring some nitro-hydrochloric acid into a test tube to complete a reaction.

The telephone tinkled and he laid down the bottle of acid on his desk, while he moved a few steps to answer the call.

Whoever the speaker was, Craig seemed deeply interested, and, not knowing who was talking on the wire, I was eager to learn whether it was anyone connected with the case of the Clutching Hand.

"Yes, this is Mr. Kennedy," I heard Craig say.

I moved over toward him and whispered eagerly, "Is there anything new?"

A little impatient at being interrupted, Kennedy waved me off. It occurred to me that he might need a pad and pencil to make a note of some information and I reached over the desk for them.

As I did so my arm inadvertently struck the bottle of acid, knocking it over on the top of the desk. Its contents streamed out saturating the telephone wires before I could prevent it. In trying to right the bottle my hand came in contact with the acid which burned like liquid fire, and I cried out in pain.

Craig hastily laid down the receiver, seized me and rushed me to the back of the laboratory where he drenched my hand with a neutralizing liquid.

Arthur B. Reeve

He bound up the wounds caused by the acid, which proved to be slight, after all, and then returned to the telephone.

To his evident annoyance, he discovered that the acid had burned through the wires and cut off all connection.

Though I did not know it, my hand was, in a sense at least, the hand of fate.

At the other end of the line, Elaine was listening impatiently for a response to her first eager words of inquiry. She was astounded to find, at last, that Kennedy had apparently left the telephone without any explanation or apology.

"Why—he rang off," she exclaimed angrily to herself, as she hung up the receiver and left the room.

She rejoined her Aunt Josephine and Bennett who had been chatting together in the drawing room, still wondering at the queer rebuff she had, seemingly, experienced.

Bennett rose to go, and, as he parted from Elaine, found an opportunity to whisper a few words reminding her of her promised reply on the morrow.

Piqued, at Kennedy, she flashed Bennett a meaning glance which gave him to understand that his suit was not hopeless.

In the center of a devious and winding way, quite unknown to all except those who knew the innermost secrets of the Chinese quarter and even unknown to the police, there was a dingy tenement house, apparently inhabited by hardworking Chinamen, but in reality the headquarters of the notorious devil worshippers, a sect of Satanists, banned even in the Celestial Empire.

The followers of the cult comprised some of the most dangerous Chinese criminals, thugs, and assassins, besides a number of dangerous characters who belonged to various Chinese secret societies. At the head of this formidable organization was Long Sin, the high priest of the Devil God, and Long Sin had, as we knew, already joined forces with the notorious Clutching Hand.

The room in which the uncanny rites of the devil worshippers were conducted was a large apartment decorated in Chinese style, with highly colored portraits of some of the devil deities and costly silken hangings. Beside a large dais depended a huge Chinese gong.

On the dais itself stood, or rather sat, an ugly looking figure covered with some sort of metallic plating. It almost seemed to be the mummy of a Chinaman covered with gold leaf. It was thin and shrunken, entirely nude.

Into this room came Long Sin attired in an elaborate silken robe. He advanced and kowtowed before the dais with its strange figure, and laid down an offering before it, consisting of punk sticks, little dishes of Chinese cakes, rice, a jar of oil, and some cooked chicken and pork. Then he bowed and kowtowed again.

This performance was witnessed by twenty or thirty Chinamen who knelt in the rear of the room. As Long Sin finished his devotions they filed past the dais, bowing and scraping with every sign of abject reverence both for the devil deity and his high priest.

At the same time an aged Chinaman carrying a prayer wheel entered the place and after prostrating himself devoutly placed the machine on a sort of low stool or tabourette and began turning it slowly, muttering. Each revolution of this curious wheel was supposed to offer a prayer to the god of the netherworld.

A few moments later, Long Sin, who had been bowing before the metallic figure in deepest reverence, suddenly sprang to his feet. His glazed eye and excited manner indicated that he had received a message from the lips of the strange idol.

The worshippers who had prostrated themselves in awe at the sight of their high priest in the unholy frenzy, all rose to their feet and crowded forward. At the same time Long Sin advanced a step to meet them, holding his arms outstretched as if to compel silence while he delivered his message.

Long Sin struck several blows on the resounding gong and then raised his voice in solemn tones.

"Ksing Chau, the Terrible, demands a consort. She is to be foreign—fair of face and with golden hair."

Amazed at this unexpected message, the Chinamen prostrated themselves again and their unhallowed devotions terminated a few moments later amid suppressed excitement as they filed out.

At the same time, in a room of the adjoining house, the Clutching Hand himself was busily engaged making the most elaborate preparations for some nefarious scheme which his fertile mind had evolved.

The room had been fitted up as a medium's seance parlor, with black hangings on the walls, while at one side there was a square cabinet of black cloth, with a guitar lying before it.

Two of the Clutching Hand's most trusted confederates and a

hard-faced woman of middle age, dressed in plain black, were putting the finishing touches to this apartment, when their Chief entered.

Clutching Hand gazed about the room, now and then giving an order or two to make more effective the setting for the purpose which he had in mind.

Finally he nodded in approval and stepped over to the fire place where logs were burning brightly in a grate.

Pressing a spring in the mantelpiece, the master criminal effected an instant transformation. The logs in the fireplace, still burning, disappeared immediately through the side of the brick tiling and a metal sheet covered them. An aperture opened at the back, as if by magic.

Through this opening Clutching Hand made his way quickly and disappeared.

Emerging on the other side of the peculiar fireplace, Clutching Hand pushed aside a curtain which barred the way and looked into the Chinese temple, taking up a position behind the metallic figure on the dais.

The Chinamen had by this time finished their devotions, if such they might be called, and the last one was leaving, while Long Sin stood alone on the dais.

The noise of the departing Satanists had scarcely died away when Clutching Hand stepped out.

"Follow me," he ordered hoarsely seizing Long Sin by the arm and leading him away.

They passed through the passageway of the fireplace and,

having entered the seance room, Clutching Hand began briefly explaining the purpose of the preparations that had been made. Long Sin wagged his head in voluble approval.

As Clutching Hand finished, the Chinaman turned to the hard-faced woman who was to act the part of medium and added some directions to those Clutching Hand had already given.

The medium nodded acquiescence, and a moment later, left the room to carry out some ingenious plot framed by the master mind of the criminal world.

* * * * *

Elaine was standing in the library gazing sadly at Kennedy's portrait, thinking over recent events and above all the rebuff over the telephone which she supposed she had received.

It all seemed so unreal to her. Surely, she felt in her heart, she could not have been so mistaken in the man. Yet the facts seemed to speak for themselves.

In spite of it all, she was almost about to kiss the portrait when something seemed to stay her hands. Instead she laid the picture down, with a sigh.

A moment later, Jennings entered with a card on a salver. Elaine took it and saw with surprise the name of her caller:

MADAME SAVETSKY, MEDIUM

Beneath the engraved name were the words written in ink, "I have a message from the spirit of your father."

"Yes, I will see her," cried Elaine eagerly, in response to the butler's inquiry.

She followed Jennings into the adjoining room and there found herself face to face with the hard-featured woman who had only a few moments before left the Clutching Hand.

Elaine looked rather than spoke her inquiry.

"Your father, my dear," purred the medium with a great pretence of suppressed excitement, "appeared to me, the other night, from the spirit world. I was in a trance and he asked me to deliver a message to you."

"What was the message?" asked Elaine breathlessly, now aroused to intense interest.

"I must go into a trance again to get it," replied the insinuating Savetsky, "and if you like I can try it at once, provided we can be left alone long enough."

"Please—don't wait," urged Elaine, pulling the portieres of the doors closer, as if that might insure privacy.

Seated in her chair, the medium muttered wildly for a few moments, rolled her eyes and with some convulsive movements pretended to go into a trance.

Savetsky seemed about to speak and Elaine, in the highest state of nervous tension, listened, trying to make something of the gibberish mutterings.

Suddenly the curtains were pushed aside and Aunt Josephine and Bennett, who had just come in, entered.

"I can do nothing here," exclaimed Savetsky, starting up and looking about severely. "You must come to my seance chamber where we shall not be interrupted."

"I will," cried Elaine, vexed at the intrusion at that moment. "I must have that message—I must."

"What's all this, Elaine?" demanded Aunt Josephine.

Hurriedly, Elaine poured forth to her aunt and Bennett the story of the medium's visit and the promised message from her father in the other world.

Aunt Josephine, who was not one easily to be imposed on, strongly objected to Elaine's proposal to accompany Savetsky to the seance chamber, but Elaine would not be denied. She pleaded with her aunt, urging that she be allowed to go.

"It might be safe for Elaine to go," Bennett finally suggested to Aunt Josephine, "if you and I accompanied her."

All this time the medium was listening closely to the conversation. Elaine looked at her inquiringly. With a shrug, she indicated that she had no objection to having Elaine escorted to the parlor by her friends.

At last Aunt Josephine, influenced by Elaine's pleadings and Bennett's suggestion, gave in and agreed to join in the visit.

A few moments later, in the Dodge car, Elaine, the medium, and her two escorts started for the Chinese quarter.

* * * * *

At the house, the medium opened the door with her key and ushered in her three visitors.

Long Sin who had been watching for their arrival from the

window now hastily withdrew from the seance room and disappeared behind the black curtains.

Entering the room the medium at once prepared for the seance by pulling down the window shades. Then she seated herself in a chair beside the cabinet, and appeared to fall off slowly into a trance.

Her strange proceedings were watched with the greatest curiosity by Elaine as well as Aunt Josephine and Bennett, who had taken seats placed at one side of the room.

The room itself was dimly lighted, and the curtains of the cabinet seemed, in the obscurity, to sway back and forth as if stirred by some ghostly breeze.

All of them were now quite on edge with excitement.

Suddenly an indistinct face was seen to be peering through the black curtains, as it were.

The guitar, as if lifted by an invisible hand, left the cabinet, floated about close to the ceiling, and returned again. It was eerie.

At last a voice, deep, sepulchral, was heard in slow and solemn tones.

"I am Eeko—the spirit of Taylor Dodge. I will give no message until one named Josephine leaves the room."

No sooner had the words been uttered than the medium came writhing out of her trance.

"What happened?" she asked, looking at Elaine.

Elaine reported the spirit's words.

"We can get nothing if your Aunt stays here," Savetsky added, insisting that Aunt Josephine must go. "Your father cannot speak while she is present."

Aunt Josephine, annoyed by what she had heard, indignantly refused to go and was deaf to all Elaine's pleadings.

"I think it will be all right," finally acquiesced Bennett, seeing how bent Elaine was on securing the message. "I'll stay and protect her."

Aunt Josephine finally agreed. "Very well, then," she protested, marching out of the room in a high state of indignation.

She had scarcely left the house, however, when she began to suspect that all was not as it ought to be. In fact, the idea had no sooner occurred to her than she decided to call on Kennedy and she ordered the chauffeur to take her as quickly as possible to the laboratory.

* * * * *

Kennedy had not been in the laboratory all the day, after my experience with the acid and I was impatiently awaiting his arrival. At last there came a knock at the door and I opened it hurriedly. There was a messenger boy who handed me a note. I tore it open. It was from Kennedy and read, "I shall probably be away for two or three days. Call up Elaine and tell her to beware of a certain Madame Savetsky."

I was still puzzling over the note and was just about to call up Elaine when the speaking tube was blown and to my surprise I found it was Aunt Josephine who had called.

"Where is Mr. Kennedy?" she asked, greatly agitated.

"He has gone away for a few days," I replied blankly. "Is there anything I can do?"

She was very excited and hastily related what had happened at the parlor of the medium.

"What was her name?" I asked anxiously.

"Madame Savetsky," she replied, to my surprise.

Astounded, I picked up Craig's note from the desk and handed it to her without a word. She read it with breathless eagerness.

"Come back there with me, please," she begged, almost frantic with fear now. "Something terrible may have happened."

* * * * *

Aunt Josephine had hardly left Savetsky when the trance was resumed and, in a few minutes, there came all sorts of super-natural manifestations. The table beside Elaine began to turn and articles on it dropped to the floor. Violent rappings followed in various parts of the room. Both Elaine and Bennett who sat together in silence were much impressed by the marvellous phenomena—not being able to see, in the darkness, the concealed wires that made them possible.

Suddenly, from the mysterious shadows of the cabinet, there appeared the spirit of Long Sin, whose death Elaine still believed she had caused when Adventuress Mary had lured her to the apartment.

Elaine was trembling with fear at the apparition.

As before, a strange voice sounded in the depths of the cabinet and again a message was heard, in low, solemn tones.

"I am Keka, and I have with me Long Sin. His blood cries for vengeance."

Elaine was overcome with horror at the words.

From the cabinet ran a thick stream of red, like blood, from which she recoiled, shuddering.

Then a dim, ghostly figure, apparently that of Long Sin, appeared. The face was horribly distorted. It seemed to breathe the very odor of the grave.

With arms outstretched, the figure glided from the cabinet and approached Elaine. She shrank back further in fright, too horrified even to scream.

At the same moment, the medium drew a vapor pistol from her dress, and, as the ghost of Long Sin leaped at Elaine, Savetsky darted forward and shot a stream of vapor full in Bennett's face.

Bennett dropped unconscious, the lights in the darkened room flashed up, and several of the men of the Clutching Hand rushed in.

Quickly the fireplace was turned on its cleverly constructed hinges, revealing the hidden passage.

Before any effective resistance could be made, Elaine and Bennett were hustled through the passage, securely bound, and placed on a divan in a curtained chamber back of the altar of the devil worshippers.

There they lay when Long Sin, now in his priestly robes, entered. He looked at them a moment. Then he left the room with a sinister laugh.

* * * * *

It was at that moment that I, little dreaming of what had been taking place, arrived with Aunt Josephine at the house of the medium.

She answered my ring and admitted us. To our surprise, the seance room was empty.

"Where is the young lady who was here?" I asked.

"Miss Dodge and the gentleman just left a few minutes ago," the medium explained, as we looked about.

She seemed eager to satisfy us that Elaine was not there. Apparently there was no excuse for disputing her word, but, as we turned to leave, I happened to notice a torn handkerchief lying on the floor near the fireplace. It flashed over me that perhaps it might afford a clue.

As I passed it, I purposely dropped my soft hat over it and picked up the hat, securing the handkerchief without attracting Savetsky's attention.

Aunt Josephine was keen now for returning home to find out whether Elaine was there or not. No sooner had she entered the car and driven off, than I examined the handkerchief. It was torn, as if it had been crushed in the hand during a struggle and wrenched away. I looked closer. In the corner was the initial, "E."

That was enough. Without losing another precious moment I hurried around to the nearest police station, where I happened to be known, having had several assignments for the Star in that part of the city, and gave an alarm.

The sergeant detailed several roundsmen, and a man in plainclothes, and together we returned to the house, laying a careful plan to surround it secretly, while the plainclothesman and I obtained admittance.

* * * * *

Meanwhile, the Chinese devil worshippers had again gathered in their cursed temple and Long Sin, in his priestly robe, appeared on the dais.

The worshippers kowtowed reverently to him, while at the back again stood the aged Chinaman patiently turning his prayer wheel.

Two braziers, or smoke pots, had been placed on the dais, one of which Long Sin touched with a stick causing it to burst out into dense fumes.

Standing before them, he chanted in nasal tones, "The white consort of the great Ksing Chau has been found. It is his will that she now be made his."

As he finished intoning the message, Long Sin signaled to two young Chinamen to go into the anteroom. A moment later they returned with Elaine.

Frightened though she was, Elaine made no attempt to struggle, even when they had cut her bonds. She was busily engaged in seeking some method of escape. Her eyes travelled ever the place quickly. Apparently, there was no means of exit that was not guarded. Long Sin saw her look, and smiled quietly.

They had carried her up to the dais, and now Long Sin faced her and sternly ordered her to kowtow to the gruesome metallic figure.

She refused, but instantly the Chinamen seized her arm and twisted it, until they had compelled her to fall to her knees.

Having forced her to kowtow, Long Sin turned to the assembled devil dancers.

"With magic and rare drugs," he chanted, "she shall be made to pass beyond and her body encased in precious gold shall be the consort of Ksing Chau—forever and ever."

He made another sign and several pots and braziers were brought out and placed on the dais beside Elaine. She was, by this time, completely overcome by the horror of the situation. There was apparently no escape.

With callous deviltry, the oriental satanists had made every arrangement for embalming and preserving the body of Elaine. Pots filled with sticky black material were slowly heated, amid weird incantations, while other Chinamen laid out innumerable sheets of gold leaf.

At last all seemed to be in readiness to proceed.

"Hold her," ordered Long Sin in guttural Chinese to the two attendants, as he approached her.

Long Sin held in his hand a small, profusely decorated pot

from which smoke was escaping. As he approached he passed this receptacle under her nose once, twice, three times.

Gradually Elaine fell into unconsciousness.

* * * * *

While Elaine was facing death in the power of the devil worshippers, I had reached the house of Savetsky next door with the police, and the place had been quietly surrounded.

With the plainclothesman, a daring and intelligent fellow, I went to the door and rang the bell.

"What can I do for you?" asked the medium, admitting us.

"My friend, here," I parleyed, "is in great business trouble. Can your controlling spirit give him advice?"

We had managed to gain the interior of the seance room, and I suppose there was nothing else for her to say, under the circumstances, but, "Why—yes,—if the conditions are good, the control can probably tell us just what he wants to know."

Savetsky set to work preparing the room for a seance. As she moved over to the window to pull down the shades, she must have caught sight of one or two of the policemen who had incautiously exposed themselves from the hiding places in which I had disposed them before we entered. At any rate, Savetsky did not lose a jot of her remarkable composure.

"I'm sorry," she remarked merely, "but I'm afraid my control is weak and cannot work today."

She took a step toward the door, motioning us to leave.

Neither of us paid any attention to that hint, but remained seated as we had been before.

"Go!" she exclaimed at length, for the first time showing a trace of nervousness.

Evidently her suspicions had been fully confirmed by our actions. We tried to argue with her to gain time. But it was of no use.

Almost before I knew what she was doing, she made a dash for something in the corner of the room. It was time for open action, and I seized her quickly.

My detective was on his feet in an instant.

"I'll take care of her," he ground out, seizing her wrists in his vice-like grasp. "You give the signal."

I rushed to the window, threw up the shade and opened the sash, waving our preconcerted sign, turning again toward the room.

With a sudden accession of desperate strength, Savetsky broke away from the plainclothesman and again attempted to get at something concealed on the wall. I had turned just in time to fling myself between her and whatever object she had in mind.

As the detective took her again and twisted her arm until she cried out in pain, I hastily investigated the wall. She had evidently been attempting to press a button that rang a concealed bell.

What did it all mean?

Arthur B. Reeve

Elaine, now completely unconscious, was being held by the Chinamen, while her arm was smeared with sticky black material from the cauldron by Long Sin. As the high priest of Satan worked, the devil worshippers kowtowed obediently.

Suddenly the aged Chinaman with the prayer wheel stopped his incessant, impious turning, and rising, held up his hand as if to command attention.

Amid a general exclamation of wonder, he walked to the dais and mounted it, turning and facing the worshippers.

"This is nonsense," he cried in a loud tone. "Why should our great Ksing Chau desire a white devil? I, a great grandfather, demand to know."

The effect on the worshippers was electric. They paused in their obeisance and stared at the speaker, then at their high priest.

Shaking with rage, Long Sin ordered the intruder off the dais. But the aged devotee refused to go.

"Throw him out," he ordered his attendants.

For answer, as the two young Chinamen approached, the old Chinaman threw them down to the floor with a quick jiu-jitsu movement. His strength seemed miraculous for so aged a man.

Furious now beyond expression, Long Sin stepped forward himself. He seized the beard and queue of the intruder. To his utter amazement, they came off!

It was Kennedy!

With his automatic drawn, before the astounded devil dancers could recover themselves, Craig stood at bay.

Long Sin leaped behind the big gong. As the Chinamen rushed forward to seize him, Kennedy shot the leader of Long Sin's attendants and struck down the other with a blow. The rush was checked for the moment. But the odds were fearful.

Kennedy seized Elaine's yielding body and, pushing back the curtains to the anteroom, succeeded in gaining it, and locking the door into the main temple.

Bennett was still lying on the floor tightly bound. With a few deft cuts by a Chinese knife which he had picked up, Kennedy released him.

At the same time, Chinamen were trying to batter down the door, Kennedy's last bulwark. It was swaying under their repeated blows.

Kennedy rushed to the door and fired through it at random to check the attack for a few moments.

* * * * *

While Kennedy was thus besieged by the devil worshippers in the anteroom, several policemen and detectives gathered in the seance room with us, next door, where Savetsky was held a defiant and mute prisoner.

I had discovered the bell, and, taking that as a guide, I started to trace the course of a wire which ran alongside the wall, feeling certain that it would give me a clue to some adjoining room to which Elaine might possibly have been taken.

Arthur B. Reeve

To the fireplace I traced the bell, and, in pulling on the wire, I luckily pressed a secret spring. To my amazement, the whole fireplace swung out of sight and disclosed a secret passageway.

I looked through it.

It was almost at that precise instant that the door of the anteroom burst open and the Chinamen swarmed in, urged on by the insane exhortations of Long Sin.

To my utter amazement, I recognized Kennedy's voice.

In the first onslaught, Craig shot one Chinaman dead, then closed with the others, slashing right and left with the Chinese knife he had picked up.

Bennett came to his aid, but was immediately overcome by two Chinamen, who evidently had been detailed for that purpose.

Meanwhile, Kennedy and the others were engaged in a terrible life and death struggle. They fought all over the room, dismantling it, and even tearing the hangings from the wall.

It was just as the Chinese was about to overpower him that I led the police and detectives through the passageway of the fireplace.

It was a glorious fight that followed. Long Sin and his Chinamen were no match for the police and were soon completely routed, the police striking furiously in all directions and clearing the room.

Instantly, Kennedy thought of the fair object of all this melee.

He rushed to the divan on which he had placed Elaine.

She was slowly returning to consciousness.

As she opened her eyes, for an instant, she gazed at Craig, then at Bennett. Still not comprehending just what had happened, she gave her hand to Bennett. Bennett lifted her to her feet and slowly assisted her as she tried to walk away.

Kennedy watched them, more stupefied than if he had been struck over the head by Long Sin.

* * * * *

Police and detectives were now taking the captured Chinamen away, as Bennett, his arm about Elaine, led her gently out.

A young detective had slipped the bracelets over Long Sin's wrist, and I was standing beside him.

Kennedy, in a daze at the sight of Elaine and Bennett, passed us, scarcely noticing who we were.

As Craig collected his scattered forces, Long Sin motioned to him, as if he had a message to deliver.

Kennedy frowned suspiciously. He was about to turn away, when the Chinaman began pleading earnestly for a chance to say a few words.

"Step aside for a moment, you fellows, won't you please," Craig asked. "I will hear what you have to say, Long Sin."

Long Sin looked about craftily.

"What is it?" prompted Craig, seeing that at last they were all alone.

Long Sin again looked around.

"Swear that I will go free and not suffer," Long Sin whispered, "and I will betray the great Clutching Hand."

Kennedy studied the Chinaman keenly for a moment. Then, seemingly satisfied with the scrutiny, he nodded slowly assent.

As Craig did so, I saw Long Sin lean over and whisper into Kennedy's ear.

Craig started back in horror and surprise.

CHAPTER XIV

THE RECKONING

Pacing up and down his den in the heart of Chinatown, Long Sin was thinking over his bargain with Kennedy to betray the infamous Clutching Hand.

It was a small room in a small and unpretentious house, but it adequately expressed the character of the subtle Oriental. The den was lavishly furnished, while the guileful Long Sin himself wore a richly figured lounging gown of the finest and costliest silk, chosen for the express purpose of harmonizing with the luxurious Far Eastern hangings and furniture so as to impress his followers and those whom he might choose as visitors.

At length he seated himself at a teakwood table, still deliberating over the promise he had been forced to make to Kennedy. He sat for some moments, deeply absorbed in thought.

Suddenly an idea seemed to strike him. Lifting a little hammer, he struck a Chinese gong on the table at his side. At the same time, he leaned over and turned a knob at the side of a large roll-top desk.

Arthur B. Reeve

A few seconds later a sort of hatchway, covered by a rug on the floor, in one corner of the room, was slowly lifted and Long Sin's secretary, a sallow, cadaverous Chinaman, appeared from below. He stepped noiselessly into the room and shuffled across to Long Sin.

Long Sin scowled, as though something had interfered with his own plans, but tore open the envelope without a word, spreading out on his lap the sheet of paper it contained.

The letter bore a typewritten message, all in capitals, which read:

"BE AT HEADQUARTERS AT 12. DESTROY THIS IMMEDIATELY."

At the bottom of the note appeared the sinister signature of the Clutching Hand.

As soon as he had finished reading the note, the Chinaman turned to his obsequious secretary, who stood motionless, with folded arms and head meekly bent.

"Very well," he said with an imperious wave of his hand. "You may go."

Bowing low again, the secretary shuffled across and down again through the hatchway, closing the door as he descended.

Long Sin read the note once more, while his inscrutable face assumed an expression of malicious cunning. Then he glanced at his heavy gold watch.

With an air of deliberation, he reached for a match and struck it. He had just placed the paper in the flame when suddenly he seemed to change his mind. He hastily blew out the match which had destroyed only a corner of the paper, then folded the note carefully and placed it in his pocket.

A few moments later, with a malignant chuckle, Long Sin rose slowly and left the room.

* * * * *

Meanwhile, the master criminal was busily engaged in putting the finishing touches to a final scheme of fiendish ingenuity for the absolute destruction of Craig Kennedy.

He had been at work in a small room, fitted up as a sort of laboratory, in the mysterious house which now served as his headquarters.

On all sides were shelves filled with bottles of deadly liquids and scientific apparatus for crime. Jars of picric acid, nitric acid, carboys of other chemicals, packages labelled gun-powder, gun cotton and nitroglycerine, as well as carefully stoppered bottles of prussic acid, and the cyanides, arsenic and other poisons made the place bear the look of a veritable devil's workshop.

Clutching Hand, at a bench in one corner, had just completed an infernal machine of diabolical cunning, and was wrapping it carefully in paper to make an innocent package.

He was interrupted by a knock at the door. Laying down the bomb he went to answer the summons with a stealthy movement. There stood Long Sin, who had disguised himself as a Chinese laundryman.

"On time—good!" growled Clutching Hand surlily as he closed the door with equal care.

No time was wasted in useless formalities.

"This is a bomb," he went on, pointing to the package. "Carry it carefully. On no account let it slip, or you are a dead man. It must be in Kennedy's laboratory before night. Understand? Can you arrange it?"

Long Sin looked the dangerous package over, then with an impassive look, replied, "Have no fear. I can do it. It will be in the laboratory within an hour. Trust me."

Long Sin nodded sagely, while Clutching Hand growled his approval as he opened the door and let out the Chinaman. Long Sin departed as stealthily as he had come, the frightful engine of destruction hugged up carefully under his wide-sleeved coolie shirt.

For a moment Clutching Hand gave himself up to the exquisite contemplation of what he had just done, then turned to clean up his workshop.

* * * * *

In Kennedy's laboratory I was watching Craig make some experiments with a new X-ray apparatus which had just arrived, occasionally looking through the fluoroscope when he was examining some unusually interesting object.

We were oblivious to the passage of time, and only a call over our speaking tube diverted our attention.

I opened the door and a few seconds later Long Sin himself entered.

Kennedy looked up inquiringly as the Chinaman approached, holding out a package which he carried.

"A bomb," he said, in the most matter of fact way. "I promised to have it placed in your laboratory before night."

The placid air with which the grotesque looking Chinaman imparted this astounding information was in itself preposterous. His actions and words as he laid the package down gingerly on the laboratory table indicated that he was telling the truth.

Kennedy and I stared at each other in blank amazement for a moment. Then the humor of the thing struck us both and we laughed outright.

Clutching Hand had told him to deliver it—and he had done so!

Hastily I filled a pail with water and brought it to Kennedy.

"If it is really a bomb," I remarked, "why not put the thing out of commission?"

"No, no, Walter," he cried quickly, shaking his head. "If it's a chemical bomb, the water might be just the thing to make the chemicals run together and set it off. No, let us see what the new X-ray machine can tell us, first."

He took the bomb and carefully placed it under the wonderful rays, then with the fluoroscope over his eyes studied the shadow cast by the rays on its sensitive screen. For several minutes he continued safely studying it from every angle, until he thoroughly understood it.

"It's a bomb, sure enough," Craig exclaimed, looking up from it at last to me. "It's timed by an ingenious and noiseless little piece of clockwork, in there, too. And it's powerful enough to blow us all, the laboratory included, to

Arthur B. Reeve

kingdom come."

As he spoke, and before I could remonstrate with him, he took the infernal machine and placed it on a table where he set to work on the most delicate and dangerous piece of dissection of which I have ever heard.

Carefully unwrapping the bomb and unscrewing one part while he held another firm, he finally took out of it a bottle of liquid and some powder. Then he placed a few grains of the powder on a dish and dropped on it a drop or two of the liquid. There was a bright flash, as the powder ignited instantly.

"Just what I expected," commented Kennedy with a nod, as he examined the clever workmanship of the bomb.

One thing that interested him was that part of the contents had been wrapped in paper to keep them in place. This paper he was now carefully examining with a hand lens.

As nearly as I could make it out, the paper contained part of a typewritten chemical formula, which read:

TINCTURE OF IODINE

THREE PARTS OF—

He looked up from his study of the microscope to Long Sin.

"Tell me just how it happened that you got this bomb," he asked.

Without hesitation, the Chinaman recited the circumstances, beginning with the note by which he had been summoned.

"A note?" repeated Kennedy, eagerly. "Was it typewritten?"

Long Sin reached into his pocket and produced the note itself, which he had not burned.

As Craig studied the typewritten message from the Clutching Hand I could see that he was growing more and more excited.

"At last he has given us something typewritten," he exclaimed. "To most people, I suppose, it seems that typewriting is the best way to conceal identity. But there are a thousand and one ways of identifying typewriting. Clutching Hand knew that. That was why he was so careful to order this note destroyed. As for the bomb, he figured that it would destroy itself."

He was placing one piece of typewriting after another under the lens, scrutinizing each letter closely.

"Look, Walter," he remarked at length, taking a fine tipped pencil and pointing at the distinguishing marks as he talked, "You will notice that all the 'T's' in this note are battered and faint as well as just a trifle out of alignment. Now I will place the paper from the bomb under the lens and you will also see that the 'T's' in the scrap of formula have exactly the same appearance. That indicated, without the possibility of a doubt, taken in connection with a score of other peculiarities in the letters which I could pick out that both were written on the same typewriter. I have selected the 'T' because it is the most marked."

I strained my eyes to look. Sure enough, Kennedy was right. There was that unmistakable identity between the T's in the formula and the note.

　　　　Arthur B. Reeve

Kennedy had been gazing at the floor, his face puckered in thought as I looked. Suddenly he slapped his hands together, as if he had made a great discovery.

"I've struck it!" he exclaimed, jumping up. "I was wondering where I had seen typewriting that reminds me of this. Walter, get on your coat and hat. We are on the right trail at last."

With Long Sin we hurried out of the laboratory, leaving him at the nearest taxicab stand, where we jumped into a waiting car.

"It is the clue of the battered 'T's,'" Craig muttered.

* * * * *

Aunt Josephine was in the library knitting when the butler, Jennings, announced us. We were admitted at once, for Aunt Josephine had never quite understood what was the trouble between Elaine and Craig, and had a high regard for him.

"Where is—Miss Dodge?" inquired Kennedy, with suppressed excitement as we entered.

"I think she's out shopping and I don't know just when she will be back," answered Aunt Josephine, with some surprise. "Why? Is it anything important—any news?"

"Very important," returned Kennedy excitedly. "I think I have the best clue yet. Only—it will be necessary to look through some of the household correspondence immediately to see whether there are certain letters. I wouldn't be surprised if she had some—perhaps not very personal—but I MUST see them."

Aunt Josephine seemed nonplussed at first. I thought she was going to refuse to allow Craig to proceed. But finally she assented.

Kennedy lost no time. He went to a desk where Elaine generally sat, and quickly took out several typewritten letters. He examined them closely, rejecting one after another, until finally he came to one that seemed to interest him.

He separated it from the rest and fell to studying it, comparing it with the paper from the bomb and the note which Long Sin had received from the Clutching Hand. Then he folded the letter so that both the signature and the address could not be read by us.

A portion of the letter, I recall, read something like this:

"This is his contention: whereas TRUTH is the only goal and MATTER is non-existent—

"Look at this, Walter," remarked Craig, with difficulty restraining himself, "What do you make of it?"

A glance at the typewriting was sufficient to show me that Kennedy had indeed made an important discovery. The writing of the letter which he had just found in Elaine's desk corresponded in every respect with that in the Clutching Hand note and that on the bomb formula. In each instance there were the same faintness, the same crooked alignment, the same battered appearance of all the letter T's.

We stared at each other almost too dazed to speak.

* * * * *

At that moment we were startled by the sudden appearance of Elaine herself, who had come in unexpectedly from her shopping expedition.

She entered the room carrying in her arms a huge bunch of roses which she had evidently just received. Her face was half buried in the fragrant blossoms, but was fairer than even they in their selected elegance.

The moment she saw Craig, however, she stopped short with a look of great surprise. Kennedy, on his part, who was seated at the desk still tracing out the similarities of the letters, stood up, half hesitating what to say. He bowed and she returned his salutation with a very cool nod.

Her keen eye had not missed the fact that several of her letters lay scattered over the top of the desk.

"What are you doing with my letters, Mr. Kennedy?" she asked, in an astonished tone, evidently resenting the uncere-moniousness with which he had apparently been overhauling her correspondence.

As guardedly as possible, Kennedy met her inquiry, which I could not myself blame her for making.

"I beg pardon, Miss Dodge," he said, "but a matter has just come up which necessitated merely a cursory examination of some purely formal letters which might have an important bearing on the discovery of the Clutching Hand. Your Aunt had no idea where you were, nor of when you might return, and the absolute necessity for haste in such an important matter is my only excuse for examining a few minor letters without first obtaining your permission."

She said nothing. At another time, such an explanation would have been instantly accepted. Now, however, it was different.

Kennedy read the look on her face, and an instant later turned to Aunt Josephine and myself.

"I would very much appreciate a chance to say a few words to Miss Dodge alone," he intimated. "I have had no such opportunity for some time. If you would be so kind as to leave us in the library—for a few minutes—"

He did not finish the sentence. Aunt Josephine had already begun to withdraw and I followed.

* * * * *

For a moment or two, Craig and Elaine looked at each other, neither saying a word, each wondering just what was in the other's mind. Kennedy was wondering if there was any X-ray that might read a woman's heart, as he was accustomed to read others of nature's secrets.

He cleared his throat, the obvious manner of covering up his emotion.

"Elaine," he said at length, dropping the recent return to "Miss Dodge," for the moment, "Elaine, is there any truth in this morning's newspaper report of—of you?"

She had dropped her eyes. But he persisted, taking a newspaper clipping from his pocket and handing it to her.

Her hand trembled as she glanced over the item:

SOCIETY NOTES

Dame Rumor is connecting the name of Miss Elaine Dodge, the heiress, with that of Perry Bennett, the famous young lawyer. The announcement of an engagement between them at any time would not surprise—

Elaine read no further. She handed back the clipping to Kennedy. As her eyes met his, she noticed his expression of deep concern, and hesitated with the reply she had evidently been just about to make.

Still, as she lowered her head, it seemed to give silent confirmation to the truth of the newspaper report.

Kennedy said nothing. But his eyes continued to study her face, even when it was averted.

He suppressed his feelings with a great effort, then, without a word, bowed and left the room.

"Walter," he exclaimed as he rejoined us in the drawing room, where I was chatting with Aunt Josephine, "we must be off again. The trail follows still further."

I rose and much to the increased mystification of Aunt Josephine, left the house.

An hour or so later, Elaine, whose mind was now in a whirl from what had happened, decided to call on Perry Bennett.

Two or three clerks were in the outer office when she arrived, but the office boy, laying down a dime novel, rose to meet her and informed her that Mr. Bennett was alone.

As Elaine entered his private office, Bennett rose to greet her effusively and they exchanged a few words.

"I mustn't forget to thank you for those lovely roses you sent me," she exclaimed at length. "They were beautiful and I appreciated them ever so much."

Bennett acknowledged her thanks with a smile, she sat down familiarly on his desk, and they plunged into a vein of social gossip.

A moment later, Bennett led the conversation around until he found an opportunity to make a tactful allusion to the report of their engagement in the morning papers.

He had leaned over and now attempted to take her hand. She withdrew it, however. There was something about his touch which, try as she might, she could not like. Was it mere prejudice, or was it her keen woman's intuition?

Bennett looked at her a moment, suppressing a momentary flash of anger that had reddened his face, and controlled himself as if by a superhuman effort.

"I believe you really love that man Kennedy," he exclaimed, in a tone that was almost a hiss. "But I tell you, Elaine, he is all bluff. Why, he has been after that Clutching Hand now for three months—and what has he accomplished? Nothing!"

He paused. Through Elaine's mind there flashed the contrast with Kennedy's even temper and deferential manner. In spite of their quarrel and the coolness, she found herself resenting the remark. Still she said nothing, though her expressive face showed much.

Bennett, by another effort, seemed to grip his temper again. He paced up and down the room. Then he changed the subject abruptly, and the conversation was resumed with some constraint.

* * * * *

While Elaine and Bennett were talking, Kennedy and I had

entered the office.

Craig stopped the boy who was about to announce us and asked for Bennett's secretary instead, much to my astonishment.

The boy merely indicated the door of one of the other private offices, and we entered.

We found the secretary, hard at work at the typewriter, copying a legal document. Without a word, Kennedy at once locked the door.

The secretary rose in surprise, but Craig paid no attention to him. Instead he calmly walked over to the machine and began to examine it.

"Might I ask—" began the secretary.

"You keep quiet," ordered Kennedy, with a nod to me to watch the fellow. "You are under arrest—and the less you say, the better for you."

I shall never forget the look that crossed the secretary's face. Was it the surprise of an innocent man?

Taking the man's place at the machine, Kennedy removed the legal paper that was in it and put in a new sheet. Then he tapped out, as we watched:

BE AT HEADQUARTERS AT 12. DESTROY THIS IMMEDIATELY

TINCTURE OF IODINE

THREE PARTS OF—

This is his contention:—whereas TRUTH is the only goal and MATTER is non-existent—

T T T T

"Look, Walter," he exclaimed as he drew out the paper from the machine.

I bent over and together we compared the T's with those in the Clutching Hand letter, the paper from the bomb and the letter which Craig had taken from Elaine's desk.

As Craig pointed out the resemblances with a pencil, my amazement gradually changed into comprehension and comprehension into conviction. The meaning of it all began to dawn on me.

The writing was identical. There were no differences!

* * * * *

While we were locked in the secretary's office, Bennett and Elaine were continuing their chat on various social topics. Suddenly, however, with a glance at the clock, Bennett told Elaine that he had an important letter to dictate, and that it must go off at once.

She said that she would excuse him a few minutes and he pressed a button to call his secretary.

Of course the secretary did not appear. Bennett left his office, with some annoyance, and went into the adjoining room the door to which Kennedy had not locked.

He hesitated a moment, then opened the door quietly. To his astonishment, he saw Kennedy, the secretary, and myself apparently making a close examination of the typewriter.

Gliding rather than walking back into his own office, he closed the door and locked it. Almost instantly, fear and fury at the presence of his hated rival, Kennedy, turned Bennett, as it were, from the Jekyll of a polished lawyer and lover of Elaine into an insanely jealous and revengeful Mr. Hyde. The strain was more than his warped mind could bear.

With a look of intense horror and loathing, Elaine watched him slowly change from the composed, calm, intellectual Bennett she knew and respected into a repulsive, mad figure of a man.

His stature even seemed to be altered. He seemed to shrivel up and become deformed. His face was terribly distorted.

And his long, sinewy hand slowly twisted and bent until he became the personal embodiment of the Clutching Hand.

As Elaine, transfixed with terror, watched Bennett's astounding metamorphosis, he ran to the door leading to the outer office and hastily locked that, also.

Then, with his eyes gleaming with rage and his hands working in murderous frenzy, he crouched, nearer and nearer, towards Elaine.

She shrank back, screaming again and again in terror.

He WAS the Clutching Hand!

* * * * *

In spite of closed doors, we could now plainly hear Elaine's shrieks. Craig, the secretary and myself made a rush for the door to Bennett's private office. Finding it locked, we began to batter it.

By this time, however, Bennett had hurled himself upon Elaine and was slowly choking her.

Kennedy quickly found that it was impossible to batter down the door in time by any ordinary means. Quickly he seized the typewriter and hurled it through the panels. Then he thrust his hand through the opening and turned the catch.

As we flung ourselves into the room, Bennett rushed into a closet in a corner, slamming the door behind him. It was composed of sheet iron and effectually prevented anyone from breaking through. Kennedy and I tried vainly, however, to pry it open.

While we were thus endeavoring to force an entrance, Bennett, in a sort of closet, had put on the coat, hat and mask which he invariably wore in the character of the Clutching Hand. Then he cautiously opened a secret door in the back of the closet and slowly made an exit.

* * * * *

Meanwhile, the secretary had been doing his best to revive Elaine, who was lying in a chair, hysterical and half unconscious from the terrible shock she had experienced.

Intent on discovering Bennett's whereabouts, Kennedy and I examined the wall of the office, thinking there might possibly be some button or secret spring which would open the closet door.

While we were doing so, the door of a large safe in the secretary's office gradually opened and the Clutching Hand

Arthur B. Reeve

emerged from it, stepping carefully towards the door leading to the outer office, intent on escaping in that direction.

At that moment, I caught sight of him, and leaping into the secretary's office, I drew my revolver and ordered him to throw up his hands. He obeyed. Holding up both hands, he slowly drew near the door to his private office.

Suddenly he dropped one hand and pressed a hidden spring in the wall.

Instantly a heavy iron door shot out and closed over the wooden door. Entrance to the private office was absolutely cut off.

With an angry snarl, the Clutching Hand leaped at me.

As he did so, I fired twice.

He staggered back.

* * * * *

The shots were heard by Kennedy and Elaine, as well as the secretary, and at the same instant they discovered the iron door which barred the entrance to the secretary's office.

Rushing into the outer office, they found the clerks excitedly attempting to open the door of the secretary's office which was locked. Kennedy drew a revolver and shot through the lock, bursting open the door.

They rushed into the room.

Clutching Hand was apparently seated in a chair at a desk, his face buried in his arms, while I was apparently disappearing through the door.

Kennedy and the clerks pounced upon the figure in the chair and tore off his mask. To their astonishment, they discovered that it was myself!

My shots had missed and Clutching Hand had leaped on me with maddened fury.

Dressed in my coat and hat, which he had deftly removed after overpowering me and substituting his own clothes, Clutching Hand had by this time climbed through the window of the outer office and was making his way down the fire escape to the street. He reached the foot of the iron steps leaped off and ran quickly away.

Shouting a few directions to the secretary, the clerks and Elaine, Kennedy climbed through the window and darted down the fire escape in swift pursuit.

The Clutching Hand, however, managed to elude capture again. Turning the street corner he leaped into a taxi which happened to be standing there, and, hastily giving the driver directions, was driven rapidly away. By the time Kennedy reached the street Clutching Hand had disappeared.

* * * * *

While these exciting events were occurring in Bennett's office some queer doings were in progress in the heart of Chinatown.

Deep underground, in one of the catacombs known only to the innermost members of the Chinese secret societies, was Long Sin's servant, Tong Wah, popularly known as "the hider," engaged in some mysterious work.

A sinister-looking Chinaman, dressed in coolie costume, he was standing at a table in a dim and musty, high-ceilinged chamber, faced with stone and brick. Before him were several odd shaped Chinese vials, and from these he was carefully measuring certain proportions, as if concocting some powerful potion.

He stepped back and looked around suspiciously as he suddenly heard footsteps above. The next moment Long Sin, who had entered through a trap door, climbed down a long ladder and walked into the room.

Approaching Tong Wah, he asked: "When will the death-drink be ready?"

"It is now prepared," was the reply.

Long Sin took the bowl in which the liquor had been mixed, and, having examined it, he gave a nod and a grunt of satisfaction. Then he mounted the ladder again and disappeared.

As soon as he had gone Tong Wah, picking up several of the vials, went out through an iron door at the end of the room.

A few minutes later the Clutching Hand drove up to Long Sin's house in the taxicab and, after paying the chauffeur, went to the door and knocked sharply.

In response to his knocking Long Sin appeared on the threshold and motioned to Bennett to come in, evidently astonished to see him.

As he entered, Bennett made a secret sign and said: "I am the Clutching Hand. Kennedy is close on my trail, and I have come to be hidden."

In a tone which betrayed alarm and fear the Chinaman intimated that he had no place in which Bennett could be concealed with any degree of safety.

For a moment Bennett glared savagely at Long Sin.

"I possess hidden plunder worth seven million dollars," he pleaded quickly, "and if by your aid I can make a getaway, a seventh is yours."

The Chinaman's cupidity was clearly excited by Bennett's offer, while the bare mention of the amount at stake was sufficient to overcome all his scruples.

After exchanging a few words he finally agreed to all the Clutching Hand said. Opening a trap door in the floor of the room in which they were standing, he led Bennett down a step-ladder into the subterranean chamber in which Tong Wah had so recently been preparing his mysterious potion. As Bennett sank into a chair and passed his hands over his brow in utter weariness, Long Sin poured into a cup some of the liquor of death which Tong Wah had mixed. He handed it to Bennett, who drank it eagerly.

"How do you propose to help me to escape?" asked Bennett huskily.

Without a word Long Sin went to the wall, and, grasping one of the stones, pressed it back, opening a large receptacle, in which there were two glass coffins apparently containing two dead Chinamen. Pulling out the coffins, he pushed them before Bennett, who rose to his feet and gazed upon them with wonder.

Long Sin broke the silence: "These men," he said, "are not dead; but they have been in this condition for many months.

It is what is called in your language suspended animation."

"Is that what you intend to do with me?" asked Bennett, shrinking back in terror.

The Chinaman nodded in affirmation as he pushed back the coffins.

Overcome by the horror of the idea Bennett, with a groan, sank back into the chair, shaking his head as if to indicate that the plan was far too terrible to carry out.

With a sinister smile and a shrug of his shoulders Long Sin pointed to the cup from which Bennett had drunk.

"But, dear master," he remarked suavely, "you have already drunk a full dose of the potion which causes insensibility, and it is overcoming you. Even now," he added, "you are too weak to rise."

Bennett made frantic efforts to move from his seat, but the potion was already taking effect, and through sheer weakness he found he was unable to get on his feet in spite of all his struggles.

With a malicious chuckle Long Sin moved closer to his victim and spoke again.

"Divulge where your seven million dollars are hidden," he suggested craftily, "and I will give you an antidote."

By this time Bennett, who was becoming more rigid each moment, was unable to speak, but by a movement of his head and an expression in his eyes he indicated that he was ready to agree to the Chinaman's proposal.

"Where have you hidden the seven million dollars?" repeated Long Sin.

Slowly, and after a desperate struggle, Bennett managed to raise one hand and pointed to his breast pocket. The Chinaman instantly thrust in his hand and drew out a map.

For some moments Long Sin examined the map intently, and, with a grin of satisfaction, he placed it in his own pocket. Then he mixed what he declared was a sure antidote, and, pouring some of the liquor into a cup, he held it to Bennett's lips.

As Bennett opened his mouth to drink it, Long Sin with a laugh slowly pulled the cup away and poured its contents on the floor.

Bennett's body had now become still more rigid. Every sign of intelligence had left his face, and although his eyes did not close, a blank stare came over his countenance, indicating plainly that the drug had destroyed all consciousness.

* * * * *

By this time, I was slowly recovering my senses in the secretary's office, where Bennett had left me in the disguise of the Clutching Hand. Elaine, the secretary, and the clerks were gathered round me, doing all they could to revive me.

Meanwhile, Kennedy had enlisted the aid of two detectives and was scouring the city for a trace of Bennett or the taxicab in which he had fled.

Somehow, Kennedy suspected, instinctively, that Long Sin might give a clue to Bennett's whereabouts, and a few moments later, we were all on our way in a car to Long Sin's house.

Though we did not know it, Long Sin, at the moment when Kennedy knocked at his door, was feeling in his inside pocket to see that the map he had taken from Bennett was perfectly safe. Finding that he had it, he smiled with his peculiar oriental guile. Then he opened the door, and stood for a moment, silent.

"Where is Bennett?" demanded Kennedy.

Long Sin eyed us all, then with a placid smile, said, "Follow me. I will show you."

He opened a trap door, and we climbed down after Craig, entering a subterranean chamber, led by Long Sin.

There was Bennett seated rigidly in the chair beside the table from which the vials and cups, about which we then knew nothing, had been removed.

"How did it happen?" asked Kennedy.

"He came here," replied Long Sin, with a wave of his hand, "and before I could stop him he did away with himself."

In dumb show, the Chinaman indicated that Bennett had taken poison.

"Well, we've got him," mused Kennedy, shaking his head sadly, adding, after a pause, "but he is dead."

Elaine, who had followed us down, covered her eyes with her hands, and was sobbing convulsively. I thought she would faint, but Kennedy led her gently away into an upper room.

As he placed her in an easy chair, he bent over her, soothingly.

"Did you—did you—really—love him?" he asked in a low tone, nodding in the direction from which he had led her.

Still shuddering, and with an eager look at Kennedy, Elaine shook her beautiful head.

Then, slowly rising to her feet, she looked at Craig appealingly. For a moment he looked down into her two great lakes of eyes.

"Forgive me," murmured Elaine, holding out her hand. Then she added in a voice tense with emotion, "Thank you for saving me."

Kennedy took her hand. For a moment he held it. Then he drew her towards him, unresisting.

THE END

Arthur B. Reeve

ABOUT THE AUTHOR

Arthur Benjamin Reeve (October 15, 1880 - August 9, 1936) was an American mystery writer. He is best known for creating the series character Professor Craig Kennedy, sometimes called "The American Sherlock Holmes," and his Dr Watson-like sidekick Walter Jameson, a newspaper reporter, in eighteen detective novels. The bulk of Reeve's fame is based on the 82 Craig Kennedy stories, published in Cosmopolitan magazine between 1910 and 1918.

He graduated from Princeton and attended New York Law School. He worked as an editor and journalist before Craig Kennedy propelled him to national fame in 1911. Raised in Brooklyn, he lived most of his professional life at various addresses near the Long Island Sound.

Starting with The Exploits of Elaine (1914), Reeve began authoring screenplays. His film career reached its peak in 1919-20, when his name appeared on seven films, most of them serials, three of them starring Harry Houdini.

In the 1930's, Reeve rejuvenated his career by becoming an anti-rackets crusader. He had a national radio show from July 1930 to March 1931; he published a history of the rackets titled The Golden Age of Crime; and the focus of his Craig Kennedy stories completed the transition from "scientific detective" work to a racket-busting milieu.

Other books by this author

Constance Dunlap

The Gold of the Gods

The Master Mystery

Guy Garrick

The Film Mystery

Arthur B. Reeve

Choose from Thousands of 1stWorldLibrary Classics By

A. M. Barnard
Ada Leverson
Adolphus William Ward
Aesop
Agatha Christie
Alexander Aaronsohn
Alexander Kielland
Alexandre Dumas
Alfred Gatty
Alfred Ollivant
Alice Duer Miller
Alice Turner Curtis
Alice Dunbar
Allen Chapman
Alleyne Ireland
Ambrose Bierce
Amelia E. Barr
Amory H. Bradford
Andrew Lang
Andrew McFarland Davis
Andy Adams
Angela Brazil
Anna Alice Chapin
Anna Sewell
Annie Besant
Annie Hamilton Donnell
Annie Payson Call
Annie Roe Carr
Annonaymous
Anton Chekhov
Archibald Lee Fletcher
Arnold Bennett
Arthur C. Benson
Arthur Conan Doyle
Arthur M. Winfield
Arthur Ransome
Arthur Schnitzler
Arthur Train
Atticus
B.H. Baden-Powell
B. M. Bower
B. C. Chatterjee
Baroness Emmuska Orczy
Baroness Orczy
Basil King
Bayard Taylor
Ben Macomber
Bertha Muzzy Bower
Bjornstjerne Bjornson

Booth Tarkington
Boyd Cable
Bram Stoker
C. Collodi
C. E. Orr
C. M. Ingleby
Carolyn Wells
Catherine Parr Traill
Charles A. Eastman
Charles Amory Beach
Charles Dickens
Charles Dudley Warner
Charles Farrar Browne
Charles Ives
Charles Kingsley
Charles Klein
Charles Hanson Towne
Charles Lathrop Pack
Charles Romyn Dake
Charles Whibley
Charles Willing Beale
Charlotte M. Braeme
Charlotte M. Yonge
Charlotte Perkins Stetson
Clair W. Hayes
Clarence Day Jr.
Clarence E. Mulford
Clemence Housman
Confucius
Coningsby Dawson
Cornelis DeWitt Wilcox
Cyril Burleigh
D. H. Lawrence
Daniel Defoe
David Garnett
Dinah Craik
Don Carlos Janes
Donald Keyhoe
Dorothy Kilner
Dougan Clark
Douglas Fairbanks
E. Nesbit
E. P. Roe
E. Phillips Oppenheim
E. S. Brooks
Earl Barnes
Edgar Rice Burroughs
Edith Van Dyne
Edith Wharton

Edward Everett Hale
Edward J. O'Biren
Edward S. Ellis
Edwin L. Arnold
Eleanor Atkins
Eleanor Hallowell Abbott
Eliot Gregory
Elizabeth Gaskell
Elizabeth McCracken
Elizabeth Von Arnim
Ellem Key
Emerson Hough
Emilie F. Carlen
Emily Bronte
Emily Dickinson
Enid Bagnold
Enilor Macartney Lane
Erasmus W. Jones
Ernie Howard Pie
Ethel May Dell
Ethel Turner
Ethel Watts Mumford
Eugene Sue
Eugenie Foa
Eugene Wood
Eustace Hale Ball
Evelyn Everett-green
Everard Cotes
F. H. Cheley
F. J. Cross
F. Marion Crawford
Fannie E. Newberry
Federick Austin Ogg
Ferdinand Ossendowski
Fergus Hume
Florence A. Kilpatrick
Fremont B. Deering
Francis Bacon
Francis Darwin
Frances Hodgson Burnett
Frances Parkinson Keyes
Frank Gee Patchin
Frank Harris
Frank Jewett Mather
Frank L. Packard
Frank V. Webster
Frederic Stewart Isham
Frederick Trevor Hill
Frederick Winslow Taylor

Friedrich Kerst
Friedrich Nietzsche
Fyodor Dostoyevsky
G.A. Henty
G.K. Chesterton
Gabrielle E. Jackson
Garrett P. Serviss
Gaston Leroux
George A. Warren
George Ade
Geroge Bernard Shaw
George Cary Eggleston
George Durston
George Ebers
George Eliot
George Gissing
George MacDonald
George Meredith
George Orwell
George Sylvester Viereck
George Tucker
George W. Cable
George Wharton James
Gertrude Atherton
Gordon Casserly
Grace E. King
Grace Gallatin
Grace Greenwood
Grant Allen
Guillermo A. Sherwell
Gulielma Zollinger
Gustav Flaubert
H. A. Cody
H. B. Irving
H. C. Bailey
H. G. Wells
H. H. Munro
H. Irving Hancock
H. R. Naylor
H. Rider Haggard
H. W. C. Davis
Haldeman Julius
Hall Caine
Hamilton Wright Mabie
Hans Christian Andersen
Harold Avery
Harold McGrath
Harriet Beecher Stowe
Harry Castlemon
Harry Coghill
Harry Houidini

Hayden Carruth
Helent Hunt Jackson
Helen Nicolay
Hendrik Conscience
Hendy David Thoreau
Henri Barbusse
Henrik Ibsen
Henry Adams
Henry Ford
Henry Frost
Henry James
Henry Jones Ford
Henry Seton Merriman
Henry W Longfellow
Herbert A. Giles
Herbert Carter
Herbert N. Casson
Herman Hesse
Hildegard G. Frey
Homer
Honore De Balzac
Horace B. Day
Horace Walpole
Horatio Alger Jr.
Howard Pyle
Howard R. Garis
Hugh Lofting
Hugh Walpole
Humphry Ward
Ian Maclaren
Inez Haynes Gillmore
Irving Bacheller
Isabel Cecilia Williams
Isabel Hornibrook
Israel Abrahams
Ivan Turgenev
J. G.Austin
J. Henri Fabre
J. M. Barrie
J. M. Walsh
J. Macdonald Oxley
J. R. Miller
J. S. Fletcher
J. S. Knowles
J. Storer Clouston
J. W. Duffield
Jack London
Jacob Abbott
James Allen
James Andrews
James Baldwin

James Branch Cabell
James DeMille
James Joyce
James Lane Allen
James Lane Allen
James Oliver Curwood
James Oppenheim
James Otis
James R. Driscoll
Jane Abbott
Jane Austen
Jane L. Stewart
Janet Aldridge
Jens Peter Jacobsen
Jerome K. Jerome
Jessie Graham Flower
John Buchan
John Burroughs
John Cournos
John F. Kennedy
John Gay
John Glasworthy
John Habberton
John Joy Bell
John Kendrick Bangs
John Milton
John Philip Sousa
John Taintor Foote
Jonas Lauritz Idemil Lie
Jonathan Swift
Joseph A. Altsheler
Joseph Carey
Joseph Conrad
Joseph E. Badger Jr
Joseph Hergesheimer
Joseph Jacobs
Jules Vernes
Julian Hawthrone
Julie A Lippmann
Justin Huntly McCarthy
Kakuzo Okakura
Karle Wilson Baker
Kate Chopin
Kenneth Grahame
Kenneth McGaffey
Kate Langley Bosher
Kate Langley Bosher
Katherine Cecil Thurston
Katherine Stokes
L. A. Abbot
L. T. Meade

L. Frank Baum
Latta Griswold
Laura Dent Crane
Laura Lee Hope
Laurence Housman
Lawrence Beasley
Leo Tolstoy
Leonid Andreyev
Lewis Carroll
Lewis Sperry Chafer
Lilian Bell
Lloyd Osbourne
Louis Hughes
Louis Joseph Vance
Louis Tracy
Louisa May Alcott
Lucy Fitch Perkins
Lucy Maud Montgomery
Luther Benson
Lydia Miller Middleton
Lyndon Orr
M. Corvus
M. H. Adams
Margaret E. Sangster
Margret Howth
Margaret Vandercook
Margaret W. Hungerford
Margret Penrose
Maria Edgeworth
Maria Thompson Daviess
Mariano Azuela
Marion Polk Angellotti
Mark Overton
Mark Twain
Mary Austin
Mary Catherine Crowley
Mary Cole
Mary Hastings Bradley
Mary Roberts Rinehart
Mary Rowlandson
M. Wollstonecraft Shelley
Maud Lindsay
Max Beerbohm
Myra Kelly
Nathaniel Hawthrone
Nicolo Machiavelli
O. F. Walton
Oscar Wilde
Owen Johnson
P.G. Wodehouse
Paul and Mabel Thorne

Paul G. Tomlinson
Paul Severing
Percy Brebner
Percy Keese Fitzhugh
Peter B. Kyne
Plato
Quincy Allen
R. Derby Holmes
R. L. Stevenson
R. S. Ball
Rabindranath Tagore
Rahul Alvares
Ralph Bonehill
Ralph Henry Barbour
Ralph Victor
Ralph Waldo Emmerson
Rene Descartes
Ray Cummings
Rex Beach
Rex E. Beach
Richard Harding Davis
Richard Jefferies
Richard Le Gallienne
Robert Barr
Robert Frost
Robert Gordon Anderson
Robert L. Drake
Robert Lansing
Robert Lynd
Robert Michael Ballantyne
Robert W. Chambers
Rosa Nouchette Carey
Rudyard Kipling
Saint Augustine
Samuel B. Allison
Samuel Hopkins Adams
Sarah Bernhardt
Sarah C. Hallowell
Selma Lagerlof
Sherwood Anderson
Sigmund Freud
Standish O'Grady
Stanley Weyman
Stella Benson
Stella M. Francis
Stephen Crane
Stewart Edward White
Stijn Streuvels
Swami Abhedananda
Swami Parmananda
T. S. Ackland

T. S. Arthur
The Princess Der Ling
Thomas A. Janvier
Thomas A Kempis
Thomas Anderton
Thomas Bailey Aldrich
Thomas Bulfinch
Thomas De Quincey
Thomas Dixon
Thomas H. Huxley
Thomas Hardy
Thomas More
Thornton W. Burgess
U. S. Grant
Upton Sinclair
Valentine Williams
Various Authors
Vaughan Kester
Victor Appleton
Victor G. Durham
Victoria Cross
Virginia Woolf
Wadsworth Camp
Walter Camp
Walter Scott
Washington Irving
Wilbur Lawton
Wilkie Collins
Willa Cather
Willard F. Baker
William Dean Howells
William le Queux
W. Makepeace Thackeray
William W. Walter
William Shakespeare
Winston Churchill
Yei Theodora Ozaki
Yogi Ramacharaka
Young E. Allison
Zane Grey

www.ingramcontent.com/pod-product-compliance
Lightning Source LLC
Chambersburg PA
CBHW050544260626
47157CB00002B/425